MV

40X210

D1006845

THE *Fat* INNKEEPER

ALAN RUSSELL

THE MYSTERIOUS PRESS

Published by Warner Books

Mysterious Press books are published by Warner Books, Inc.,
1271 Avenue of the Americas, New York, NY 10020.

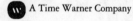 A Time Warner Company

The Mysterious Press name and logo are registered trademarks of Warner Books, Inc.

Printed in the United States of America

First printing: April 1995

10 9 8 7 6 5 4 3 2 1

Library of Congress Cataloging-in-Publication Data
Russell, Alan
    The fat innkeeper / Alan Russell.
        P.   cm.
    ISBN 0-89296-539-8
    1. Hotels—California—La Jolla—Employees—Fiction.   2. House detectives—
California—La Jolla—Fiction.   3. La Jolla (Calif.)—Fiction.   I. Title.
PS3568.U7654F38   1995
813'.54—dc20   94-31061
                                                                         CIP

To the memory of my mother, Carolyn Lois Falconi
Russell, and to the grandson she never got the chance to spoil,
Hart Crane Russell.

Chapter One

The Hotel California's mailer had announced: Grunion Fun! There were a lot of things about the promotion Am Caulfield didn't like. Most Americans, he was sure, were as suspicious of exclamation points as he was. And just how much hype did a two-ounce toothless fish merit? These weren't killer whales or great white sharks or smiling dolphins—these were grunion.

Grunion wouldn't look too out of place in a sardine can, but they distinguish themselves from other fish in ways that humans find fascinating (or at least a subspecies of humans—*Southernus californicatus*). Birds do it, and bees do it, but not like grunion. The fish come ashore to spawn on California's and Mexico's coastal beaches, with the height of the so-called grunion runs occurring in April and May. Spring is announced in San Diego not by an explosion of greenery, or a rise in temperature, but by the pronouncement of grunion runs. Local news, always hard-pressed to make exciting weather forecasts, invariably turns to grunion-run prognostications to use up air time. The grunion visits are predictable in that they occur only at night during the full moon, and happen within several hours of the evening's high tide.

As a native San Diegan, Am had grown up as a surf rat and experienced his share of grunion runs. He had watched the curious and the hopeful turn out to the beaches, had even tried to snatch a few grunion (it is legal to catch grunion with your hands, but about as easy as holding on to a greased pig). Nature's display usually brought families, the adults content to hunker around fire rings to wait for the fishy fireworks, their children running around laughing and screaming.

That, in Am's mind, was how it should be, but it certainly wasn't that way tonight, at least not along the stretch of beach in front of the Hotel California known as the La Jolla Strand. What marketing had done was to turn something special into a three-ring aquarium. Not that reality has ever stood in the way of any good promotion. The Hotel's mailer had allowed a few paeans to nature, but basically promised sex on the beach, and plenty of it.

Those in the hotel business often try to claim a kinship with show business. Though Am believed the relationship between hotels and show business was overstated (at least on the hotel end—it wasn't as if he had ever heard Robert Redford or his ilk going around saying, "Acting is very much like the hotel business"), he still wasn't one to discount the two cardinal rules of performance: You never follow an animal act, and you never count on Mother Nature. When first informed about Grunion Fun! Am had pointed out the potential dangers of violating not one, but both of those rules. The marketing people had not been inclined to listen to his warnings. What was the security director of the Hotel doing critiquing their work? Why wasn't the man trying to track down lost towels? In so many words they told Am to "go fish."

Over two hundred guests of the Hotel California were trying to do just that. They had taken the promotion's bait, but the grunion weren't cooperating. For hours now, the guests had been waiting for the grunion, assured that the fish did indeed have reservations. Bermuda shorts and dark socks didn't identify the guests as out-of-towners, but their "official" grunion catching equipment, which consisted of complimentary neon buckets, flashlights, and Greek fishing caps emblazoned with the Hotel logo, did advertise that they weren't locals. Zen question, thought Am: Who are the real fish?

It was clear the guests were beyond restless. They had come for fun. They had paid good money for fun. And hadn't fun been promised? Wasn't that how the weekend had been advertised? After "cavorting with nature," after watching "the wet and the wild," there was supposed to be a *fabulous fish fry*. ("We like grunion," the brochure had gushed, "especially with onion.") The participants had been primed for a spectacle, for the "the slippery, sliding, spawning grunion" (there had been fold-out pictures to prove it). The veritable piscine orgy had been played up like the goings-on of a Bangkok brothel. To Am's mind, the scribed spectacle of fish writhing in the sand brought up visions of *From Here to Eternity*. He was surprised that "Love Is a Many Splendored Thing" wasn't being piped out to the beach.

The May fog was rolling in a lot faster than any grunion. The pimple on San Diego's mostly perfect climate is that a marine layer likes to hang around the coast for much of May and June, what the locals call "June Gloom." It's not something the Chamber of Commerce is likely to promote, but if you pine for London fog, you need only to travel to San Diego during late spring or early summer.

"Damn fog," complained one of the Hotel's grunion runners. "Getting so we won't even be able to see the fish. That is if they *do* turn up."

There were a few surly grunts of agreement. Am was glad the fog had grown thick enough to obscure his identifying Hotel blue blazer and name tag. You call weather information, you get a recording. You find a hotel employee, you have an ear to complain to.

"Where are those fish?" groused another would-be grunion runner.

"Fish," shouted a voice (the fog was getting thicker by the moment—so the caller had become just that, a voice, and a neon bucket), mimicking the call of a fishmonger. "Hey, fish!"

Another voice took up the call, and then another. "Fish," everyone started calling, "Fish."

Waiting for Godot this wasn't. It must have looked quaint from the Hotel California's four restaurants: the fog rolling in, the revelers on the beach with their pant legs rolled up, and the flashlights probing the incoming waves in search of the elusive grunion. From Am's perspective, it had the makings of a riot.

"Fish! Fish! Fish!"

Enough voices had now joined in with the calling to challenge the roar of the surf. But the chorus wasn't quite loud enough to drown out all sounds.

"Isn't it exciting, Am?"

Mary Mason (aka Typhoid Mary) was the Hotel's social director. In another life she had to have been the activity director for the *Titanic*. With the ship sinking, she had likely suggested that everyone gather for snow cones.

"Grunion Fun!" said Am through clenched teeth. "There are few enough natural phenomena in Southern California, if you discount earthquakes and mudslides. This all seems very wrong to me."

Why did this promotion bother him more than others? Hotels, even venerable hotels like the Hotel California, resorted to such fanfare to keep heads in beds. Given any holiday, even an obscure one, the Hotel had some event. There were promotions offered for Groundhog Day ("Who cares about some woodchuck's shadow? Get rid of your own shadows with a complimentary facial in our spa") to Guy Fawkes Day (special prices on English beer and a fireworks display that ended with a bang). The Hotel had Easter Bunny Hops, and Santa arriving on a surfboard. You do those kinds of things when you are trying to fill 712 rooms 365 days a year. And when you run out of holidays, you scratch your head and create events. Last week someone had suggested, half-seriously, a Muzak-appreciation festival.

"You're a party pooper, Am Caulfield."

"Apparently I'm not the only one. The grunion aren't coming."

"No one guarantees when the grunion will arrive," said Mary. "There's just an ETA."

She sounded like a flight attendant. It was probably a position to which Mary had aspired. He could feel the jet nosediving, could picture Mary still offering earphones for the in-flight movie.

"Fish . . . fish . . . fish . . ."

The chanting had changed, and to Am's ear, not for the better. The raucousness was gone, replaced by something different, something deeper, something more dangerous. Grunion Fun! had probably appealed to the same kind of crowd that would have turned out for a witches' Sabbath. The calling was slower now, and more insistent. It sounded like a summoning.

"Maybe next year we should try Grunion Gun!" said Am. "All we need is an NRA mailing list and a few hundred handguns. The object will be for everyone to shoot at the fishies as they come ashore."

Mary ignored Am's grousing, but finally awakened to the chanting all around her, the voices crying out from the fog. A little defensiveness (or was that fear?) crept into her Pollyanna voice: "I don't know what everyone is getting so antsy about. There's still the fish fry whether anyone catches any grunion or not."

The banquet was to take place in the Montezuma Room, with the evening to be highlighted by a reading from *The Old Man and the Sea*. To Am, it was all about as natural as mauve shoes.

"Fish . . . fish . . . fish . . ."

The voices were coming into their own, like a pack of howling dogs harkening back to an age before rubber bones and squeak toys. There was something primeval about the chant. The Druids probably chanted like that. From grunion run, thought Am, to a gathering of the neophyte occult.

"Fish . . . fish . . . fish . . ."

The offshore breeze picked up. It had been blowing out, but now the wind was pushing back at them. Mary had lined the beach with tiki torches. They were by no means Am's favorite prop, but he wasn't altogether happy to see them blown out. Clouds and the fog obscured the full moon; suddenly the street-lamps lining the boardwalk couldn't be seen. Am's senses were short-circuited. It felt as if he was on the set of a Halloween slasher movie. He caught glimpses of the fluorescent pails. Pushed by the wind, they looked like dancing will-o'-the-wisps. Shrouded beams of flashlights ineffectively challenged the fog, weakly signaling more than illuminating.

He could feel the ocean's pounding through his feet, could feel its pushing through the heavy sea air. Others were aware of its strong rhythm, their chanting/groaning called out in time with the waves, as evocative as galley slaves at the oars.

Everyone caught the scent at the same time. There were glad cries. Surely the grunion were running; by the ubiquitous smell, there was an ocean full of them. But the promise changed along with the scent. The hint became an olfactory fist, a reckoning of decay and death and brine turned rancid. The smell became an assault. The neon grunion buckets were raised not for fish, but to lips, and it wasn't grunion that were deposited within.

No more chants, there was only retching. Delivered from the sea were not a horde of six-inch grunion, but a solitary leviathan.

Chapter Two

"Call me fucking Ishmael," said Am.

The whale wasn't white; the fog had lifted enough for Am to see it was a dark gray. Handkerchief over nose, he made his approach. The dead whale was its own monument. In a body of water, it is difficult to gauge how immense these mammals are. Am suspected it was a gray whale (also called California gray whale, though mostly by Californians). From the shores of La Jolla Strand, he had often witnessed their spouting plumes off in the distance. Their annual migration is one of nature's great commutes, the whales traveling over five thousand miles, from the Arctic Ocean to the Gulf of California.

The whale was half in the water and half out. The strong surging of the ocean could neither take the whale closer to shore, nor return it to the sea. The whale was firmly landlocked. Am had heard of living whales beaching themselves, but this one had been dead upon arrival.

The beach was deserted; fear, confusion, and most of all, the smell, dispersing the crowd. As safety and security director of the Hotel, Am knew he should be tending to the scattered guests, but having endured their grumbling, and even worse, their chanting, he didn't have much sympathy for them. Let them eat fish, he thought. He doubted if many of the Grunion Fun!ners would be going to the fish fry.

Alone with the whale, with the huge presence, Am asked, "What happened to you?"

His voice was masked by the cries of birds. Hundreds of gulls had appeared, and they were sounding the dinner bell for thousands more. One of the mighty had fallen, reason for lesser beasts to rejoice. At least most of them. Curiosity, and sympathy, propelled Am past the shoreline. It was a different kind of whale watching than he was used to. San Diego has a flotilla of whale boats that carry curious people, not harpoons. Am walked into the waves, unmindful of the water, searching for some visible wound on the whale, something to account for its death, but there was nothing he could see.

The whale had died on its way back to the Arctic Ocean. Gray whales migrate in pods, staying close to the coastal waters. Am couldn't help but wonder about the whale's end. Had the creature died alone? Am had seen film footage of cetaceans helping their young and their injured. He wondered if the pod had slowed down for this one, had helped the whale into shallower waters. Maybe he was being anthropomorphic. Somewhere in Am's old record collection were a few whale-song albums. He felt an urge to play one, to broadcast it over loudspeakers. It would be an appropriate dirge, even if it couldn't be heard at the moment. The gulls were beyond raucous, acting and sounding like humans confronted with a thirty-ton ice-cream sundae.

Am raised his arms and shook them, shooing off the birds closest to him. Thinking of the whale songs made him nostalgic. In the seventies, when a record track was more important than a career track, he had enjoyed sipping wine with friends and listening to the whales. The otherworldly calling of the giants had spurred on some discussions that went deep into the night—and sometimes other nocturnal activities as well. He remembered making love, half of his ear to the whale's cries, the other half to his partner's. Their eldritch chorus had transported him. It was a special moment; almost, if he dared to admit it, a holy one. Wine, woman, and whale song. The trinity sounded contrived, but it wasn't. The trinity sounded dated, and it was.

His hand moved, and surprised him. We're taught to avoid the dead, but Am reached out to the whale. What was he grasping at, old memories? The blubber didn't feel as he expected. There was a firmness to it, a roughness that went beyond the barnacles, hitchhikers that had attached themselves by the thousands. The crustaceans had gone along for the long ride, but now that was over.

Sighing, Am withdrew his fingers. Making love while listening to whale calls was one thing, but walking out into the surf to commune with a dead whale was another. He started back to the Hotel, every step a fight not to lose his shoes to the grasping combination of water and sand. A movement, a flash of a match, startled him. He forgot to keep his toes curled hard into his shoes, and forfeited one to the muck. A wave came in and tried to claim the shoe, and a tug of war ensued before Am triumphed, coming up with his footwear and some seaweed.

Should he put the shoe on, or go barefoot? It wasn't a hard choice. Barefoot, pants rolled up, Am felt better. He looked around for the light-bearer. Even over the waft of whale, he smelled a cigarette burning. The figure was

standing in the leviathan's shadow. Am wondered how long
he had been under scrutiny. Whoever was there didn't seem
to be bothered by the whale smell. Odor or not, Am knew
the curious would soon arrive; as many, and as loud, as the
gulls.

Am needed to make some calls: to the lifeguards; the
neighboring Scripps Institution of Oceanography; Sea
World; the half-dozen bureaucracies of the city that would
involve themselves in beached whaledom. There would certainly be enough whale to go around for everyone. What he
feared most was that there might be too much. The clean-
up job was likely to be the whale of a tale.

"Good evening."

Am turned. The smoker had stepped away from the
whale's shadow. He cast quite a shadow himself. The man
was round, and somehow familiar. The shadow nodded to
Am, and he found himself nodding back. Confronting Hiroshi Yamada, the Fat Innkeeper, was almost as surprising
as confronting the whale. Hiroshi was the new owner of the
Hotel California, or at least the son of the absentee owner.
At the beginning of the year (not as, as Am was wont to observe, December 7, 1941) he had arrived at the Hotel with
a coterie of countrymen from Japan. This was the first time
Am had seen him alone. Much like Mary and her trailing
lamb, wherever Hiroshi went, the other Japanese were sure
to go. It was almost as if they were joined at the hip, but
sour grapes might have colored that observation. One of
Hiroshi's cohorts, Makato Takei, had taken over Am's former position of assistant general manager. Musical-chairs
management had relegated Am into his current post, a fit
he thought as complimentary as an East European suit.

Hiroshi pointed to the whale. "The whale must have just died," he said. "I see no signs of deterioration."

"Nor I," Am said.

Yamada's English was very good. Usually, one of the Fat Innkeeper's underlings did his speaking for him. Yamada took a deep breath. To all appearances, he liked what he smelled. His body expanded, especially his neck. Yamada was about thirty years old, not so much fat as large. He was built like a mini sumo wrestler, his more than two hundred pounds spread over a five-foot-eight-inch body.

"Do you think the Hotel should look into salvaging the whale?"

"Salvaging?" The whale wasn't some galleon filled with gold or silver. Am couldn't understand what Yamada was saying.

The Japanese man translated his English: "Make use of it."

He said the words very slowly. The slowness, Am suspected, was for his benefit. Belatedly, he understood Yamada's implication and all but shouted, "No!"

The Fat Innkeeper opened his eyes wide with surprise. Too late, Am remembered that the Japanese avoided confrontation whenever possible. They didn't even like to use the word "no," much preferring that their disapproval be understood without their having to express it openly. In that regard, the Japanese culture was much like the hotel culture, with the altogether too direct word of "no" rarely uttered to a guest.

Dumb, thought Am, reconsidering what he had done. It is bad enough to contradict a boss, but to defy a Japanese boss directly goes against all the conventions in that culture. The Japanese way would be to speak in nuances, to skate the issue and try to finesse the point subtly. But how do you skate around, let alone finesse, a dead whale?

His friend Sharon had advised Am that when talking with the Japanese he should start with a point of agreement, a safe topic, and try to build on common ground. Practice *nemawashi,* she said, root-binding. By not taking any firm stands, by hearing and listening, direct arguments could be avoided. Maybe, thought Am, he and Sharon should have been practicing *nemawashi.* Their relationship was a long-distance one now, conducted mostly over the telephone. Sharon had been working for Yamada Enterprises for over three years, and had learned much of the Japanese way. Under her surreptitious tutelage, Am was trying to navigate the cultural minefield.

Okay, he thought. How do you root-bind when you feel root-bound? Maybe he should comment on the eau de whale, crinkle his nose and say, "Sure stinks, don't it?" But one man's meat is another man's poison. There were cheeses that Am thought tasted worse than last week's socks that were considered epicurean delights. And what about Napoleon's letter to Josephine? "I will return in a week. Do not bathe."

"The whale came a long way," said Am.

Hiroshi nodded. "Yes."

"Those who live along this coast have sort of adopted these whales," said Am. "They think of them as . . ."

Dogs? No. In some parts of the orient, dogs are admired more on the plate than on the leash. And besides, a dog was too small and too domesticated. ". . . spirits."

The Japanese understood about spirits. Am had prepared for the Yamada takeover differently from anyone else. Some of the Hotel staff had studied the Japanese language and

culture, but Am had read Japanese folktales, believing that
a country's folktales are the Cliff Notes to its soul.

"Yes," said the Fat Innkeeper, still nodding. "Such a large
animal would have a large spirit. And a generous one, to
come ashore to us in this way."

If a cow died on Am's doorstep, mightn't he view it as
manna from heaven? This was a hundred cows, and then
some. Hell, this was a barbecue roast for the city of La
Jolla—that is, if any La Jollans had a propensity for whale
blubber. But how do you explain Bambi-syndrome in
Japanese? Was there a way to announce delicately that a
public-relations disaster would ensue if Yamada carved
steaks out of the whale? God, Greenpeace would be picket-
ing before the night was out.

"Yes, the spirit decided to call." Decided to leave his
thirty-ton carcass as a hell of a calling card. "Now we have
to respect the vessel left to us."

The Fat Innkeeper thought about that for a bit. He was
still offering a small smile, still trying to understand why
this great bounty from the sea couldn't be utilized, couldn't
be cubed and served with a little seaweed and soy sauce.

"But since the vessel is landlocked now," Hiroshi said,
"and will never sail again, its useless wood could warm the
house."

Even without a Japanese translator, Am figured the
roundabout interpretation was, "Let's do some carving, and
store some whale in the walk-in."

He wiped perspiration from his forehead. How do you
genteelly explain that sacred cows aren't to be butchered?
"The little children," Am said, "that go to Sea World might
want to come see this one instead."

Hiroshi still didn't look convinced. Spirits and little kiddies hadn't yet moved him, and Am wondered what would. He also wondered what Ikkyu-san would have done. The hero of many Japanese folktales, Ikkyu was a combination acolyte/jester who was always finding himself in difficult, if not impossible, positions.

Am's favorite Ikkyu story had the acolyte traveling with a priest to a temple. The call of nature struck Ikkyu, and he started to open the front of his kimono at the side of the road, when the priest admonished him to stop, as the deity of the road was there. Farther up the road they came to a field, and Ikkyu again prepared to urinate, but the priest stopped him once more. "You can't go there!" he was told. "You'll violate the deity of the harvest." They continued along, the acolyte's bladder pressing him further, when they came to a river. Ikkyu was about to relieve himself into the water when the priest angrily told him, "The water deity is in the river. Nobody would ever do it there!" The acolyte hurried forward, and stopped by a large boulder, but again he was interrupted by the priest, who chided him for even thinking of violating the deity in the large rock. A desperate Ikkyu looked around for some spot that wasn't holy. Then a thought came to him. He scrambled up the boulder and started peeing on the head of the priest. "What are you doing?" cried the priest. "There is no *kami* on your head," said Ikkyu-san, and continued right on urinating.

The story was special to Am even before he explored the footnote, and the pun, surrounding *kami*, a word that means both "deity" and "hair." The priest's tonsure must have looked like an especially attractive target. Am figured that if he was to survive under Japanese ownership, Ikkyu was as good a role model as any. At the moment, though, he decided it would be better to act like the priest.

"To many," said Am, "the whale is holy."

Hiroshi looked at the whale, a distinct longing to his glance. Then he turned back to Am. "You will take care of it?" he asked.

"I will," said Am.

The two men looked at one another. For once, the Fat Innkeeper's phalanx of fellow countrymen was not between him and one of the *gaijin*—a word, and a Japanese philosophy, that translated to "outside person." Sharon said that the Japanese felt that the rest of the world was deprived in that they had not been born Japanese, a severe disability to their way of thinking. And though they might be living in foreign lands, in their own mind they were never the outside person. They were *wareware Nihonjin*—we Japanese.

Reaching into his shirt pocket, Hiroshi pulled out one of his business cards. The importance of the transaction Sharon had only recently explained to Am. "There is a ritual to *meishi*," she said, "the exchange of calling cards. You are supposed to accept the card and look at it, and make some comment. You don't just take a card and stick it in your wallet. That's an insult. You're giving the person your backside, and not the attention they deserve."

The card was outstretched toward him, hanging there like an executioner's ax, a reminder of his misplaced intentions. Am accepted the card, offered a nod that was close to a bow, and then dug out his wallet. Maybe he had an old business card. That's how he could save face. His heart was pounding, and his throat was tight. He had resented having to get bilingual business cards, English on the one side, Japanese on the other, and walked around the security hut muttering, "This is still the U.S.A., isn't it?" The land of the free, and the brave. And the foolish.

There were no old cards, only plenty of the new. He had to play the cards, bluff it out. Am handed Hiroshi a card, English side up, his title of safety and security director clearly displayed. But Yamada wasn't content with only the English version. He turned the card over.

Good job, Ikkyu-san, thought Am. This time you just pissed into the wind.

The Fat Innkeeper did a double-take. So much for the stereotype of orientals being inscrutable. He stared at the card, his eyes wide, then looked back to Am.

"So," he said, "you are a samurai?"

It had seemed like the right thing to do at the time. Until Sharon's lecture, Am hadn't known that the Japanese collected business cards as boys did baseball cards, hadn't been aware of their importance. Like most impetuous acts, he hadn't thought ahead, had neglected to consider what he would do when asked for a business card from someone who was Japanese. He thought of trying to explain to Hiroshi that it had taken all of his willpower not to identify himself as House Dick on the English side of the card, but figured something would be lost in that translation. Like his job.

"Yes," Am finally said. "I am a samurai."

The Fat Innkeeper didn't respond right away. He regarded Am for several moments, then finally gave the tiniest of nods, turned, and began to walk away.

Am let out a lot of silent air. Why hadn't he made it easier on himself and just announced he was the son of God? To the Japanese, samurais are icons. The warrior myth is not one they take lightly. Samurai films are their westerns, and their shrines. Japanese executives often take up swordplay and archery, sports drawn from the samurai tradition.

Some consider the samurai mentality to be a major part of the Japanese psyche.

He breathed deeply, took in a lot of whale, and gagged slightly. What a night.

A wave surprised him. Sometimes sets are that way, a dozen anemic waves and then suddenly one or two big breaks. This wave broke at his knee level, and then pushed forward. When it receded, it left behind hundreds, no, thousands, of grunion.

In the moonlight, the grunion spun their fantasy for an audience of one. The females buried themselves in the sand, their tails down. There was wriggling, and dancing, and flashing of silver. It was better than advertised, better than Grunion Fun!

A minute later, and the vision had passed. Another wave had come in, and the grunion had ridden off with it. With their departure, Am hurried off. He was afraid if he stayed, Ahab's leg would be the next thing to turn up on the beach.

Chapter Three

"Quis custodiet ipsos custodes?" whispered Am. He didn't bother with the English translation—Who is to guard the guards themselves?—but instead stealthily slid a key into a lock and opened the door to the Hotel's main spa.

The spa attendants were gone, which was just as Am had expected and wanted. He was tired of smelling like the catch of the day, and needed a break from the whale duties. Am figured he had earned a hot shower, a whirlpool, a steambath, and a massage on one of the vibrating tables, to be followed by a wallow in the spa's lotions and potions and powders. The whale predicament had officially been handed over to legal representatives from the city of San Diego. Saved from sushi, but not the sharks. That didn't mean the problem had been taken care of, far from it, but now the Hotel could point to the city and self-righteously say, "It's their job."

"Am, this is Central, do you copy?"

The voice came booming out of Am's walkie-talkie. Damn. Why hadn't he been smart enough to turn the thing off? "Central" was Fred, the dispatcher from security, a retired carpenter who had seen entirely too many episodes of

"Rescue 911." Fred described fender benders like the down-ing of the *Hindenburg*.

Am picked up his walkie-talkie. "Unless Jonah is giving a press conference on the beach," he said, "I'd suggest you call Stephenson."

Fred sounded even more excited than usual. "We have a code red, Am! We need you ASAP up to room 374. Do you copy?"

"On my way," said Am.

"Ten-four," said Fred, sounding not a little deflated. He continually coached Am to respond, "I read you," or "Over and out," or "That's a ten-four," and would have preferred Am reiterating the room number with a "That's a three-Thomas, seven-Sam, four-Frank," but try as he might, Am still couldn't bring himself to speak that way.

Code red, he thought. What the hell was a code red? That was one of the things he should know. After five months in his new post he thought he had that rainbow chart down, but damned if he wasn't mentally color-blind at the moment. The colors were representative of situations, codes that allowed security to communicate without the guests, or anyone, monitoring, knowing what they were talking about. Code red. Was that a fire? No, that was code orange. A noisy drunk? No, that fell under the disturbance category, a code blue. Red was, was . . . Am's brain cells were derailed by the squishing sound of his footfalls, and his skin being rubbed raw by the wet and chafing pants. If he didn't get out of the wet clothes soon, his whole body was going to be a code red.

Maybe there should be a new code, Am thought, code gray—a gray whale on the beach. The thought must have eased up his subconscious, as suddenly he remembered what code red signified. "Color me stupid," he said aloud. Code red meant that a call had been made to the paramedics, and that someone was in need of medical attention. He started running faster, the squishing sounds dogging him.

There were at least fifty people crowded inside room 374, all of them blocking his way. Am knew that announcing he was hotel security wouldn't exactly bring a Moseslike parting of the crowd. The public has about as much respect for a house dick as they do crossing guards. Am circumvented that by acting like an impatient plainclothesman, his method acting based on the time he had interrupted a cop at his coffee and learned that was about as advisable as taking a bone from a strange dog. With a grim expression, and a loud, flat voice, Am announced that a pathway for the paramedics had to be cleared. He was pleased with the crowd's quick response, though he was unsure whether it was his posing, his words, or his smell that opened the passage. Or maybe, he decided after a look, everyone had just seen enough of the corpse.

Two Hotel employees were still trying to revive the dead man, but Am figured they'd have a better chance with the whale. When someone's dying or dead, that's not the best time to gauge an age, but Am estimated the victim was about sixty. His guesswork came between the CPR efforts. It didn't appear that rigor mortis had yet set in. The man's features were contorted, his struggle to live still apparent on his face. His eyes, even behind thick-rimmed glasses, were bulging. The glasses reminded Am of barnacles still holding on.

"I'd call it a deathbed conversion," said a pipe-smoking man standing near to Am, his voice conversational.

"No doubt about it," replied a woman with a red hat that was as loud as her voice.

From Am's rather limited experience, he had found that death brings a quiet to a room. It was generally a time for reflection. But those gathered seemed to think it was time for a party.

A very tall man raised his arms, flapped them slowly up and down. "His gravity is turned off now. Do you remember that?"

"Do I?" said a very wrinkled, very small, woman. "It was like being unshackled."

A bearded man smiled. " 'Be positive.' What fine last words. The great skeptic has spoken."

"Be positive," repeated most of those in the room.

A woman with Bette Davis's voice, but alas, not her eyes, asked, "And that's all he said, Jack?"

Heads turned, and Am followed their direction. Jack was seated in a chair, taking more stock of the ocean view than the goings-on in the room. Standing next to him was T.K. Washington, one of the Hotel desk clerks. T.K. was an aspiring comic, and hardly a bastion of propriety, but even he looked shocked at the cavalier attitudes of those in the room. He caught Am's eyes and shook his head.

"What?" Jack was awakening to the question. He smiled, a gentle smile. Jack looked like a poet. Not a good poet, but one of those people who while away their time hanging around coffeehouses and occasionally, but only very occasionally, scribbling around the edges of a piece of paper. Jack was about thirty, blond and blue-eyed, but he didn't so much exude Nordic stock as he did white bread.

"She asked," said the old woman, "if the only thing that Doubting Thomas said was, 'Be positive.' "

"That was it," said Jack. "He was on the ground, and I went to him. He could barely get those words out. And then he died."

He said it as if the dying part were a happy ending. Judging from the little noises of his listeners, they agreed.

The arrival of the paramedics interrupted Jack's story-telling, but not the festivities. "Ah, the belated cavalry," said the woman in the red hat.

"A day late and a dollar short," said Prince Albert in the Can.

"You needn't bother," advised Bette Davis, not meanly, but more as a matter-of-fact observation to the uniformed figures rushing by her.

"I remember watching the paramedics work on me," said the bearded man.

"So do I," said the tall man.

At least, thought Am, the big guy wasn't flapping his arms anymore.

"They worked so hard. I thought it would be wrong to leave with their putting in so much effort. But everything was such a glorious show."

The words sounded wistful, spoken as you would of a first love.

"Thank God you arrived," said Helen Dunning, giving up her breathing station to one of the paramedics. Helen was the manager on duty that night, and it showed. Her forehead was soaked with perspiration, and her long, sandy-blond hair clung to her head as if she had just showered. Helen's makeup was gone, but even had it been in place it wouldn't have masked the look of loathing she gave to the crowd.

In her hand she held the plastic resuscitator tube she had

tried to breathe life through. Helen looked at the object blankly, then, without really thinking, tossed it high over her shoulder. Several people vied to catch it.

Am wasn't one of them. He shouldered his way through the crowd and reached her side. "Hey, are you okay?"

"I'm just giving them the bridal bouquet," she said, her voice somewhere between weepy and hysterical.

Am put an arm around Helen, and moved her away from both the living and the dead. "What happened?" he asked.

She took a few moments to swallow and focus. "A guest called the operator from an elevator. Apparently him," she said, pointing to Jack. "He said he needed someone to come up right away to Dr. Kingsbury's room, said he thought he was having a seizure or something.

"I told T.K. to run up to the room and check out the situation, and the next thing I know T.K. is calling me and saying that we've got a man dying. I could deal with that, or I thought I could, but what really unsettled me was this group. Macario from maintenance was nearby, so I grabbed him. He was doing heart massage, and I was doing mouth-to-mouth, and all the while these people kept wandering in. This man's death seemed to be an excuse for a party. A few of them even had the nerve to call their friends and tell them to come over. Armchair quarterbacks are one thing, but these are armchair morticians. Some of them told me to relax, that he was dead already. Others were more blunt. One man said my 'huffing and puffing' was disturbing the vortex. As far as I'm concerned, they're all ghouls."

Her accusation was loud, but with all the conversations going on, no one seemed to notice. "Let's go outside," said Am. "Get a breath of fresh air."

Helen didn't argue, let herself be led through the room.

Out in the hallway she took several deep breaths. Some
color started returning to her face. "It's not going to be a
happy ending for him, is it?" she asked.

"I don't think so," said Am.

Long sigh. "I think I need some coffee, or something."

"You want company?"

"No. Thanks, though. But stop by later, okay? We'll
need to compare notes before writing up our reports."

There would certainly be enough of those, thought Am.
"Will do," he said, offering her a last comforting hug.

Helen walked away, albeit a little unsteadily. When she
turned the corner, Am started back to the room. He needed
statements, and witnesses. It was time to take control of the
situation. A clatter of wheels and a shouted "Step aside"
made Am jump out of the way of the gurney. The elevator,
he thought, kicking himself as he ran after the paramedics.
He should have positioned someone to hold the elevator
doors open for them. But his guilt, and his running, proved
unnecessary. A familiar figure was already holding the elevator doors. When the gurney was safely inside, the doorman gave up his post and started slowly walking toward
Am. It was the walk of an old west sheriff ready for a showdown. There was no love lost between Am and Detective
McHugh of the San Diego Police Department. McHugh
considered Am the worst kind of amateur sleuth—a lucky
one.

As the detective approached him, Am was sure that
McHugh's sky blue eyes were seeing too much: Am's still
wet shoes and trousers, his unbuckled belt (damn, thought
Am, I forgot to fasten it back in the spa), and his disheveled
condition. McHugh had the unhurried pace of a man who

has been on the planet for a half a century, and seen enough not to be in a rush to see any more.

Behind Am came the sounds of laughter and convivial conversation. The closer the detective approached, the more his frown intensified. He paused before continuing toward the room, stood next to Am and said, "Isn't it a little early to be throwing a wake, Caulfield?"

Then, seemingly puzzled, he sniffed the air, disdainfully snorted, and walked by.

Chapter Four

Whenever anything unpleasant happens at a hotel, be it accident, injury, or even death, some manager somewhere has the undesirable job of asking questions. Am knew the difficulties of such interrogations. Offering sympathy was important, but not to the point of endorsing any liability on the part of the property. Though obtaining answers in the face of pain or grief is often difficult, it is also necessary. It is amazing how frequently a story changes, especially after a consultation with a lawyer. A guest that admitted to breaking his leg after tripping over his own feet suddenly remembers that the fall didn't occur in his room, but over a loose section of carpeting out in the hallway. Filling out an accident report and getting a signed statement are often safeguards against a lawsuit.

This wasn't the first time Am had encountered death at the Hotel. With seven hundred and twelve rooms, four restaurants, six lounges, and fourteen meeting rooms, it wasn't surprising that death sometimes called. But this was not like any other death that Am remembered. There was no weeping, or gnashing of teeth. No one seemed particularly bothered, or even put on a pretense of being mournful.

Getting anyone to talk about the late Dr. Thomas Kingsbury was not a problem. Stopping them was more difficult.

Am had heard of Kingsbury. He was one of those figures
who popped up every so often in a magazine like *People,* or
on some television interview. Kingsbury was a doctor and a
scientist of not a little fame, but the general public knew of
him not so much for his own discoveries, but for his cru-
sades into exposing the deceits of what he called "pseudo-
science." Kingsbury did not believe in much. He doubted
saints, but not sinners, and liked nothing better than de-
bunking the paranormal. The doctor had made a career of
exposing bogus telepaths, evangelical healers, and mediums, and relished taking on what he called "the modern
witch-doctor establishments," targets which ranged from
tarot readers to government economists.

It wasn't a vacation that had brought Kingsbury to the
Hotel California. He had been attending the Union of
Near-Death Experiences Retreat (UNDER). Belatedly, he
had something in common with its other attendees.

UNDER had officially welcomed Kingsbury's scrutiny,
had promised they would do all they could to facilitate his
inquiries. They were certain he could root around all he
wanted and still not denigrate their collective experience.
Lazarus wasn't the only one with a story to tell. They had
been dead, all of them, and were convinced they had
glimpsed their afterlife.

Kingsbury had sent lengthy medical questionnaires to all
of the attendees of the UNDER conference, and had scheduled "post-mortem interviews" with sixty of the conventioneers. The questionnaires had delved into physical
histories, with emphasis on the circumstances of their
"deaths." The medical questions stretched over a number of

pages, "an inquiry," one participant told Am, "that was a good precursor to being a medical cadaver."

The doctor had died halfway through the four-day conference. Although he had attended some of the workshops and heard some of the talks, most of his time had been spent interviewing what he liked to call "zombies," or "the undead." Am had the feeling he would have gotten along very well with Dr. Kingsbury.

"He was a funny guy," said the Bette Davis voice, whose real name was Norma, "not what I expected. In the middle of a bunch of serious questions he asked me, 'Now, how many fairies do you think can dance on the head of a pin?' And when we finished up, he said, 'Does anyone else in your family besides you suffer delusions, or visions?' I kind of figured he'd be a stuffed shirt, but he wasn't."

If you could forgive the anticlimax of Norma's eyes (they were close-set and dishwater brown—the antithesis of Bette Davis's), she was rather attractive, an athletic-looking forty with a quick smile. "Do you think he was flirting with you?" asked Am.

"I would hope so," she said, flashing a smile. "He mentioned to me in a very professional voice that there were tangible and consistent changes with those who had had near-death experiences, changes that didn't seem to be gender-related, except in the preferred manner of dying. Men, he said, almost universally professed to wanting to go out with a bang, and I don't mean dynamite."

"And that's not a female goal?"

"Not according to Dr. Kingsbury," she said, being purposely ambiguous.

"So you thought his observation was inappropriate?"

"I didn't say that," said Norma. "I'm just saying he

raised a flag. When men talk about sex, no matter what the guise, I think there's often an ulterior motive."

Am didn't know how he should respond. Damned if he did, damned if he didn't. "So," he said, "at the risk of sounding like a pickup line, just how did you die?"

She laughed. "The pickup line would have been: 'Didn't we meet once? Wasn't it at Saint Peter's gate?' "

"I'll have to remember that."

"Car accident," she said.

How, wondered Am, had Kingsbury died? Heart attack, probably. Apparently, he wasn't the only one interested in that question. He could hear McHugh questioning several people, among them T.K. Why was the detective taking such an interest in this death? And how was it that McHugh had arrived at the hotel so soon after Kingsbury's death?

As if to emphasize that riddle, McHugh announced, "I want all nonessential personnel to clear the room."

That's the tone of voice, thought Am. That's it exactly. The one that says, police business, goddammit.

"See you later," said Norma.

"In this life, or the next?" asked Am.

The room rapidly cleared, leaving only McHugh, T.K., two uniformed officers, and Am. The detective offered Am a less-than-hospitable side glance that clearly signaled he was not one of those considered essential to the case. For several seconds Am stood his ground, time enough to realize he was in an untenable position. He couldn't force McHugh to tell him anything, and he wasn't about to truckle. If the detective didn't want him there, then he would have to gather information in a roundabout way.

Slowly, and with what he considered dignity, Am began his exit from the room. His departure didn't go unnoticed.

"Do me a favor, Caulfield," said McHugh, walking up to him.

Willing to be wooed, Am stopped to listen.

"I understand two of your staff tried to revive Kingsbury," said the detective. "I'd like to talk to them."

Gofer, thought Am. Glumly, he nodded.

"Oh, and Caulfield?" asked the detective. Am stopped in the hallway, just outside the door to the room. He looked at McHugh with what he thought was the appropriate disinterest, but the detective, intent on applying some plastic coverlets to the doorknobs, spoke to Am without even looking at him.

"The next time there's a murder at this hotel," he said, "do me a favor and secure the crime scene."

"Murder?" asked Am, but he was too late. The door had already closed on him.

Chapter Five

McHugh's announcement was an effective attention-getter. Am wondered whether his remark was a hateful joke, a way for the detective to get back at him by playing with his mind. If that was his intent, the ruse was an elaborate one. Room 374 had been sealed off to all but SDPD with yellow crime-scene tape that prevented entry. The display was not a motif in keeping with a five-star hotel, especially not The Hotel, which was always written in the uppercase, and pronounced the same way. The Hotel had been around for more than a century. It epitomized Southern California class, if that wasn't an oxymoron. Murder at the Hotel was about as acceptable as franks and beans being offered as the nightly special in one of its restaurants. Maybe with a French name, thought Am, you could get away with the franks and beans, but murder allowed no euphemisms.

Should he call the Fat Innkeeper? Am had been debating that for the half hour since room 374's door had been closed to him. He had delivered Helen Dunning and Macario Lopez to the room, and had almost asked McHugh to allow him participation in the investigation, but pride had held back that request. Am had settled down the hallway within

viewing range of the door, anxious to hear the goings-on
from T.K., Helen, or Macario as soon as they were released.
It was a difficult wait because he couldn't do anything in
the interim, not even share his worry.

Am started pacing again. At least he wasn't squeaking
anymore, even if his shoes and socks were still wet. It felt as
if there were something wet and gummy between his toes,
but though he had probed with his fingers he hadn't found
anything other than a matted sock. There was really no re-
course but to take the damn sock off.

Leaning against a wall, Am removed first his shoes, and
then his stocking. Massaging his toes was the highlight of
his evening. He didn't want to put the sock back on immediately, especially in its wet state, but neither did he want
to wring it out on the carpeting. There wasn't a bathroom
nearby, but there was a terra-cotta ashtray not ten steps off.
He hopped over, then started squeezing the water out of the
stocking. The droplets did a good job of making a puddle
out of the Hotel imprimatur minted into the fine sand.

His other foot demanded equal time, so Am repeated the
process. His toes started to come to life again. If only he
could discreetly remove his underwear. Murder at the Hotel
was bad enough. Facing it with wet underwear was next to
unbearable.

"Am! Hey, Am!"

T.K.'s voice was unmistakable, catching Am between
rubbing his toes and dreaming of a thorough scratching.
Socks in one hand, shoes in the other, Am felt like a hobo
posing for some artistic brush. T.K. wasn't the only witness
to the spectacle; Helen and Macario were also walking toward him.

His first impulse was to try and put his socks on while

standing up, but he thought better of that. The Hotel was rife with intimate sitting areas, benches usually sandwiched between a decorative urn on one side and a flower display on the other. Am spotted one. It was just outside of room 374, but it was occupied. McHugh was sitting there watching him.

"Hey, Am," said T.K. as he pulled up to him. "Big Brother figured you'd be waiting. He says he'd like to talk with you now. That is if you're done with your laundry."

Am couldn't be sure whether the line was T.K.'s or McHugh's, but he didn't appreciate it either way. Everyone was standing around watching him with curiosity. There is nothing so difficult as putting on stockings while under inspection. Ask any lover who has ever tried to make a graceful midnight retreat.

"Perhaps," said Am, his sock unable to surmount his heel despite his exertions, "it would be better if I was to talk with all of you a little later."

The tone of his voice was such as to make them move along and not look back. McHugh was too far away to hear, but not to watch. The more Am struggled with the sock, the more the detective shook his head.

The hell with it, thought Am. He stuffed the stockings into his pockets, then stepped into his shoes.

And found that damn piece of seaweed.

He didn't pause, didn't give McHugh the satisfaction of seeing his expression change. Shoes untied, he continued forward.

Chapter Six

In the middle of the Fat Innkeeper's office was a map of the earth. What was disconcerting about this map was that Japan implicitly dominated the rest of the world. The Land of the Rising sun was set center-stage, and larger than life, its dimensions not drawn to scale with the rest of the planet. Am kept staring at the map. It was hard for him getting used to seeing the United States positioned off to the side.

Guess I'll have to orient myself, he thought.

Like any messenger with bad news, Am waited pensively. Mr. Takei had intercepted his call to the Fat Innkeeper. No one had yet seen Takei smile. He was considered to be the power behind the throne, speaking for Hiroshi Yamada while directing policies and work to be done. It was hard to see his eyes, hidden as they were behind his thick glasses. He was thin and pale, quite the opposite of the Fat Innkeeper.

Am inwardly winced. That nickname was going to catch up with him. It wasn't really his fault; it was Richard's. It was dangerous to have a friend like Richard. The man was entirely too smart, a research scientist at the Scripps Institution of Oceanography, who habitually applied marine nicknames to almost everyone. Most of the time the nicknames were only used by, and only made sense to, Richard. Though Richard had bestowed hundreds of aquatic nicknames, the Fat Innkeeper was the first to catch on. It was, Am supposed, an improvement on some of Yamada's earlier nicknames. The staff had initially referred to him as "yo' mama," or "the fat Jap"; now, there was something almost nostalgic about those names. Ask a Hotel employee who Hiroshi Yamada was, and you might draw a blank, but ask anyone on staff who was the Fat Innkeeper and they could tell you. Most could even give you his scientific name: *Urechis caupo.*

Richard said the appellation had come to him almost like a burning bush (further interrogation revealed his inspiration arrived shortly after his sixth gin and tonic). He had heard some of the Hotel gossip about Hiroshi, and when he had seen him on the evening news, "everything clicked." Archimedes yelled, "Eureka." Richard yelled, "Urechis." Archimedes was thinking about gold; Richard was contemplating a sea worm.

That's what a fat innkeeper is, an invertebrate that lives in a U-shaped burrow, but not alone. The innkeeper shares his lodge with other guests ("symbionts" was Richard's preferred term), including some species of pea crab, small bivalves, and different species of worms and goby fish.

The convivial innkeeper sees to the needs of its guests ("commensals," Richard was quick to tell anyone, was the better word) through its fussy eating habits. The twenty-inch worm sports a ring of mucus glands around the top of its trunk, glands it expands against the side of the burrow. A mucus net is sent out that filters out tiny organisms and particles flowing through its den. As the filter fills, the worm moves forward and devours the bag and its contents—or some of them. The larger detrital matter, and whatever other food the innkeeper eschews, passes down the line to its tenants.

Richard had called and told Am about his fat-innkeeper revelation, then had supplied him with articles, pictures, drawings, and assorted miscellaneous information about *Urechis caupo*. Am had made a few copies for his co-workers, and then watched everything snowball. The most popular off-duty staff shirt featured a fat innkeeper sitting contentedly in its burrow. Even the perennial Hotel California softball team had changed its name. Now they were the Urechis Caupos, with their nickname "the worms." The new name hadn't helped the team. They were still in last place.

Somehow it heartened Am to think that out in the ocean there were invertebrates essentially practicing his own trade. It allowed him the kind of connection that mystics would have ascribed as demonstrating the universality in all nature, but all the same, Am wished he had never heard of the fat innkeeper. Everyone attributed the naming to him. Court jesters (let alone the palace guard) know better than to dub their rulers "stinky," or "slimy," or worst of all— "wormy." That was essentially what Am had done. He had figured (or more likely, hoped) Hiroshi's nickname would be short-lived, but now it was part of the Hotel nomenclature. Sometimes nicknames do stick—like his own. His real name was Ian, but that had been in another life, before hotels. Now he was Am, an abbreviation of the assistant manager he had once been.

The door opened and the Fat Innkeeper ("Mr. Yamada,

dammit," Am reminded himself) entered the room, followed by Takei, Matsuda, and Fujimoto. Contrary to popular opinion, the three men really didn't look that much alike (Sharon said most Japanese were convinced all Americans looked alike, so apparently it's a universal prejudice), even though all of them were roughly the same age, around forty-five, and wore the same dark suits and red ties. Takei, in charge of daily operations, was the thinnest of the lot, his face almost skeletal. Matsuda was the numbers man, the chief financial officer who supervised the Hotel finances. He had more gray hairs than the others, and a nose that was big by Japanese standards. Fujimoto oversaw the food-and-beverage operations, and was the sportiest of the three. Am suspected he sometimes moussed his hair, and on a few occasions he'd even been spotted wearing paisley ties.

Am jumped to his feet, and walked toward the men. He hadn't expected all of the Japanese bigwigs to be meeting with him, but he wasn't totally surprised either. The Three Musketeers might have coined the phrase, "One for all, and all for one," but the Japanese live it. The Fat Innkeeper made the introductions. The Hotel has more than a thousand employees, so it wasn't too surprising that Am had never talked with Matsuda or Fujimoto. Takei was another story, if not a more pleasant one. Am thought the man more termite than human, so great was his love for paper. Takei was always asking for reports and contingency plans from security. Am admired his diligence, but he was tired of reinventing the wheel. Takei loved minutiae, seemed delighted to come up with more "what ifs" than Rod Serling. He had planned for countless disasters. Sharon said there were several reasons for this: the Japanese pursuit of perfection; their need for a sense of control; and, most of all, the

almost instinctive Japanese fear that there is trouble waiting around the corner. It is as if they always expect, she
said, the worst. Takei had wanted to see earthquake plans,
and fire-safety procedures. They'd gone over how to deal
with bomb threats and power failures. About the only
thing they hadn't put down on paper was what to do in the
event of a murder. Welcome to America.

The Fat Innkeeper announced the Japanese names first,
then he offered up Am's name and his position. With the
timing of a veteran performer, and the accompaniment of a
slight smile, Hiroshi then added, "He is also the Hotel
samurai."

The Fat Innkeeper explained further in Japanese. Paranoia is always quick to surface when you're being discussed
in a language you don't understand. When he finished, no
one was laughing. Not that Am ever expected belly laughter out of this group, but the silence weighed in as more
oppressive than usual. The only noise was from Takei. Almost so as not to be noticed, he was sucking air through his
teeth. Am had been warned that such inhalation was the
Japanese equivalent of a Bronx cheer, though in their usual
understated way.

"Your business cards," said Takei at last, "are open to
misinterpretation."

That was about as straightforwardly censurious as the
Japanese were ever likely to get. When in doubt, Sharon
had told him, employ *sumimasen*—apology without end.
But Am wasn't about to play Uriah Heep for anyone.

"I will discard the old cards immediately," he said, "and
have new ones made up at my own expense."

And I'll try to suppress the suddenly very strong urge,

thought Am, to have the new cards announce myself as a proctologist in Japanese.

It wasn't *sumimasen,* but no one objected to his solution. Am waited for the other men to find their seats, Sharon's words again in his ears: "Sometimes they play a form of musical chairs. They know who belongs in the seat of honor, but there's often a hierarchical infighting for the other chairs."

Am's mother had taught him to say please and thank you. He knew to excuse himself after inadvertently belching, kept his nails clean, and closed his mouth when he chewed. Am was good about cleaning up after himself, and the sermon of his youth had been, "Treat others as you would like to be treated yourself." He didn't spit in public, and didn't even much spit in private. Having been able to impart those behaviors onto him, Am's mother had reckoned herself a success. Mom hadn't prepared him to be Japanese.

He took the last seat. The meeting didn't begin with a call to business, or an agenda. The Fat Innkeeper commented about the heavy fog, and Am found himself explaining about the coastal marine layer. It was something, Am figured, that Hiroshi was already acquainted with. The Japanese way was scripted; he had only to remember his part. An American owner probably would have asked, "What the hell happened in room three seven four?" Hiroshi would get to the same question, but not without the proper sacrament. What Am feared, though, was that they might talk to cross-purposes. Sometimes even the Japanese didn't understand one another, losing their way among the etiquette.

The talk of fog was winding down. Am wondered if it

was time to bring up the death of Dr. Kingsbury. It was tiring to have to think before speaking, definitely not in keeping with the American way.

"In this country," said Am, "every year the hotel industry puts up guests for more than a billion room nights."

Am let the figure sink in. "By the odds of probability alone," he said, "sometimes bad things happen."

First the Fat Innkeeper nodded, then the other three dark heads followed. They had found that all-important point of agreement. "Tell us about the bad thing that happened," said Hiroshi.

They heard about Kingsbury, and his death, and McHugh's suspicions that he might have been murdered. "The detective had received a call from Dr. Kingsbury the day before he died," said Am. "They set up a meeting for eight o'clock tonight. Although Kingsbury wouldn't detail the specifics of their proposed get-together, he did tell McHugh that a fraud was being perpetrated, and that he had uncovered enough incriminating information to warrant a police investigation.

"McHugh tried to get him to say more over the phone, but Kingsbury prevailed upon him for a face-to-face. The detective got the feeling that the doctor might have been fishing, seeing if he really did have a crime the police would be interested in pursuing. McHugh sensed that Kingsbury wanted the police involved for the sake of a public forum. That's one thing the good doctor always excelled at—getting publicity."

"Dr. Kings-bur-y," said the Fat Innkeeper, stretching out his name to three words. "I have heard of him."

"He was also known as Tommy Gunn the Magician," said Am, rhyming the name with his stage profession.

"Kingsbury studied magic and illusion to learn the tricks of the trade, to get an understanding of just how people could be fooled. It was his life's work to expose the charlatans and reveal their staged miracles.

"Kingsbury was staying at the Hotel as part of the UNDER convention, a gathering of those who have had near-death experiences. Supposedly, he was skeptical of the 'proof' of life after death that these near-death groups have been circulating."

"What kind of proof?" asked Hiroshi.

"Many who have almost died claim similar experiences. Most remember leaving their bodies and traveling toward a bright light. Some say they talked with friends and relatives on what they call 'the other side.' Many reminisce about the overwhelming peace they perceived when they were clinically dead, and claim that anyone who has had a near-death experience no longer fears death."

"You have not told us how this doctor magician died," said Takei.

Am sensed the other man's hostility, even if his animosity wasn't exactly manifested in word or deed. Maybe Takei didn't like the idea of a *gaijin* lecturing them. Maybe it grated against him that Am had once been in charge of many of his own duties.

"That's because neither I, nor the authorities, yet know," said Am. "Detective McHugh said that Kingsbury's death looked suspicious, and he's seen a lot more bodies than I ever have. The autopsy will tell us if he's right."

"So, all this alarm might be unnecessary?" Takei's question wasn't a question.

"That's right. Even Kingsbury's dying words seem to support a natural death. Some of the UNDER people now believe he joined their movement at the end, even publicly endorsed their cause.

"His last words were 'Be positive.' That goes hand in hand with the near-death experience."

The men were silent, lost in contemplation of Kingsbury's last words. Norma had told Am that Thomas Edison's final utterance was "It is very beautiful over there." She said she had seen that beauty. The only last words Am knew were those of Eugene O'Neill as he expired in Boston's Shelton Hotel: "I knew it. I knew it. Born in a hotel room—and God damn it—died in a hotel room." Am had half a mind to usurp O'Neill's words on his own deathbed.

"It is fortunate," said Takei, "that we have a samurai to deal with this situation. You know *bushido,* of course?"

Am wondered if it was a form of martial arts. The Fat Innkeeper decided to interpret. "*Bushido* is the way of the warrior, of the samurai. It is a manner of living, of acting, of being. *Bushido* is a discipline, a code of bravery. It is a way, and a truth, and an inner guide."

Bushido sounds like bullshit, thought Am.

"But no samurai," said Hiroshi with that little half-Buddha smile of his, "however noble and determined, has ever conquered death."

"I don't intend to be the first," said Am. "But I do intend to get better acquainted."

Chapter Seven

It is against the nature of most men to accept the fact that they are not qualified to do something. Prop a beer in their hands, steer the conversation in the right direction, and before long they'll wax eloquent on the finer points of brain surgery, battlefield tactics, nuclear engineering, coaching a football team, and the most elementary task of all, how to run the country. The wonderful thing about being an armchair quarterback is that you're not called to go out on the field. So just how, thought Am, had he managed to get himself in the middle of a very visible situation in which he had absolutely no idea how to proceed? It wouldn't do to tell the Fat Innkeeper and his cronies that he was content to let the police handle the investigation. He could just see Takei raising a damning eyebrow at that one. To concede without trying wouldn't be the samurai way.

Am's ruminating was taking place in his own bathtub. Hot water, he thought, seemed to be his proper medium that day. Am eased his shoulders and neck farther into the water. His tub wasn't nearly as large as those in the Hotel spa. It wasn't filled with milk and/or herbs, and there wasn't an attendant waiting to offer the requisite pampering (a bathing session one copywriter had alliteratively labeled as the "electrolyte enrapturement experience"). But for all the Hotel's touting of their "ultimate liquid escape," they didn't, to Am's knowledge, offer a rubber ducky. The yellow duck was placidly floating, stirred by the small waves of Am's movements. It was alone in the water tonight. Am had opted not to bring out the floating whale that usually accompanied it.

He reached for the duck, and squeezed. The resulting quack sounded somewhat waterlogged. Certified in lifesaving techniques, Am worked on the victim, draining water out of the duck. Along its underside he felt raised ridges and investigated what was there: "Made in Japan."

"My geisha house and welcome to it," he said, then tossed the duck aside. It quacked, much more assertively this time, on impact with the floor. That, or it laughed.

Am sank even farther into the tub, imagined himself an alligator with only eyes and nose clearing the liquid. The warm water took away some of the harder edges of the day, but he couldn't drift very far from his concerns. A guest had died at his Hotel. He wanted McHugh to be wrong, hoped the autopsy would prove Kingsbury's death was the result of natural causes, but his instincts told him that was wishful thinking.

While the medical examiner was figuring out how Kingsbury died, maybe Am should be considering why he died. Cops were always looking for motives, and Am decided that would be his first order of business in the morning. If *bushido* couldn't solve the case, then maybe Yankee ingenuity could.

As if to emphasize that point, Am reached for a small pump. San Diego averages less than ten inches of rain in a year, and Am had decided to irrigate his garden through his baths. Tubing ran from the pump into the garden below. The so-called gray water wasn't exactly legal, but his plants were thriving. He dried himself off while the pump made short work of his bath. The strangling calls of a pump going dry prompted him to turn it off. Perhaps because Am's fingers had been underwater for so long, they were unusually sensitive. On the underside of the pump was a small metal plate with upraised bumps, the embellishments of identification. He stopped himself from looking to see where the pump was made, afraid to discover that he was sharing his bathtub with all of Japan. Who would have guessed World War II would have paled against the larger conflict, the rubber-ducky war?

Am's bedtime dilemma was whether to call Sharon. It was late, but he knew she'd be up. She said women had to work twice as hard as men to get ahead. Whether that was true or not, Am couldn't say; he only knew her work was like the old rhyme—never done. Did he resent her for that? Did it injure his male pride that he was the one who kept calling her and not vice versa? Sharon had told him that she didn't have time for a relationship. He had made that same speech once or twice himself. The shoe was on the other foot, and the phone was in the other hand. He called anyway.

She answered on the first ring. That was at least some consolation. Sharon was in British Columbia, part of a negotiations team looking to purchase another hotel for Yamada Enterprises, or at least one of its subsidiaries. The family business, the *doozuku gaisha,* was immense and still expanding. Sharon had said an anthropologist would be hard-pressed to figure out all the familial players and relationships in the company. She had told him that if you analyzed the *shinseki,* the networks of households, you could find scores of businesses. They were bedfellows—literally. Like royal lineages of old, marriages of ranking families were arranged to strengthen positions. By American thinking, the result was almost incestuous. It was also tough to beat. These days American firms never compete against one company; they compete against a consortium. In Japan, whenever an important marriage is announced, the newspapers routinely document the network of *shinseki.* Marriages can mean a mating of major automotive and electronic concerns, with kissing cousins in chemicals and computers and other enterprises—even hotels.

"Interrupting your metamorphosis?" asked Am. He liked to tease Sharon that she was turning Japanese.

"Call me Madama Butterfly," she said.

"That explains it," he said. "Today felt like an opera."

"Do tell. Or would you prefer singing?"

"Wailing," he emphasized, then explained, letting out his whale song.

He talked about life and death, about business and business cards, and working in an "occupied Hotel." Am and Sharon had met at the Hotel California. She had arrived as a hospitality spy, had worked there gathering information before Am found her out. He still insisted that what she had done was unethical; she conceded only some gray area. The Japanese had to know everything about any business they were interested in buying, she had explained. It was almost a compulsion with them. According to her, the Japanese loved data more than sushi, and their information networks rivaled those of the CIA, KGB, British Intelligence, and Mossad. These days, though, Sharon's Mata Hari days were over, unless helping Am figure out how to navigate the

Japanese cultural maze qualified her as a double agent. Her advice came with a price, though, payment doled out by Am in the form of a Japanese folktale. Sometimes she called him "My Scheherazade-zuki." It was about as close to an endearment as she was offering these days.

"Kipling was right," finished Am in his lament, "when he said, 'Oh, East is East, and West is West, and never the twain shall meet.' "

"I suppose you're talking about the same Kipling," said Sharon, "who in one sentence managed to be sexist, racist and imperialist, when he wrote, 'Take up the White man's burden.' "

"Change the word 'white' to 'yellow' and we have the unspoken mind-set of the Japanese, don't we?"

"The Japanese don't think of themselves as being yellow," said Sharon. "They consider themselves wheat-colored."

"Wheat-colored," said Am. "I supposed that makes sense. Don't they always go around saying America is their granary?"

The exact quote, oft repeated in Japan, is that Europe is their boutique, and America their farm.

"And you don't like being a farm boy?"

"I don't like being treated like a boy."

She had told him before that the Japanese were the most prejudiced race on the planet, had even conceded that many of their business designs were imperialistic in nature. And yet Sharon admired many things about Japan and the Japanese, including their accomplishments, their drive, their industriousness, their innate curiosity, and their culture.

"Then don't act like the American stereotype that they believe in: loud, whining, and uneducated."

"What? And disappoint them?"

Sharon had told him before how the Japanese public schools ran 240 calendar days per year, as opposed to 180 days in the United States. She had a lot of facts like those at her command, enough for him to refer to her sometimes as "Tokyo Rose."

She was pragmatic, with a business head, and he was the philosopher and dreamer. Her roots were East Coast and upper class. He had never lived more than half a mile from the Pacific. And yet Am remembered how only a few months back they had connected. They had—had— twained. Oh, how they had twained. Maybe Kipling was wrong. Sharon must have felt his hope and his ache.

"I have no time for *ren'ai*, Am Caulfield," she said. "You have to start going out with other women."

"What's *ren'ai?*"

"Romantic love," she said.

"I'm surprised the Japanese even have a word for such a thing," he said.

"Don't stoop to their level," she said. "Don't automatically assume the worst. Surprise them, farm boy. Who knows? Maybe they'll even surprise you."

"Is this sayonara?"

"Not before my folktale."

"You wouldn't consider phone sex instead?"

She didn't answer. Eventually, Am told her about the two elderly neighbors, the one honest and good, and the other black-hearted and evil. They saw each other on the road just before the new year, and the subject of their new year's dream was raised. For the Japanese, the first dream of the new year is very propitious, foretelling what is to be.

"A few days later," Am said, "the neighbors saw each

other again and compared their dreams. The honest old man said that he had dreamed that luck would come to him from the heavens, while the vile old man said in his dream he had seen that luck would come to him from the earth.

"That very day the honest old man started tilling the earth on a field he shared with the evil old man, only to find a huge jar full of coins. He decided that this was the fulfillment of his neighbor's dream, and that the right thing for him to do was to go and tell him about his find. He tromped next door and told the evil old man about the booty that awaited him, then went home to warm himself in front of a fire.

"The evil man hurried over to the site. As he turned the buried jar toward him, he was overjoyed to hear the sound of clinking gold. But instead of finding coins inside it, he found it was full of writhing snakes. Vowing revenge, the evil man carried the jar over to his neighbor's house. He climbed a ladder that was propped alongside the house and, straining with his load, made it up to the roof. Looking down through the smoke vent, the evil old man could see his neighbor and his wife warming themselves. The sight incensed him. He hoisted the jar up over his head and decided to dump all the snakes atop the good man and his wife. But when he overturned the container, it wasn't snakes that fell into the room, but coins of silver and gold.

" 'Isn't it wonderful!' cried the honest old man, as the room filled with lucre. 'First our neighbor receives his luck from the earth, and now we receive our luck from heaven!' "

Sharon didn't say anything for several moments. Maybe, Am thought, he could have chosen a better story. With a little doubt, and a little defensiveness, Am announced,

"Japanese folktales aren't necessarily like Aesop's, or Hans Christian Andersen's."

"I wouldn't expect them to be," said Sharon. "I was just thinking about the story. Thank you for sharing your pennies from heaven."

Cued, he offered his own good-bye. He wanted to tell Sharon that she had been his new year's dream, but that would have been a lie. If he remembered correctly, he had dreamed about the Hotel. Was it a sweet dream? He couldn't recall, could only remember his having to work through a hangover the next day.

Chapter Eight

Mass transit is not something considered synonymous with Southern California, but it was Am's preferred method of getting to work, partly because he enjoyed the pleasant bus ride along the coast, and partly because he didn't have to explain himself to Annette. But today he needed to drive, reason enough to plead.

"Going to La Jolla Strand," he told his car, using the same kind of tone you would to mollify the gods.

Annette was a 1951 Ford Station Wagon, but not just any station wagon. She was a "woody," a wood-paneled wagon. Am had bought her under false pretenses, had figured only to hold on to her a few months before getting a nice return on his investment. That never happened. Anyone who owns a collectible soon learns that Emily Post could have written a three-volume set on dos and don'ts. Am figured that owning a Frank Lloyd Wright house was about the same thing as owning a woody in Southern California. You don't add an indoor Jacuzzi or a sundeck to a Wright house. It's inviolable. And you don't just treat a woody like you would any car. Am claimed he would have sold Annette years back if it hadn't been for his neighbor

Jimbo, who liked nothing better than working on her and keeping her in "bitchin' trim." Whenever Am mentioned that he was thinking of selling her, people responded as if he were spitting on the flag. They didn't know about, or wouldn't believe, her quirk. Annette drove fine if you didn't take her far from the coast, preferably within sight of it. Stray from that route, and she quickly let you know you were on the road to hell.

Luckily, the drive from Del Mar to La Jolla is most easily navigated along the coast. Annette cantered along Old 101, her V-8 purring and easily taking the grade up Torrey Pines. Temperamental? she seemed to be saying. Not me.

The scenic drive was lost on Am that morning. He had risen very early and purchased copies of the San Diego *Union-Tribune,* the *Los Angeles Times,* and the *Blade-Citizen.* All three newspapers had devoted a good deal of black ink to the life and times of Dr. Thomas Kingsbury. Or was that lives and times? Kingsbury had been a doctor, a researcher, a magician, and a psychic/paranormal investigator. "When I was a healer," he was quoted as saying, "it was unacceptable for me to give up on a patient. I resented being stymied by the incurable, and the unknown. I went into research to open doors. I went into the miracles business. That's when I really started to resent the phonies. I saw too many scientists giving their all only to be eclipsed by pseudo-science charlatans. I saw the sick being preyed upon, false hopes being dangled for dollars. Every society needs their Totos pulling back the curtains on disingenuous wizards. I made it my mission to promote reason and rationality, and expose snake oil and cosmic dust."

The portraits the newspapers provided made Am wonder just whose death he was investigating. Was it Dr. Thomas Kingsbury, dedicated hematologist; Thomas Kingsbury,

M.D., research scientist; Tommy Gunn the Magician; or Dr. Tom, the avenging angel? The man was a Rubik's cube. He had won a slew of awards, most for research unpronounceable to laymen; work with globulins, glutinins, hemoglobins, leukocytes, and polymerization. Kingsbury evidently never met a blood disease he wasn't interested in. Maybe that's why he had so vigorously pursued the claims of the exploitive paranormal; he couldn't stand bloodsuckers.

There had been occasional patches of fog along the drive, at first innocuous wisps, but a gray layer by the time Annette crossed the borders of north La Jolla. The June Gloom had staked its position along the coast as firmly as a desert dweller on a beach holiday. Am caught his first glimpse of the Hotel just above Scripps Institution of Oceanography, its telltale red tile roof a beacon through the haze. The Hotel stretched along the expanse of La Jolla Strand, forty acres of beach-front property. It had been housing guests for more than a hundred years, and during that time had undergone numerous expansions and renovations. What hadn't changed was the resort's many charms. A masterpiece does not age; it just adds myths.

Am parked Annette in Outer Mongolia, the employee parking lot that was far away from the Hotel, but relatively close to the security hut. He took a shortcut, a trail of his own making, cutting through the more circuitous flower-lined pathways. The Hotel's gardens were famous, from its towering palms to its colorful peonies. No walkway was without bird-of-paradise or hibiscus; no trellis without bougainvillea or mandevilla; no trail without roses or orchids. Any stroll was a floral seduction, the intoxicating scents of jasmine, honeysuckle, and gardenias commanding visitors to do as they should—stop and smell the flowers.

Am noticed the fragrances, but having served in the Hotel California's service for ten years, he was not so easily waylaid. He had bitten of the Hotel's apple long ago, thought of himself as far removed from innocence, but maybe he'd need to do some more chewing to get further knowledge of evil, and an understanding of why Dr. Kingsbury had been murdered.

The security hut was not on any recommended Hotel tour. It was removed from both the gardens and the ocean, no mean feat, as most of the Hotel managed both floral and aquatic vistas. Am was sure the location wasn't some accident. He suspected there was a direct correlation between the perceived importance of departments and their housing. The executive offices were fit to receive dignitaries, and had ocean views. The quarters for sales and marketing were expansive, with museum-like displays; purchasing and accounting, located in the back of the house, looked high-tech enough to be a bookie operation; and catering, in its garden setting, was a cornucopia of exhibitions, with pictures of food, weddings, and meeting rooms, and samples of fruits, chocolates, and cookies. ("Offer them most of the seven sins when they walk in," the catering manager had once explained, "and you'll book the function every time.")

Where was the security hut? It was the last stop on a poorly asphalted path (only legs, or utility carts, could navigate it) closed to guests. Its nearest neighbors were groundskeeping and gardening, but it was clear those two departments considered security the country cousin. Am's predecessor in his job, Chief Horton, had often proclaimed, "In the priority of things, security at the Hotel is considered lower than a snake's fart." The Chief had always found it difficult to speak without some reference to flatulence.

The transition from hotel management to hotel security had not been an easy one for Am. He was used to being involved in the important decisions of the property. Formerly, he had to be concerned about everything that went on in the Hotel, a situation almost analogous to trying to control the workings of a mini-city. His responsibilities were now much more limited, even if many departmental heads were still in the habit of calling on him for help. He had considered resigning, but had found it difficult to end his relationship with the Hotel, telling himself it wasn't quite the right time yet. "I haven't suffered enough," he said, usually with a laugh, an explanation that sufficed for most. The truth was an onion he didn't pick at. From the first, he had felt at home in the Hotel. As it had done to so many others, the Hotel had enchanted him.

Am walked into the security hut. Flanders was on dispatch. He had gone through most of a box of jelly doughnuts sitting in front of him; strawberry, from the look of his shirt. Flanders looked like John Belushi in his last days; bloated, unkempt, and borderline demented.

"Do not pass go," said Flanders. "Do not collect two hundred dollars. General Tojo's called three times in the last five minutes. He wants you over in the executive offices pronto, Tonto."

Tojo, aka Takei. "Did he say what he wanted?" asked Am.

"No," said Flanders. "But by the teakettle sounds coming out of his teeth, I'd say it was your ass."

Yes, thought Am, the Hotel enchanted him. The only problem was that he could never be sure if it was a good spell or a bad spell.

Chapter Nine

One thing that could be said for Takei, no matter how early you arrived at work, he was already there toiling away. As far as Am was concerned, that was reason enough to dislike him.

Takei was waiting for him outside the executive offices. He didn't try and hide his anger, didn't try to ritualize his displeasure. The man was almost turning American, and Am wasn't sure he liked that.

"When I arrive," he said, "I find another young man sitting in my office."

So, thought Am. Someone had finally beaten Takei to work.

"He had the same story as the others," said Takei. "I tell him there is a mistake, and that he should remove himself from my office, but he will not leave."

That was a first, thought Am. His predecessors had quickly vacated Takei's office when asked to leave.

"He say that he was hired as the manager," said Takei. "I tell him more than a few times that that position is already taken."

Takei's tone was firm. The unsaid echo was there might be an opening in security very soon.

"I'll take care of it," said Am.

"You tell me that before, three, four times. Did you call the authorities like I suggest? The FBI?"

Am got the feeling that Efrem Zimbalist, Jr., was still headlining on reruns in Japan. "We're talking about serial hiring," said Am, "not serial murdering."

Takei's face went white. "This is not a funny thing," he said, "even if everyone seems to think so."

Somewhere in that somber statement Am heard a child's cry of "Everybody is laughing at me." That explained why, from appearances at least, Takei was more alarmed about this situation than he was by Dr. Kingsbury's death. In Japan few things are more important than saving face.

"I'll get back your office for you," said Am. "And I'll try to get answers. Maybe this one noticed more than the others."

"If he did not, what will you do?"

Am almost said, "I'll perform *seppuku* in the lobby," but instead replied, "I'll come up with a new plan."

It would have been more accurate had Am announced he would simply come up with a plan. What he had been hoping was the practical joker would tire of his game. But this prankster was single-minded, if nothing else.

The kid was sitting in Takei's leather chair. He looked as Am expected, about eighteen or nineteen, and still in the market for acne cream. Diana Wade was talking to him, trying to put the young man at ease. Takei's administrative assistant was getting all too used to these kinds of situations, and was hard-pressed not to show her amusement.

"Hi, Di," Am said.

Diana was new to the Hotel, one of the few recent additions that Am approved of. She was a single mother successfully raising two young boys, which meant she was basically unflappable. Her job, Am had heard her say, was the easy part of her day.

"Hi, Am. I've got another new boss. This one's named Larry Young."

The kid was the fourth GM to announce himself in the past month. There was a similarity to all of the pretenders to the throne. They were eighteen to twenty years old, equal parts cocksure and unsure. All of them had applied for a job at the Hotel, any job. Apparently someone had managed to purloin their applications. The young men had been called and arrangements made to meet them at a site off the property. The mystery interviewer had been uniformly impressed with all of the candidates. Their intelligence, their acumen, and their character had in every instance astounded the bogus human-resources director. He had told the applicants that they were not just suited for any job, but the top job. They were to be hired as general manager. It was the kind of story which only a young man could believe, could swallow without too many questions. It didn't totally surprise them that someone else confirmed what they had always suspected: they were very special.

"Hi, Larry," said Am. "My name is Am."

Am offered his hand, but it wasn't accepted enthusiastically. "Mr. Fletcher," said Larry, "warned me about you. He said I shouldn't listen to either you or Mr. Takei."

"Fletcher" was elaborating on his practical joke. That wasn't good news as far as Am was concerned. Now he was even coaching the pretenders to the throne. The kid was wearing his defensiveness. It fit about as well as his sports jacket, which was a couple of sizes too large for him, probably his father's. The tie he was wearing had gone out of style about the year he was born.

"What else did Fletcher tell you?" asked Am.

"That you and others would be jealous. That you'd try and confuse me, and trick me into thinking there had been some mistake about my being hired."

"And what were you supposed to do while all this trickery was going on?"

"Remain in this office and wait for Mr. Yamada. He's going to explain everything to all of you."

Am sighed. The staff thought these periodic visits by the "new" managers were hilarious, but the joke wasn't only on Takei; the kid was involved too. He was serious, and his lip was trembling a little. Everything was going like the script he had been presented, a script Am was beginning to resent more and more.

"And what did Mr. Fletcher tell you to do if we insisted you leave this office?"

Larry was never going to be wearing a Phi Beta Kappa key, but he seemed a nice enough fellow. He hadn't yet learned business poker, how to hold cards, and bluff, and up the ante. "He said that I should refuse. That I was just to wait for Mr. Yamada."

Fletcher undoubtedly thought that involving the Fat Innkeeper would make his joke that much more special.

"And now that you're sitting here, Larry, does that advice, or anything else Mr. Fletcher told you, make any sense?"

The teen didn't respond, but he sure did seem to be thinking. He face showed his growing doubts.

"We don't know who this Mr. Fletcher is," said Am.

"The only thing we do know is that he is obviously angry with the Hotel, and is using young men like you to get back at us. I could call for help. There are a few people on this staff who'd probably enjoy dragging you screaming out of this office, but that's not what I want to do."

The kid sank into the chair. "I just came here looking for a job," Larry said. "A good job."

Fletcher had played on a universal fantasy. The Horatio Alger rags-to-riches through hard-work stories have never been as popular in this country as the Rita Hayworth fables. To be human is to await discovery, whether at a Schwab's drugstore or at a bus stop. Larry had been seduced by a Publishers Clearing House mentality, the idea that fate's finger had just been itching to tap him on the shoulder. Naïveté was the only requirement for the "job" he had landed.

"I can't promise you a job," said Am, "good or otherwise. But I can get you an interview with Linda Gold, the Hotel's *real* human-resources director."

Am's offer didn't immediately win the kid over. Maybe he really was GM material. But it did prevail over the histrionics that Fletcher obviously wanted. Larry reluctantly rose from his chair. He'd recover. We all find out about Santa Claus someday.

"No one's in personnel yet," said Am. "How about I buy you a cup of coffee first?"

Larry preferred cocoa to coffee, and asked for extra marshmallow topping. At first he was quiet, perhaps a little ashamed, but then he began to open up to Am, asking him questions about the Hotel. Am forgot about Larry's youthfulness, and how his belief system was still intact. Am didn't take things with a grain of salt, just assumed he was dealing with Lot's wife unless he discovered otherwise. When Larry asked him how long he had worked in the hotel business, Am told him he wasn't sure whether he should answer in human years or dog years. His cynical assessments on life, and the hotel industry in general, scared Larry.

"I'm beginning to think," said the young man, "that I shouldn't apply for any job here."

The kid's solemn pronouncement made Am feel like a pretty bad career counselor. "Look," he said, "if you're a people junkie, working in hotels can be a great job. Next to being a parish priest, I can't think of another profession that allows you to help mankind more. At times you feel like you're being paid to be a good Samaritan. It's a job where the psychic income can be very high. Recently I helped Dr. Jonas Salk book some rooms for his friends. No, I didn't create the polio vaccine, but at the Hotel California you get to experience a lot of secondhand immortality."

"Who's Dr. Salk?" the kid asked.

God, thought Am. I'm that next generation. That's one thing Southern California doesn't give courses in—how to be middle-aged.

Am took out his notepad. It was time to play the house dick. Larry had applied for a job at the Hotel ten days ago. Human resources had supplied him with an application. He had been told to fill it out, and that he would be contacted if an opening became available. Larry had left his completed application atop an empty counter. He figured that the woman who had helped him would process it when she returned. That didn't narrow Am's list of suspects, as human resources was a frequently visited department and anyone could have walked in and picked up Larry's application.

Larry said that he had been called three days ago by a man who identified himself as Mr. Fletcher, head of human resources. He had agreed to meet with Mr. Fletcher at a nearby Denny's, was told to look for a man wearing a carnation. Fletcher had explained he liked conducting his interviews away from the Hotel so as to put the candidates at ease. Am had heard the same story from all the others Fletcher had "hired."

Fletcher always remained seated during his interviews, making it impossible for anyone to guess his height. Am couldn't be sure whether he was dealing with the same individual, or a cabal of personnel-director imitators. Copycat hirings might be a new fad for Hotel employees. So far Fletcher had been a blond, a brunet, and a redhead, and his complexion had ranged from pasty to tanned. He was said to be between forty-five and sixty-five. The only thing that had remained the same was his made-up name, and the enthusiastic use of his hands. The man liked to gesture, to use his digits in operatic form.

Any distinguishing marks? No, said the kid. Anything that made Fletcher stand out? No.

Any reason for me to be optimistic about figuring out who the imposter is? thought Am. No.

Chapter Ten

The fog was showing signs of lifting, which on this morning wasn't necessarily a very good thing.

The whale wasn't improving with age, and that was playing havoc with the Hotel. For once, Am found himself grateful for being removed from the rigors of the front desk. Beleaguered clerks had told him that virtually everyone in the Hotel was asking for new room assignments. All of the guests were convinced there had to be a better room location, somewhere upwind from the whale.

City crews were on the scene trying to figure out what to do with thirty tons of putrefying mammal. Apparently they didn't have the kind of equipment that could just raise up the whale and haul it away. The word was that some vivisection was going to be necessary. The sight of a whale being butchered on the beach would undoubtedly stir up the guest hornet nest once again.

Despite the smell, the beach was crowded with the curious. There was a lot of picture taking going on, Lilliputians excited by the presence of the whale. The park and recreation department had sequestered off the area around the whale. Yellow "Do Not Cross" tape was rapidly becoming a part of the Hotel colors. Am hoped the Hotel prankster wouldn't get it into his mind to paint a white outline of the whale in the sand after it was removed.

The boardwalk was crowded, something that usually only happened during the summer. There was gridlock along the beach wall closest to the whale. Among the spectators was a familiar face, and a familiar tail. Wallace Talbot was out for a walk with his black cocker spaniel Cinder. For more than half a century Wallace had lived at the Hotel. He acted like a character out of the silent films, was famous for his courtly gestures and fanciful ways. Wallace was wearing a colorful ascot, a French beret, and a white poplin suit. On another man the clothes might have looked foppish, but it was an outfit Wallace wore well.

Between man and dog, and trying to avoid being tripped up by the leash, was an attentive woman Am assumed was an artist. More and more painters were now seeking Wallace out. He must be gratified, thought Am, that his art was finally being recognized on a national, if not international, level. Most of Wallace's canvases featured the vistas of the La Jolla Strand. He had done more than a thousand paintings of the area, but the octogenarian claimed he had "barely scratched the surface of its possibilities." Am hoped a dead whale wasn't going to emerge from his brush anytime soon.

Am worked his way forward to say hello. As he drew nearer, he began to reevaluate his assumption that the woman was an artist. The sketchpad and brush he had thought she was holding turned out to be a pen and memo book. A purse was hanging from one shoulder, and a small tape recorder from the other.

Reporter, Am thought. Probably doing a story on Wallace Talbot. But on the odd chance she wasn't . . .

Am started to turn away, but Wallace espied him. "Holden," he yelled. "Don't be shy." To make sure of his capture, Wallace released Cinder. She went to Am straightaway, trained by the many treats he had brought her over the years. Even though his hands were empty, she was still glad to see him. She settled her head between his fingers, confident of a good scratching.

With his usual theatrical air, Wallace motioned with his arms in grand sweeps while making introductions. "Holden Caulfield," he said, "also known by the enigmatic first name of Am, I'd like you to meet Marisa Donnelly."

Am was used to Wallace calling him Holden, after *The Catcher in the Rye*'s Holden Caulfield. Salinger's character had obviously impressed Wallace, for he always gave the name special emphasis, as if it were a title. As far as Am was concerned, it was significantly better than *Urechis caupo*.

"Pleased to meet you," said Am, shaking her hand. Marisa was not the kind of woman Am usually ran away from. She was about thirty, had a smooth olive complexion, raven hair, and large green eyes. Her eyebrows were dark and thick, her hair long and slightly wavy. Marisa's white and shapely teeth, set off by rose gums, should have been used to promote some toothpaste, that, or her all-too-brief smile could have been the basis for a lot of UN accords.

"Holden is the Hotel's glue," explained Wallace. "Every great hotel needs its magic, and Holden is the magician that makes everything right."

"Security director," said Marisa, reading his name tag.

"Catcher in the rye," announced Wallace.

"Formerly assistant general manager of the Hotel," explained Am, "but currently assigned to the safety and security department." It wasn't that Am felt he had to apologize for his job, or at least not exactly. But some people assume you are what you work.

"Marisa is a reporter with the *Union-Tribune*," said Wallace.

"Formerly an editor at Harcourt Brace Jovanovich," she said.

Am felt better. He wasn't the only one explaining.

"She's out here doing a story on our unexpected visitor," explained Wallace.

"Actually," she said, "I'm here on two stories. Since I was already at the Hotel covering the UNDER convention, I was told to write a sidebar piece on the whale."

For a moment, Am almost asked her if she had written the story on Dr. Kingsbury's death. He had assumed that most of the information had come from the obituary on file. You know you've made it, he thought ruefully, when newspapers already have your obituary written up. None of the newspaper stories had even hinted that Kingsbury's death could have resulted from anything other than natural causes. That was the way McHugh wanted it, and Am as well. Reporters would only cloud the investigative waters.

"So," she said, "for the record, how have your guests been reacting to the whale?"

Am lied. He said that they had been very understanding, had been good sports about the whole thing. Why, said Am, one guest had commented that this would be some whale of a tale to tell all of his friends.

Marisa clicked off her tape recorder. "Am," she said, "must be short for Am-nesia. I just came from the front desk. There were people there asking for refunds and reduc-

tion in rates. It looked like there were droves of early check-
outs, and there was one man even threatening to sue. And
everybody, I mean everybody, wanted to move to another
room."

"Really?" said Am.

"Not going to help me win my Pulitzer, are you?"

Am tilted his head toward the unmoving mountain of
whale. "Unless you can prove that whale's Moby Dick," he
said, "I wouldn't start working on any acceptance speech."

"Maybe the autopsy will show something."

Was Am imagining it, or was there a double meaning in
her tone? And was she watching him closely to gauge his
reaction, or was that just a friendly glance?

"Sorry to dash any hopes," said Wallace, "but as both of
you surely know, the White Whale was a sperm whale,
whereas this one has already been identified as a gray
whale."

"Better luck with your next investigative story," said
Am.

"Oh," she said sweetly, sizing him up for a final harpoon,
"I haven't given up on this one yet."

Chapter Eleven

Anyone who has worked in hotels for a few years wouldn't have much trouble leaving the business to set up shop as an experienced psychic. Being a good reader of the human trade is an important part of the hotel craft. Much in the way a doctor examines patients, so does hotel staff observe guests, the body human announcing itself in various ways to both professions. In a glance, an adept clerk can often anticipate a skipper, a complainer, or a midnight party. They can sense friend or foe, and all the gray areas between, their call usually based on their five senses, though those outside the business would swear such prognosticating to be a product of their sixth sense.

Often, hotel employees can't even tell you why they anticipated a certain behavior, especially as they work in a business where there are no givens, where appearances deceive as often as they enlighten. "When a man tries to hide the fact that he's got a limp," one hotel veteran had told Am, "that limp will show up in other places." Am had learned how one guest with paint-splattered pants and a threadbare sweater had turned out to own most of Oklahoma City, while another guest, decked out with an Armani suit, and the trappings of a Rolex watch, Louis Vuitton luggage, and most of Fort Knox around his neck, was a cabdriver with a lot of debts. The revelations confirmed what Am had intuitively suspected. Gilbert and Sullivan created the lyrics, but the hotel business is often testament to them: "Things are seldom what they seem, Skim milk masquerades as cream." The consummate hotel professional has to see beyond appearance. Kingsbury, thought Am. Skim, or cream, or in between?

Detective McHugh had the resources of the San Diego Police Department behind him. He had the trace evidence team, and the forensics lab. He had local, state, and national computer banks. He had a team of investigators. Am had a hotel bill. To an experienced translator, though, hotel charges can be the Rosetta stone to a guest's soul.

Kingsbury had stayed at the Hotel for three nights, had died before he could spend his fourth night there. He had managed to dine at all four of the Hotel's restaurants, an indication that the doctor enjoyed trying new dining spots (that, or he hadn't been impressed enough with any of the Hotel eateries to want to dine in the same restaurant twice). His meals were for amounts that made Am believe the doctor had not eaten alone, something he'd have to check on.

The doctor's Hotel bill was relatively debit-free. He had availed himself of few of the Hotel's temptations, hadn't played tennis, or used the pitch and putt course, or charged in any of the Hotel's shops with the exception of the sundry store, and there for only a minimal purchase of four dollars and twenty-six cents. Kingsbury had taken no tours. He hadn't participated in aerobics, dance lessons, or jazzercize, hadn't had any facials, massages, or body wraps.

Kingsbury had managed, though, in his short stay, to

visit three of the six Hotel lounges, one of them on two occasions. He had made seven long-distance calls, and dialed
up four local numbers. He had sent three faxes, and received two in return. And he had watched one in-room
movie. Which one? Am tapped out his query. Unless requested by the guests, the movie names were not printed on
the final bill, just the charges for them. There was a reason
for that, a reason that appeared on the screen. The doctor
had taken time from his scientific inquiries to watch *Tea for
Three,* one of the soft-porn offerings currently available to
the guests.

He had been busy, thought Am. Dining, drinking, interviewing, attending the conference, getting and receiving
faxes, making calls, and even taking in a prurient picture.
And dying.

The Hotel's property-management system allowed Am a
lot of fingertip information, but he wasn't content to try
and divine everything from a video-display terminal. He
preferred looking at the paper charges, the more scribbles
and ketchup stains, the better. Before the advent of computers, Am had often read just such tea leaves to decipher
signatures, or figure out where the charge belonged. He
called up the accounting department and asked for Ward
Ankeney, the controller. Ward claimed he had been at the
Hotel "since the cigar box and pencil ledger-entry days."
Like Am, he knew there were times when the computer
couldn't tell you everything. He didn't question Am's need
to look at the charges, just said they would be available to
him by early afternoon.

Am's phone rang. The display showed that Janet DeSilva
was calling from sales and marketing. For a moment Am
was tempted to let his voice mail take a message. He had

been given the rare privilege of a few undisturbed minutes at work, and was now eager for a few more. Janet had taken over for Kim Yamamoto in sales several months earlier. Ironically Kim, who was third-generation American Japanese, had said her departure was due in part to her not wanting to work for "old world Japanese." Janet's ascendancy to sales and marketing director hadn't been without its problems. Around the Hotel, Janet was getting to be known as "Dammit, Janet." Someone had taped a sign to her door which said, *"Your* Lack of Planning Does Not Constitute *My* Emergency." Many "someones" had agreed with the short-lived editorial.

"We have a problem, Am."

"What—did another whale wash up on the beach?"

"Worse," she said.

"I'll be right over."

Chapter Twelve

Being greeted by the sounds of someone sobbing isn't the most welcoming of receptions. Kate Kennedy was at her desk making fast work of a box of tissues. Janet was hovering nearby, ostensibly offering comfort to the crying woman, but from appearances she didn't trust her hands anywhere near Kate's neck.

"Thanks for coming, Am," said Janet.

There was a third figure in the office. Melvin Carrelis was carefully taking notes. The Hotel's legal counsel met Am's eyes and nodded. Oh, God, Am thought. Whenever Melvin surfaced, it was never a happy occasion. He always wore his black suits as if to accentuate that point. Even for a lawyer, Melvin seemed slippery. He was balding, but in denial, letting the rest of his dark hair grow long. Melvin had a large nose that he liked to lead with. Whenever he talked, he moved his nose; forward, side to side, thrusting, parrying. Am had once met Mrs. Carrelis at a party. She had told him, "When I married Melvin, I thought he was a Greek god. Now I think he's a goddamn Greek." At the time of her pronouncement, Mrs. Carrelis wasn't feeling any pain.

"Kate," said Janet, "why don't you acquaint Am with the situation?"

Situation. Even Janet's delicate phrasing made it sound like a disease. A communicable disease. Kate had been with the Hotel for less than a year. She was a strawberry redhead several years removed from her sorority, but the weaning process was slow. This was the first time Am had seen Kate without a smile, and without makeup, which had been swept away by her own flood. Am had known she had freckles, but had never imagined she had so many.

"Ammididnaminto. Mishtakemymymishtake."

Kate's speech sounded vaguely Japanese. Am looked to Janet for a translation. "Kate made a mistake," she said. "We all did. A few months ago we revised some of the group contracts. In streamlining them, we omitted a few minor sections."

"Omitted," interjected Melvin, pressing his nose forward, "with the understanding that there would be an oral follow-through."

Am had the feeling that Melvin had been repeating that point over and over. Janet conceded his remark with upraised hands and a sigh. Kate chose to sob a little more.

"In the course of any booking," Janet said, "we're supposed to ask certain questions. Kate didn't ask those questions, and I didn't scrutinize her booking.

"And," she added, "Melvin deleted a line that's been in our contracts since time immemorial."

The nose recoiled slightly. "Objection," he said. (This was probably as close to a trial as Melvin had ever been.) "I was told that as a matter of course there was a line of inquiry that each sales agent had to perform. Those questions,

I was assured, were to be answered in full prior to the signing of the contract. In this instance . . ."

"They weren't," said Janet, mercifully abbreviating
Melvin's courtroom speech.

Janet handed Am the contract, and the group prospectus.
He flipped through the pages, searched for what had caused
the distress, but didn't see anything out of the ordinary.
The Swap Meat was the name of the group. They had
booked seventy-two guest rooms for three nights. They
were utilizing two meeting rooms, the Neptune room and
the Sea Horse Hall, with several meals and functions scheduled. The individuals were to pay on their own, but first-
night deposits had been tendered for all the guest rooms.
The only unusual request Am could see was that The Swap
Meat had requested as many interconnecting rooms as possible.

He handed the papers back to Janet. "What's the problem?"

"Apparently," she said, "we're hosting a swingers' convention."

"Swingers?"

"I don't mean chimps," she said. "We're talking about
mate swapping. Multiple sexual partners."

"How . . . ?" Am asked, searching out eyes while stretching the question. He must have lingered too long on Kate,
who started to blubber once again.

"Kate assumed they were a gathering of swap meet organizers," said Melvin, nose slightly up. "It wasn't a case of
them misleading. It was just that the right questions were
not asked."

By repeating that line often enough, Melvin undoubtedly hoped to construct a lead lining for his ass. For the last

five years he had been the Hotel's final word on the law, even if he wasn't exactly on the track to a Supreme Court nomination. His legal matriculation had come from a downtown San Diego law-degree mill. Somehow he had passed the state bar. In a weak moment, Melvin had once admitted it had taken him "several attempts."

Am made the mistake of turning back to Kate, heard her sobs start to redouble, and then settled for Janet. "It was one of Kate's first sales," said Kim. "We went over the importance of getting the money in advance, of making out a rooming list, and having the contract signed. I remember complimenting her on the booking. We booked them at full price."

In most hotels there is a rack rate, and then a tiered tariff structure. Travelers often avail themselves of the corporate rate, or commercial rate, or group rate, or any of a dozen other enticing names that signify a special rate. Some hotels resemble flea markets more than inns, where the negotiating of a room rate compares (sometimes unfavorably) to dealing with the vendors along Avenida Revolución in Tijuana. Am had heard of one hotelier that had sought professional help for a persistent nightmare. In the man's dream his guests were gathered at the hotel lounge, where the subject of room rates surfaced, and comparisons were made. The wide disparity of the rates proved not only a revelation to the guests, but a cause for anger. Everyone thought they had the "special special," just as everyone thinks he knows where the pea is in a shell game. Fueled by righteous indignation, the guests began to riot. After breaking glasses and ravaging the bar, the lynch mob converged on the lobby. The hotelier apparently always awakened just as his office was being stormed.

"Why wasn't a history done on this group?" asked Am.

Before a hotel accepts business, it wants to make sure potential clients are solvent. Hotels also like to be reassured that their property will still be standing by the time the group leaves (though Am was willing to bet that most hotels would take a chance on booking Attila and his Huns, given a sizable cash deposit). As a matter of course, sales departments do a background check on those properties where groups have stayed before, attempting to determine if there were any problems associated with their stay. Many headaches are averted through such calls.

"We did a history on them," said Janet. "They last stayed at the Briar Inn. Their controller would only say that there was no damage, and that they paid their bill in full upon departure."

"Where's the Briar Inn?" asked Am. "In Sodom and Gomorrah?"

No one answered, unless Kate's wailing qualified as such.

Am turned to counsel. "So where's our loophole for terminating this gathering?" he asked.

Melvin avoided any eye contact. Even his nose movement was minimal. "Legally," he said, "we are setting ourselves up for the losing end of a lawsuit if we try to breach the contract, especially at this late date."

"Don't we have some kind of morals clause in our contract?"

"Hotels are hardly the bastions of morality," said Melvin.

"They're setting up the Neptune Room now," Janet said. "They're making it into an . . . orgy room."

"What?"

"I saw them getting it ready. That's when I discovered what was going on. I went there to meet with the two

group leaders, Mr. and Mrs. Lanier. They were busy putting
mats down on the floor, which I thought was a little unusual. Then I noticed the sounds coming from the four
large-screen televisions. Adult films were playing on all of
the monitors. The Laniers were oblivious, treated all the
screaming and groaning like it was elevator music, but you
should have seen all that was going on."

For a moment, Am was afraid that Janet was going to go
into details, but she caught herself, shook her head, and
tried to regain her thoughts.

"You know," asked Janet, "how they say you can't see the
forest for the trees? Well, I was so taken aback it took me a
while to see everything in front of me. Then I noticed that
the north side of the room had four tables full of sexual
paraphernalia. Some of the props are rather pronounced."

Am couldn't help it. He groaned.

"I was too shocked to talk. And being propositioned,
twice, in my very short time there, didn't help me get my
voice back.

"The offers came from *both* Mr. and Mrs. Lanier," she
said, with not a little emphasis.

Am didn't have a "tsk tsk" left in him. His mouth was
dry and his armpits were wet. The idea of the Neptune
Room being used for an orgy wasn't a pleasant one. Royalty
had been feted in the room. The worst thing Am had ever
heard happening in the Neptune Room was the food fight
between the eastern and western account representatives of
a major pharmaceutical company. It was said that the east
had won, but only because they commandeered the dessert
trays first.

The Neptune Room was part of the so-called Seven Seas,
seven meeting rooms of nautical names located on the north

side of the Hotel. Of all the Seven Sea banquet rooms, the Neptune Room was probably the least secluded. It had huge bay windows on both its west and east sides, and a lot of walk-by traffic. By keeping the curtains closed, the Hotel could try and control the sights, but how were they going to control the sounds? The sexcapades wouldn't go unnoticed. Explaining to guests would be bad enough, but what about the press? Given the questionable nature of Dr. Kingsbury's death, Am expected the Hotel would soon be awash with reporters. Damn if it didn't already have one nosing around. Am remembered the firm set of Marisa's jaw. She was on the hunt for something. A sex scandal would probably work for her as well as a murder. The banner headlines were easy to imagine. VENERABLE HOSTELRY HOSTS ORGY! HISTORIC HOTEL A BAWDY HOUSE! There were production and copy people who went to bed at night dreaming of such a story. Odd how the sweet dreams of some are the midnight sweats of others.

Am offered a long and painful sigh. You expect crazy things to go on at a hotel. In some ways, hotels even condone them. One hotel had gone so far as to advertise, "Have Your Next Affair Here." The copy was written around a display showing an ornate function, but the double entendre left room for thought, if nothing else.

Halfway into his ulcer, Am remembered that he wasn't Hotel management any longer. No one could tell him it was in his job description to stop an orgy.

"Why'd you call me?" asked Am. "Shouldn't you be talking with Mr. Fujimoto? Or Mr. Matsuda? Or Mr. Takei? Or the shogun himself, Mr. Yamada?"

"We're afraid to," admitted Janet. "Can you see us trying to explain group sex to the Japanese?"

"They might be easier than the Southern Baptists," said Am. That flock, he remembered, was also meeting in the Seven Seas, in a room just a stone's throw away from the swingers. He hoped that geographic distance would stay only figurative.

"I thought of calling you before anyone else, Am," said Janet. "You used to come up with all those clever outs. Everyone always admired how you pulled rabbits out of hats. You had names for your solutions . . ."

"Procrustean solutions," said Am. After Procrustes, the innkeeper who made his guests fit his beds, whether by stretching them or hacking them.

"Yes," she said. "You always had the magic touch."

Flattery was getting her somewhere. Am did pride himself on being the Houdini of the hotel world, pulling off miraculous escape after miraculous escape.

"What do you think about all of this, Melvin?" Am asked.

"I'm game for trying to handle it on our own," he said. "I've been reading up on Japan. Did you know the United States has more than half a million lawyers, while Japan has less than ten thousand? Maybe I'm paranoid, but I get the feeling our own Japan Incorporated doesn't think a Hotel counsel is necessary."

Especially a Hotel counsel that screws up on contracts.

"None of us want the Hotel to suffer," said Janet.

Translation, thought Am: None of us want to lose our jobs.

"We want the buck stopped here," said Melvin, with bobbing nose.

"No," said Am. "You want the fuck stopped there."

Kate started crying again, making Am feel guilty

enough to commit himself to help. "How many of their room block," he asked, with obvious reluctance, "have already checked in?"

"About half," said Janet. "The rest are arriving today. Most are coming in on a chartered bus from Las Vegas."

Where else? thought Am. He considered, then rejected, the idea of instructing the clerks to tell the remainder of the group that there were no rooms at the inn. Enough of the swingers were already in-house to make that strategy ineffective.

"They've got some welcoming dinner, don't they?"

"Yes," said Janet. "At seven tonight in the Sea Horse Hall."

"What's the entree?"

"Chicken divan."

"Salmonella poisoning," Am said. "If we can arrange that, it should put all of them out of commission."

"Am!" said Melvin, horrified.

"It's either that," Am said, "or saltpeter."

"Be sensible," said the lawyer.

"All right. We'll advertise the orgy on our reader board, and put the concierges in charge of selling tickets to other guests."

"S-samonella sowns gootome," sniffled Kate.

"Maybe we could reason with them," said Melvin.

"Sure," Am said. "Thank you for traveling from around the country, but now that you are here, we request that you call your group sex off. Just read your Gideon Bibles, and enjoy the view."

"I can't be a part of a Lucrezia Borgia solution," said Melvin.

"I wasn't really serious," said Am. He was almost con-

vinced of that. For a few moments he thought. Or was that
prayed? Saint Julian is the patron saint of the hotel business. Am had suggested on more than a few occasions that
the Hotel should provide Julian a shrine. Or did the entire
Hotel already qualify as that?

"Did you get this group their connecting rooms?"

Janet nodded. "We have them on the second and third
floors, with blocks of connecting rooms."

"Good," Am said. "That means we can quarantine them,
station personnel around their room blocks to make sure
things don't get out of hand. The last thing we want is a
French farce being played out throughout the Hotel.

"Not that we can afford to give them the impression that
they're not welcome. That would make them dig in their
heels, and quote their constitutional rights to life, liberty,
and the pursuit of libido. Ostensibly, we'll be rolling out
the bordello red carpet, and act like they're the most welcome group we have ever had.

"Reality won't be as pleasant as our lip service. Housekeeping will have to fix their rooms up special. All the
maids should have stogies and instructions to light up as
they prepare their rooms. We'll want to leave behind the
guest rooms from hell. Dirty linen, and towels from the rag
bags. One functioning lightbulb per room, and a twenty-
five watter at that. Old socks, or worse, in strategic places.
The picture of neglect should yell out from every corner of
every one of their rooms.

"You'll also need to coordinate with the front desk. Don't
connect any phone calls to the rooms. Take messages, and
make sure they're delivered hours later. Ring the rooms, at
least those phones that are still left operational, and then
apologize for having connected to the wrong room. Have

the clerks be as inefficient as possible. Tell them I know how expert they can be at that."

Am thought a moment. He had twenty years of guest complaints to work from. "Coordinate with room service. *If* the food arrives, make sure it's late and the order is all wrong. Room service should come without cutlery. You'll need to expand the conspiracy to all departments that might be called upon to go up to those rooms. We want everyone to appear happy to help, to show the same kind of eagerness two-year-olds bring to fingerpainting, and we want them to leave the same kind of mess. Any cure is to be worse than the disease."

Kate, Janet and Melvin were madly scribbling down notes. Am found himself taking a deep breath. It wasn't easy, he decided, organizing chaos. It went against his every instinct. He felt like a watchmaker smashing a watch.

"And I," he said, "will be conspiring with engineering about how best to put their two meeting rooms out of commission."

It wasn't uncommon for all fourteen of the Hotel meeting rooms to be used on the same day. Accidents and acts of God had happened before when all of them had functions scheduled. Am had faced up to the consequences of broken pipes, gas leaks, fires, storms, vandalism, and earthquake damage, had been forced to find alternate space for the meetings by utilizing restaurant space, converting connecting suites into meeting space, and on one occasion raising a big top. He had done whatever was possible to keep the show going.

"Janet and Kate, you'll need to make it appear that every other meeting room is being used. Put some bogus names on the reader board, then have them set up and arrange for staff to sit in them. Tell the Swap Meat how sorry you are, but say that you have no alternative meeting space. Act helpless and apologetic. Tell them these things happen. And keep saying, 'Have a nice day.'

"Oh," he said, remembering. "No toilet paper in any of the rooms. None at all. Explain there's a temporary shortage."

Kate's eyes were actually dry. There was a glimmer of a smile on her face. And Janet looked hopeful. Melvin appeared the happiest of all. There was a Rudolph glow to his nose. What was being proposed wasn't illegal, but it was unethical, terrain he was quite familiar with.

"How soon," asked Janet, "before the accidents occur in their meeting rooms?"

"About as quick," said Am, "as you can say, '*Coitus interruptus*'."

Chapter Thirteen

Cotton Gibbons had a lot of rules in his life, one of them
being that he never talked with management unless absolutely necessary. The maintenance man (he thought the
term "engineer" much too highfalutin, and would be
damned before he followed the suggested personnel—no,
human-resources—guidelines, which suggested maids be
called housekeepers, dishwashers be referred to as stewards,
and front-desk clerks be called guest service agents) didn't
trust anyone who wore a tie, figuring that a tool belt was
the only proper adornment to any wardrobe. It wasn't that
Cotton was a friend to the masses; truth to tell, he was generally surly to all. But he had decided, after ten years of
avoiding talking with Am, that they should now be friends.
It was not a friendship which Am actively cultivated. Cotton's sudden congeniality was promoted by what he perceived as Am's "raw deal." The line between offering
sympathy and voicing self-pity can sometimes be a thin
one, and it was a line that Cotton often crossed over. Am's
demotion fit well into Cotton's perception of the universe,
where the non-tool-users in ties tried to screw over the op-
pressed. That the new chieftains were Japanese was proba-

bly the greatest thing that could have ever happened to Cotton. They were the culmination of his finger pointing, the visible demons to his grasping theories. There was a new bumper sticker on Cotton's three-quarter-ton Chevy pickup: STOP THE WHALE KILLERS! BOYCOTT JAPANESE GOODS. It was not a bumper sticker in keeping with the others plastered to the vehicle, most of which had been supplied by the NRA and John Birch Society, nor was the conservation message easily squared with Cotton's rifle rack. "I was going to get a bumper sticker that said, 'Buy American,'" he confessed to Am, "but I didn't think that would piss *them* off enough."

Them was the ownership, and anyone vaguely resembling the ownership. There were many orientals on the Hotel staff, including Koreans, Filipinos, Chinese, Vietnamese, and Cambodians, countries that historically have little love for Japan. That didn't make a difference to Cotton. To him, *they* were all the same. Am tried to explain that most oriental cultures were very different, and that he might as well try lumping Americans with Bulgarians as Koreans with Japanese.

"They're all the same," Cotton had repeated.

Am remembered a joke, one he hoped had a didactic theme. "Two men at a bar," he said. "Mr. Chang and Mr. Steinberg, the one oriental, the other Jewish.

"Mr. Steinberg is clearly bothered. He starts muttering to himself, and gets angrier and angrier. After chugging down a few drinks, he comes to a decision. Raising himself from his barstool, he walks over to Mr. Chang, punches him in the face, and knocks him to the floor.

"Wagging his finger in Mr. Chang's face, Mr. Steinberg righteously announced: 'That's for Pearl Harbor.'

" 'But I'm not Japanese,' shouted Mr. Chang. 'I'm Chinese.'

" 'Japanese, Vietnamese, Chinese,' said Mr. Steinberg. 'What's the difference? You're all the same.'

"Mr. Steinberg turns around and walks back to his end of the bar. Picking himself up, Mr. Chang once more sits at the bar, but this time he's the one muttering to himself. He orders a few drinks, and with each one becomes angrier and angrier. Finally, he walks across the bar, faces Mr. Steinberg, and decks him with a single punch.

"Standing over him, Mr. Chang said, 'That's for the *Titanic.*'

" 'What do you mean?' asked Mr. Steinberg. 'It was an iceberg that sank the *Titanic.*'

" 'Iceberg, Weinberg, Steinberg,' " said Mr. Chang. 'What difference does it make? You're all alike.' "

Cotton was a little slow to laugh. By Am's reckoning about two weeks slow and counting. Rednecks, he thought, they're all alike.

Am heard Cotton before he saw him, his grumbling preceding him. They had agreed to meet at the Seal Wishing Well. There were three wishing wells on the property, one of many multiple landmarks at the Hotel that had confused and averted many a rendezvous.

"Painted whore," mumbled Cotton. "Heart of dry rot."

Cotton's terms of endearment were addressed to the Hotel, the same Hotel that was generally referred to as a "Grande Dame," or a "Stately Queen." By the nature of their job, the engineering department usually sees the Hotel at its worst. Cotton took the physical failings of the Hotel as a personal affront, as if he were being personally spited.

"Problem?" asked Am.

"Problem? Nothing more than the fucking Hotel's falling down."

Cotton had studied under Chicken Little. He was thin and tall, around fifty and a long way from mellow. His hair was still more black than gray. He didn't have a red neck, but he did have plenty of nose and ear hair that, to Am's knowledge, had never been harvested.

"Got some lighting that Edison must have put in that's gone bad."

Chronologically, Cotton wasn't off the mark by much.

"And got some clogged scuppers that I'd like to drop a couple of depth charges on."

Scuppers. One of those magical words that the engineering department could talk about for hours on end. There was a general fascination over such inanimate objects that Am thought bordered on the ridiculous. Scuppers. It was a subject Am needed to nip in the bud.

"I need your help," he said.

Cotton looked disinterested. Engineering hears "help" yelled more frequently than a 911 operator.

"It has to be done on the sly."

Things were sounding better, judging by Cotton's expression.

"I need you to take out two meeting rooms: the Neptune Room and Sea Horse Hall."

"Take out?" asked Cotton.

It sounded like a hit. "With extreme prejudice," said Am, intoning CIA emphasis.

Am offered Cotton the background, and the reasons why the rooms had to be temporarily put out of service. Cotton didn't need the reasons—he needed to be restrained.

"It has to look like an accident," Am cautioned, "and you can't cause any injuries. And no real damage, nothing that we can't fix up in a day or two."

"Leave it to me," said Cotton, a look of rapture on his face.

" 'Never make a toil of pleasure,' " quoted Am, " 'as Billy Ban said when he dug his wife's grave only three feet deep.' "

Cotton suddenly looked serious. Am figured it was his talk of graves.

"Scuppers," he announced. "First I'll take care of them, then I'll get on to the other."

Cotton left a happy man. Am wasn't quite so cheerful. Maybe there was a Mrs. Billy Ban in Kingsbury's life, someone not only glad to dig his grave, but motivated enough to kill him. Am needed to know those kinds of things, and felt a sense of failure that most of the morning had passed without his having been able to delve into the doctor's death. He had been waylaid by a pretender to the throne, a decomposing whale, and an impending orgy.

Scuppers, Am thought. Given the alternatives, maybe he could understand their attraction after all.

Chapter Fourteen

The ideal bellman is a Boy Scout grown up, but still in search of merit badges. Jimmy Mazzelli had never been a Boy Scout, nor was he an ideal bellman (or even "bell captain"—his preferred and self-appointed title).

Jimmy assumed his job was a license to hustle. He ran the Hotel football pools ("administrative fees" five percent), and was willing to take any bets on the side. Jimmy made it a point to stick his nose into everything going on at the Hotel, figuring it was to his advantage to keep up on all that was going on. In that way, and that way alone, he was like the Japanese, who firmly believe that information is power.

So just what information, Am wondered, was Jimmy passing on to Marisa Donnelly?

He moved closer to hear their conversation, but didn't even get within listening range before being noticed. Jimmy was the ultimate survivalist. One moment he was talking and combing his long, slicked-back hair, and the next he was running off, comb in hand, as if he were the anchorman on a baton relay team.

There are certain professions that cause a momentary reflection, even nervousness, to the average citizenry. The sudden appearance of law-enforcement officers, the IRS, the clergy, and the Fourth Estate tend to make even the upright take stock of their failings. The presence of Marisa Donnelly made Am think about the nearness of the Neptune Room. She was less than a hundred paces away from her sexposé.

Marisa approached Am. "Tit for tat," she announced. Or had she said, "Tit for tattle?"

Regardless, she had said tit. Dammit, he thought, she knows about the impending group grope. "It's being taken care of," said Am.

Her full, dark brows furrowed and became one. "What's being taken care of?"

Then again . . . "Uh, the whale."

"The big story of the day, right?"

She had used that same intonation earlier in the morning, a slight mocking that announced *they* knew that wasn't the real truth. He shrugged, not yet willing to play along.

"It's not even the first whale to make headlines in La Jolla," she said somewhat imperiously.

La Jolla, often touted as "the American Riviera," is a coastal enclave for the wealthy. It is the kind of city where even the local McDonald's takes on airs (the village wouldn't allow a McDonald's, but they did allow a boutique McSnacks). In La Jolla, whales do not make headlines nearly as often as fat cats.

"There was another beached whale here?" he asked.

"Not exactly. In 1918 a fishing boat was perched off the La Jolla kelp beds. The boat bumped into something, and then there was an explosion. It rained whale. The victims made it sound like a Texas gusher, except in this case it was rancid oil and blubber that poured down onto the deck of their boat. The smell, they said, made everyone sick. When the fishing party docked their boat, the stink cleared the pier.

"The exploding whale was the talk of San Diego. There was only one possible explanation for what had happened. During the first World War, a schooner had been commissioned to hunt whales around San Diego. There was a national shortage of fats and oils, so whales were targeted to give their lives to the cause. To expedite the slaughter, the schooner's harpoons were rigged up with bombs that were supposed to detonate on impact. Thousands of whales were taken in that way."

"But one got away."

Marisa nodded. "They figured the harpoon must have eventually killed the whale. It likely drifted into the kelp beds, where it became entwined. The bomb finally went off when the fishing boat jarred the whale."

"Score one for the whales," said Am.

"Now two," she said.

Am offered a wry smile. He was tempted to blow the dust off one of his old whale song LPs and ask Marisa if she wanted to come over and listen to it. He was even willing to bet she had a few of the same albums.

"Most people don't know it," she said, "but there was a time when the gray whales used to come to San Diego Bay to do their breeding. They say the bay was full of whales, that is, until whale hunting became a way of life around here. For over thirty years, from the 1850s to the 1880s, whaling was a San Diego industry. On Point Loma and North Island, whales were regularly towed in, butchered, and boiled."

Am had always thought of American whaling as something that had taken place in the Atlantic, something that was distinctly eastern. Maybe, he hoped, if the whales weren't bothered for a few more decades, they'd start using San Diego Bay as their nursery once again.

"Is San Diego's whaling history going to be in your story?" he asked.

She nodded.

"You'll make a lot of people feel guilty," he said.

"That's the point of most good stories," she said.

He heard the double meaning in her tone again. "Somehow," he said, "I don't think you and Jimmy Mazzelli were talking about whales."

"We weren't."

He didn't say anything for several seconds, and neither did she. "I'm investigating some rumors that are going around," Marisa finally said.

"What rumors?"

"If you couldn't give me an honest answer about how your guests felt about the beached whale, I don't figure you as a reliable source."

Am responded defensively. "I was looking out for the Hotel's best interests."

"You were lying," she said.

Am didn't like her words, but she was right. If you can't be honest about a dead whale, then what can you be honest about? He thought of offering several excuses, but didn't. "I'm sorry," he said.

His apology surprised her. She regarded him with new interest. It's been a while, he thought, since anyone's looked me over like that.

"One hundred and eighty-two pounds," he said.

"Huh?"

"That's what I weigh. I haven't been appraised by such gimlet eyes since going up against the weight guesser at the Del Mar Fair."

"I'm trying to weigh more than pounds."

"I hope you have better luck than he did."

"Oh?"

"He made the mistake of assuming I was lighter than I am."

Am didn't tell her that the prize he had won cost the carny barker less than the price of his guess, that the booth was set up as a no-win situation for the consumer. Maybe she already knew.

"For the record," he said, "many of our guests have felt discommoded by the whale."

"You're saying there's something rotten at the Hotel California?" she asked.

She offered Shakespeare, and her undertone. He wanted more than her cryptic dance. "I said what I said," allowed Am, "which is more than you have."

The prodding worked. "I've heard," she said, "that Thomas Kingsbury's death is suspicious."

The silver lining, he supposed, was that she didn't know about the Swap Meat. "I can't comment on that," he said.

"I didn't think you would."

He noticed she said *would* instead of *could*. He also noticed she was walking away. Am studied her escaping form; in it, he saw a professional threat and a personal interest. For a moment he weighed the situation, and then he followed her. When he caught up with her he asked, "Is that how you end all of your conversations?"

"I'm late," she said.

"Sure you're not the one doing the evading this time?"

"No," said Marisa, "I'm doing my job. Part of which is to cover today's featured speaker."

It was the other part of her job, the one she wasn't elaborating upon, that interested him.

"Detective McHugh is in charge of the investigation," Am offered.

"As if that wasn't obvious hours ago," she said. "He and a few of his shadows have been nosing around none too unobtrusively. If they wanted to keep things under wraps, they haven't done a very good job of it."

"I'm worried about a premature newspaper article," he said.

"I'm worried about a dated newspaper article."

That settled, they walked into Halcyon Hall. It was one of the largest of the Hotel meeting rooms, could accommodate up to five hundred people. Almost that many were already assembled.

"Damn," said Marisa, "we'll probably have to sit in the front row."

The stage was right on top of the seats, which meant that the front rows had the same limited appeal as up-close movie-house seating. Am followed Marisa down an aisle. He noticed a few familiar faces, placed them with the Kingsbury room the night before, and belatedly remembered that Marisa was covering the UNDER Convention. One of her predictions, at least, proved to be only too correct. They ended up in the front row. Observing the speaker would require their chins to occupy that space usually reserved for their noses.

"All right," said Marisa, speaking in a voice only he

could hear. "I won't run any story until the autopsy is concluded. In turn, I expect complete cooperation from you."

"What kind of cooperation?"

"For starters, access to any and all Hotel information."

Violation of privacy, he thought. The cardinal sin in the
hotel business. Not to mention transgressing an Amend-
ment or two.

"Go on."

"And free run of the property. With your master key, and
my curiosity, we can go far."

Maybe as far as San Quentin Penitentiary, he thought.
Am didn't get a chance to answer her demands and end
their partnership even before it began. The lights in the
room dimmed. Music started to play, softly at first, then
louder. Am tried to place the music, then remembered: it
was Brahms' *German Requiem*.

The curtains opened. Spotlights played down on the
podium. A figure walked up to the microphone. Or did she
glide? She was wearing white, had on a gossamer gown
that, kitelike, unfurled around her. Her complexion was
whiter than her outfit, her cheeks that faintest of pinks,
only hinting at a coming spring. Her hair was a blond that
was almost white, her eyebrows a fine translucent sand.

The *Requiem* played on.

"Who is that?" asked Am.

"Why," said Marisa, "that's Lady Death, of course."

Chapter Fifteen

"I am the speaker for the dead," she said.

The music had stopped. Halcyon Hall was preternaturally quiet. The apparition, the Angel of Death, had everyone's attention. And she knew it.

"I have walked through the valley of the shadow of death," she said. "I have seen into that great beyond, and Chief Seattle was right: There is no death. There is only a change of worlds.

"I will tell you about the other world."

She did. Eloquently, beautifully, even passionately. She spoke of the world where, medically dead, she had journeyed. She talked of following a great white light, described the surreal landscapes she had encountered, and remembered her disappointment in being told by an unseen force that it "was not her time to die." It was clear that many in the audience were recalling their similar near-death experiences as she spoke. The more she talked, the more the crowd responded. She worked the room better than a revival-meeting preacher.

Her name wasn't Eurydice. She had lived, died, and now lived again as Angela Holliday. There was an ethereal quality to her, perhaps because of her fair complexion, perhaps because the lighting didn't give her a shadow so much as a nimbus.

"After almost dying," she said, "many of us were told that our being alive was a miracle. But I say that miracles are merely a point of view. On any given day, we experience thousands of miracles, but we rarely acknowledge them. Our vision has become jaded. We don't pause to exult in creation, and we run from introspection. We have forgotten what life is, and we are afraid to speak of death.

"In fact," she stage-whispered, "when we talk about death we are supposed to whisper, or better yet, not even talk about it. But that is not why we have gathered here. We have come to talk of death. For those who have been where I have, you will understand when I say that I embrace death, for it gave me new life. I embrace death, for it embraced me, and showed me immortality."

She walked across the stage, stood directly above Am and Marisa. Her closeness gave off a heat. Am wasn't sure whether it was all the lights, or just her light. "We are used to viewing death from a distance. Maybe you were like me. You had this tremendous experience, and you wanted to talk about it, but no one wanted to hear. 'Get on with your life,' your family and friends said, as if by saying those words they could put this thing behind you.

"But I didn't want to forget. I wanted to remember, and explore what had occurred. I took a journey and I came back changed. Life and death are not the same to me anymore.

"I am the speaker for the dead. I tell my story, and I tell yours."

The greatest applause is total silence. Angela Holliday

had that applause. She bowed, deeply, and then she left the stage. She was gone for half a minute before the clapping started. It was the kind of ovation that built over the minutes, but Lady Death didn't return for a curtain call.

"Let's go," said Marisa.

She awoke Am from his reverie and motioned for him to come along. He decided she was the kind of person who never stayed for the last few innings of a baseball game, who skipped out during the seventh-inning stretch. The idea of a stretch suddenly appealed to him. Am rolled his neck a few times, tried to work out the kinks caused by having to stare upward at Angela. The speaker had, he admitted to himself, transfixed him.

"We're going to be late," said Marisa.

"For what?"

"My interview. Heaven can wait, but from what I've heard, Angela Holliday can't."

"You're interviewing Angela Holliday?"

His excited tone annoyed her, even if she wasn't sure why. "If you can call ten minutes an interview. That's all I could wangle out of her manager. After Lady Death boots us out, I figure we can get right to work on the Kingsbury stuff."

"Imagine that," said Am, "we're going to get our own mini-tour of the Pearly Gates."

"This isn't Saint Peter we're talking about," said Marisa. "And the only tour we'll be getting is a few parceled seconds of her national book tour. It's been dubbed the Eulogy Tour. Some eulogy. Word is they gave her a half million dollar advance for her book."

"What's the name of her book?"

"*Speaker for the Dead*. Love those cheery titles."

* * *

By earthly standards, the Crown Jewel Suite was about as close to heaven as most mortals ever get. The room had housed seven presidents, two emperors, four queens, three kings, a bevy of lesser royalty, and enough Hollywood stars to fill up a minor constellation or two. It rented for three thousand dollars a night. A curator didn't come with the room, but should have.

The Crown Jewel Suite had long been the showpiece of the Hotel's interior designers, each trying to outdo the last. Most hotel managers remind designers that function should be just as important as aesthetics, a lecture usually listened to carefully, then invariably ignored. In the case of the Crown Jewel Suite, function ranked right behind whether to offer waxed or plain dental floss (it was decided that both should be in the amenity pack). The room was made up of one-of-a-kind pieces. One enthusiastic designer had said after decorating the largest of its three bathrooms, "I see not the loo, but the Louvre." For what it was worth, his toilet did make it into a number of tabletop magazines.

Mr. Hubert, a rather flamboyant gay man, had been the Hotel's primary interior designer for the past dozen years. He was a truly gifted artist, but he did have his quirky side. One of his claims to fame was that for a time he had managed to put a color motif to all seven of the Hotel floors. "The guest," he had insisted, "can have the color he wants." During the short-lived "lollipop era" (thirteen months), there were only a dozen documented requests for a floor on the basis of color. Mr. Hubert had also tried to have the Hotel carpets changed four times a year. "They should reflect the seasons," he had lectured to the owners. When reminded that San Diego doesn't really have seasons, Mr.

Hubert supposedly replied, "It is our duty to remember that the rest of the world does."

One of Mr. Hubert's favorite laments was "I am handcuffed by the museum mentality of this place." By that he meant the historical status of the Hotel prohibited him from tinkering with it very much. He derided all the "sacred-cow rooms," areas that had been the same for so long that their longevity alone dictated they could not be touched. Because guest rooms weren't sacrosanct, Mr. Hubert worked on them with abandon. His latest motif was "the five-senses appeal." Engineering, which had the onus of fixing anything wrong with the guest rooms, called Mr. Hubert's designs the "no-sense appeal."

Marisa knocked on the entry door to the Crown Jewel Suite. Am expected an attendant would do the answering, a man with small eyes and big shoulders, but it was Angela Holliday who opened her own door. She had changed clothes, was wearing jeans, a peach button-down cotton shirt, and sandals. She didn't need white wings, Am decided.

Introductions were made (Am found himself identified as "with the Hotel"), and Angela led them into the suite. She casually motioned to the wet bar and said, "Help yourself to anything you want." There was a lot they could have helped themselves to, including the requisite fruit basket, chocolates, cheese and crackers, and a fully stocked bar, but they politely declined and waited for her to sit down.

Angela chose the white leather sofa ("the next white sofa that goes in this Hotel," executive housekeeper Barbara Terry had been heard to say, "will be made of Mr. Hubert's hide"), was easily able to position her feet under her backside in that contortion which some women describe as being comfortable. From her shirt pocket she pulled out a tiny hourglass. Or maybe it was a ten-minute glass. She placed it down on the coffee table that separated her from her interviewers, the kind of coffee table that shouldn't be adorned by magazines (a bleached mahogany with beveled glass and inlaid turquoise). The hourglass granules began to fall.

"I'm sorry to have so little time to spare," she said, "but I think you'll find that most of your questions can be answered by reading my book."

She pointed to a stack of books on the coffee table. "Please. One for each of you. They're autographed."

Marisa didn't seem inclined to reach for a book, so Am took two and said thank you for both of them. The cover was mostly black, save for an ethereal, if apparently female, orator. Behind this speaker were dark, spectral masses, distinguished through the glow of their eyes. Marisa opted to open her notepad instead of the book. Her questions started without preamble, and were answered in the same manner. Am thought the Q and A was like watching a professional tennis match, his head moving back and forth while following the hurried interview format. Marisa covered the background first, took down the shortened life (death?) and times of Angela Holliday, then tried to ask a few questions that went beyond a PR profile.

"Do you like being called the Angel of Death?" she asked.

"I don't appreciate the sensationalistic aspects of the name," she said, "but it's a nickname I can live with."

Am laughed, and received an answering smile. Marisa either didn't think her response funny, or was too hard-pressed for time to chuckle.

"I heard your talk . . ."

". . . it was wonderful," said Am.

". . . today. You mentioned how your near-death experience taught you many things. What was the most important thing it taught you?"

Angela directed her answer to Am. "To not be afraid of death," she said. "It is hard to imagine how liberating that notion is. Knowing that there is life after death gave me a freedom I never had before."

"I noticed in your speech you never referred to the afterlife as 'heaven.' "

"I didn't call it 'hell' either. Death brings us to another plane. It sounds like a cliché, but that place is a far, far better place than the one we now occupy."

"That sounds like an endorsement for death."

"It's an endorsement for life, for how we should occupy this time, but don't. I was able to see what is truly important, and what isn't."

"What is important?"

"Love. Not romantic love per se, not that I knock such . . ."

Another smile for Am.

". . . but more of the philosophy of love as a guiding light. That's what we are on this planet for. Everything else, seen from a distance, is trivial. We make living complicated, but it should be simple."

"One of the criticisms of the near-death movement is that it is *too* simplistic," said Marisa. "Critics say it is just another version of the great carrot at the end of the stick, the reward in the next world."

"Critics and cynics will be with us always."

"Some of those so-called critics and cynics have gone so

far as to say the near-death philosophy is an endorsement to suicide. They claim it makes death attractive."

Angela shook her head. Vigorously. "That's nonsense. Many of the survivors of near-death experiences were specifically told it was not their time, that they had to go back, even when they didn't want to. Death is not a pie in the sky. It is not something to which we can dictate terms."

"The late Dr. Kingsbury said that he wouldn't be surprised if the near-death experience couldn't be accounted for by chemicals given off by the body during extreme trauma. He was also of the opinion that the near-death experience is now a self-fulfilling prophecy, that those on the threshold of death have certain expectations about what will occur because of what he termed the 'propaganda' of your movement."

"But in the end," said Angela, "Dr. Kingsbury became our Paul vis-à-vis his Saul of Tarsus conversion. He saw the light. Dying, he said, 'Be positive.' His last words succinctly sum up our movement. I regret that he didn't live, so as to tell all of us his experiences. I think it not inaccurate, though, to state that his was a deathbed conversion."

"Do you think . . ."

"I'm sorry," interrupted Angela, patting the tiny hourglass with her thin index finger. There were no grains of sand left. "Our time is up."

Marisa opened her mouth, but the speaker for the dead repeated the same words, pronounced them this time with a finality that went beyond ending a conversation: "Our time is up."

Chapter Sixteen

"I wanted to tell her," said Marisa, "that I had just had a near-hourglass experience. I wanted to turn that damn thing over and say, 'Look! We can keep talking. It's a miracle' "

"You saw how a television crew was already lined up outside," Am said, feeling the need to defend Angela, "and another was forming behind it."

Marisa did a cow imitation, complete with an outstretched neck and long-drawn-out *moooo*. "That makes me part of a media cattle call. You would think the press wouldn't buy into that. But over the next day or two Lady Death will be splashed all over the local news. There will be bigger lines at her book signings than at the Saint Vincent de Paul food line."

"Psychological needs of the community transcending economic needs," intoned Am. "Sounds like a good story to me. She's apparently striking a chord . . ."

"She's not Lazarus."

"She's also not your usual tour guide."

"You're right. What kind of tour guide only gives a ten-minute talk? And from that I'm supposed to fluff a major article."

"You could always excerpt from her book."

"That would mean reading it, which I am not going to do."

"Then how does your story get written?"

"I'll quote from her speech. And besides, there's always the introduction to journalism question of 'where.' Her suite was made for hyperbole. It's not exactly a Kmart showroom, is it?"

"Not quite," said Am. "And you only saw the sitting room. Behind doors number two and three were the real prizes."

"Tell me."

He did, and she started taking notes, scribbling as they walked. Am described the Italian marble-top desks, the Austrian-made Bakalowits chandeliers, the oversized down duvets, the Bugatti furniture, the four-poster honeymoon bed mounted with brocades and silk and English chintz, and the classical statuary and custom art. He also clued her into the "hidden" features of the suite, the custom-made three-inch soundproof doors, the hand-woven two-inch-thick carpeting, the air-conditioning that didn't give off the usual recycled air but instead provided fresh-chilled, the specially created potpourri placed in secreted caches around the room, the individual thermostat console at bedside, and even the two touch-control fireplaces.

"Magic Fingers?" asked Marisa.

"Sorry," said Am.

She mugged her disappointment.

"But there is an in-room spa," he said, "with twelve jet sprays. And a propensity for eating panty hose."

Marisa gave him a quizzical look.

"Last week engineering had to tear the spa up," explained Am. "Somehow a pair of panty hose ended up clogging one of the pipes. That, I'm sure, was a story in itself. A major part of this business is overcoming monkey wrenches, nylon and otherwise. Since the suite was promised for the night, a whole crew worked furiously to get it fixed. That's the problem with a unique accommodation, when another room just won't do. It's difficult enough to keep up any hotel room even when you have interchangeable parts, when the beds and bureaus and tables can be switched around between the rooms, and there are replacements waiting in storage. But one-of-a-kind rooms are a different undertaking altogether. They require incredible preventative maintenance. TQM is a religion at all great properties."

"TQM?"

"Total Quality Management," translated Am. "It used to be QA, which is Quality Assurance, but I think someone figured out that three letters sound more official than two. It all translates to having systems in place which try and ensure guest satisfaction. At the Bristol Hotel in Paris they don't disinfect the toilet seats, they remove them, scrape them, and revarnish them prior to the arrival of every new guest. And before a guest checks into the Ritz in Paris, at least half a dozen employees verify the room is letter-perfect, with inspections not only by room checkers and management, but electricians, plumbers and painters.

"A few hotels have even gone so far as to decide that the best the world has to offer isn't good enough for them. London's Savoy Hotel decided to manufacture its own beds, reputed to be the most comfortable on the planet. The Savoy considers their investment in beds—a rather sizable one—

to be in their own best interests. As any hotel employee can tell you, a guest that has failed to have a good night's sleep is about as happy as a bear denied hibernation."

They entered the main lobby. It always looked familiar to visitors, perhaps because it had been featured in dozens of movies. Hollywood thought the Hotel's lobby the embodiment of what a grand old lobby should look like, and for once Am agreed with Tinseltown's taste. The ceiling was high, not the thirty-story atriums so popular these days, but high enough to house a respectable basketball court. There were murals painted on the ceiling, most created by depression-era artists. Short on funds, the artists hadn't been short on vision. Faux gold leaf abounded, the fool's gold designs about the only things in the lobby short on bona fides. The lobby had been built with the integrity of another time, erected long before earthquake standards and building safety regulations were put on the books, but not before artisans knew how to create an enduring edifice.

The front desk was quiet, a rare occasion. A solitary guest was being helped by T.K. "Check-in hour is officially at three o'clock," he announced, "but let's see what I can do for you, Mr. Gordon."

Am didn't like T.K.'s all-too-cheery tone. It was his show-time voice. The aspiring comic was always trying out new material at the front desk. He'd been warned on several occasions that he would be trying out his material at the unemployment office if he went too far, but T.K. was irrepressible.

"Let me guess, Mr. Gordon," said T.K., flashing his white teeth in a wide smile. "You want a room with a view."

Mr. Gordon smiled back. He was more bald than not,

about sixty, had the genial, self-assured countenance of someone who had never been forced to scratch too hard for a living. He was, Am had to admit, the perfect dupe.

"Yes," said the guest. "That's exactly what my wife and I want. A room with a view."

T.K. nodded. He reached below the counter, pulled out a book, then slapped it down with a resounding thump. "That'll be six ninety-five."

Mr. Gordon was clearly confused. "What do you mean?"

"E.M. Forster," said T.K., raising up the novel for Mr. Gordon to see. "His greatest book. *A Room with a View*. As I'm sure you know, it's considered a modern classic."

T.K. offered the book to the guest. Mr. Gordon looked uneasy, even a bit afraid. "I thought we were talking about a room with . . ."

By his own admission, T.K. was "half chameleon, and half African-American." When the comedic situation called for it, he was good at exploiting white guilt. T.K. wasn't smiling, was the picture of someone trying to puzzle out an unusual situation himself. Mr. Gordon decided he didn't want to offend. He took the proffered book, thumbed a few pages.

"How much did you say?" he asked.

"Six . . ."

"Complimentary," interjected Am.

T.K. didn't miss a beat. He hadn't noticed Am's approach to the desk, but had been busted by him enough times to know his routine was at an end.

"That's right," said T.K. "It's our May special. We offer a room with a view with *A Room with a View*."

"Well," said Mr. Gordon, "that's mighty nice of you."

Am motioned for another desk clerk. He requested, and

received, a copy of the entire UNDER convention room block. There were over 150 rooms registered to the group. Why couldn't we be a normal hotel? thought Am. Why did we attract the swingers and the near dead, and not the Shriners? With Marisa looking over his shoulder, Am ran his finger down the names. He looked for and found the name of Jack Baldwin, the witness to Dr. Kingsbury's last words and last breath.

From a house phone at the front desk, Am dialed Baldwin's room. While waiting for an answer, he explained to Marisa that he had interviewed the staff the night before, "including E.M. Forster's mouthpiece" (T.K. pretended not to hear), but Baldwin had been the only one near enough to identify Kingsbury's last words.

Almost ready to hang up, Am was surprised by a late pickup. "Hello, Mr. Baldwin? My name is Am Caulfield. I'm the security director at the Hotel, and I was wondering if I could come up and talk with you about last night."

Am waited out a rather lengthy response. "I'm sorry the police haven't given you time to do even that, Mr. Baldwin," he said, "but I can assure you I'll only be a minute or two."

There was another long pause. "Which book signing is that, Mr. Baldwin?"

Shorter wait, quicker answer: "Well, believe it or not, I have her book right in my hands. It's autographed, and I'd be glad to present it to you free of charge. That's right. Thank you. I'll be right up."

Am and Marisa started to walk away, but then Am remembered something and walked back to the desk. He held out his hand pointedly to T.K.

"What?" protested the clerk.

"I thought you'd join me in our 'giving-books-to-guests' campaign," Am said.

Am continued to hold out his hand. Reluctantly, T.K. reached under the counter and pulled out another copy of *A Room with a View.*

"How'd you know?" asked T.K.

"It's human nature to repeat novel jokes," said Am.

Chapter Seventeen

"It's not very nice of me to say so," said Jack, "but I'm beginning to wish the poor man had just expired quietly."

Am apologized for his troubles. In the hotel industry, apologizing is as natural as breathing. Marisa didn't say anything. Am had introduced her as being "from the union." He didn't elaborate that she was from the *Union-Tribune*.

"Can we go over the scenario just one more time?" Am asked.

Jack ran a hand through his thinning blond hair. He was tired, and proceeded with obvious reluctance. "I had an appointment with the doctor," he said, his voice weary. "I knocked on his door. There were sounds from inside . . ."

"What kind of sounds?" asked Marisa.

"A man's voice, accompanied by thumping and thrashing sounds. Instinctively, I knew something was wrong. A heart attack, I figured, or an epileptic seizure. I considered trying to pound the door down, but I figured that would only get me a dislocated shoulder, so I attacked it instead with my fist, knocking very loudly.

"When there was still no answer, I started running down

the hall. I searched for a maid, or anyone who could get me in the room, but no one was around. The elevator was open, so I jumped inside. My original plan was to ride down to the front desk, but I had sense enough to use the telephone in the elevator. The switchboard operator told me she'd send someone up immediately."

"Did you go right back to the room?" asked Marisa.

"Yes."

"On your way there," she asked, "did you encounter anyone?"

"No. The first person I saw was the man from your staff. He almost beat me to the room."

"What happened after the door was opened?" asked Am.

"It was all a blur," said Jack. "It was clear Dr. Kingsbury was in distress. We ran to his side. Your man asked me if I knew CPR. He barely gave me time to nod, said 'Do it,' then ran to the phone.

"I was trying to remember exactly what to do. You always wonder if you'll be able to respond to an emergency. The situation confirmed what I suspected: When the going gets tough, don't count on me. It was Dr. Kingsbury who reached for me, not I for him. He could barely say the words. I wish I could duplicate his force of will during his last moments. Dying, he told me, 'Be positive.' "

"You're sure of that?" asked Marisa. "Couldn't he have said something else, something similar?"

"He said, 'Be positive,' " said Jack.

Jack's words were spoken with a firmness that surprised Am. The man looked like a dreamer, but when the occasion called for it, he could be adamant.

"He died right after saying those words," said Jack. "I saw his life force leave him."

"Was he happy at his end?" asked Am.

"Happy?" The question evidently surprised Jack. He had to think about it. "Not particularly."

"And yet he said, 'Be positive.' "

"Yes."

"So he's telling you something uplifting," said Am, "and yet he himself was . . ."

". . . not smiling beatifically," admitted Jack. "But given his situation, I'd say his schizophrenic message was justified. Part of him was dancing with angels, while another part couldn't have been very happy that he was about to die a murder victim."

Am and Marisa exchanged glances. "Murder?" she asked.

"That's what the police think," said Jack, "even if they haven't come out and admitted it."

"And what do you think?" asked Marisa.

"I don't know. But now I hope he was murdered."

"Why is that?"

"One way or another he's dead, and I'd hate to think I've been asked the same questions over and over for no reason."

"Why did Dr. Kingsbury want to talk to you?" asked Am.

"He wanted to hear about my near-death experience. He was interviewing lots of us."

"How many?"

"I couldn't tell you. I only know he had us scheduled every half hour. UNDER helped him coordinate his interview times."

"Was there a posted schedule of those interview times?"

"I think so. In my case, I was told to be at his room at eight-thirty, and I was. I should have listened to Mother, and made it a point to be socially late. Then I would have missed all the unpleasantness."

"Tell me about your near-death," said Am.

"Do you really want to hear about it?" Jack asked, sounding somewhat pleased.

He didn't need much convincing. His was a poor-little-rich-boy story, as told with popular psychological jargon. Am and Marisa heard about his low self-esteem, his dysfunctional family, and the "destructive dynamics" in his life. Jack decided to end his life by mixing alcohol and barbiturates. He did it right, he said, making a cocktail that should have killed him "three times over."

"I was clinically dead a couple of times," he said. "No heartbeat, no respiration. And I vividly remember passing over to the other side.

"I didn't have any form. No one does over there. I was this . . . ball . . . of consciousness. There were others around me, little beacons, little points of light. It was all very orderly, very beautiful, the kind of harmony that I've always wanted, but has always eluded me. My entire life I've tried to belong, and for once I felt I fit in. The only problem was, I had to die.

"I felt myself going forward. It was almost like a dance. But then my music stopped and I found my way barred. I remember suddenly encountering this force, this, for want of a better word, sun. And that great light asked me a question: 'Why are you here?' It wasn't something I could hide from, nor could I answer. I felt ashamed because I knew I shouldn't be there. It was like I had cheated. Then I was asked a second question: 'What have you done?' And I didn't have a good answer to give. Don't get me wrong: it didn't feel like I was on trial, or that I would suffer for not having accumulated enough good-guy stories, but it was more like I was being told I should have had that answer before killing myself. It became quite clear to me that I had violated some time-frame agreement, and that I had to go back to the other side.

"That was three years ago. Sometimes I feel like the redeemed Ebenezer Scrooge. I don't know if I've saved any Tiny Tims, but since my near-death experience I've changed. I'm not so introspective as I was. I've tried to look outside of myself. I suppose I've become one of those do-gooders I used to disdain, using my money to help the community, and my time to work for causes other than my own.

"What I most want," he said, "is to be able to better answer those questions the next time around."

Funny, thought Am. Both he and Marisa were operating under a similar motivation. They wanted to be able to better answer a few questions also.

Chapter Eighteen

Cotton Gibbons was used to letting his hands think for him. His tinkering was the way he put matters right in his world. He enjoyed getting lost in the mechanics of a situation and solving problems. What he didn't like were human intrusions. People weren't logical like machines. Grudgingly, he made some limited attempts at working within social conventions, but had about as much finesse as the proverbial bull in a china shop. Imagine his happiness, then, when asked to put two meeting rooms out of service.

He was almost finished fixing the scuppers. The work had gone more slowly than usual, the result of his wandering mind. It was atypical for Cotton not to be absorbed by the problem at hand, but those meeting rooms had kept intruding into his thoughts, short-circuiting his usually sure fingers. Maybe it was because Cotton wasn't in the habit of looking forward to something. He hadn't even felt this good the month before when he'd had tickets to the tractor pull and truck show at the stadium.

Too bad I couldn't just go and blow up the rooms with the perverts in them, he thought. They'll all go to hell anyway. The vision of fire and brimstone and the eternal torment of the sex maniacs inspired Cotton. He had just about settled on initiating a water leak in one of the meeting rooms, and giving off the appearance of a collapsing roof in the other, when he suddenly decided those solutions weren't good enough. They weren't quite—artistic enough. This was something that had to be done right. It needed the proper touches.

For the first time in his life, Cotton almost felt like an artist. Weren't those artsy types always yapping about their influences and motivations? He wasn't going to just take out the meeting rooms. No, he was going to make a personal statement.

He considered his palette, and the frenzied fuckers he was going to neuter. He was going to cut them off—at their knees at least. Cotton thought about fire and brimstone again. He'd been raised on visions of the Old Testament God. It would serve the bastards right, he thought, if those deviants got a taste of hell. He could be the right hand of God. He could hand out—what did they call it?— poetic justice.

The brimstone would be easy. Back in the shop were some compounds and acids full of sulfur. Rotten eggs had nothing on that stuff. Whenever he used even a dab he was always forced to listen to the comments. Why, once Chief Horton had been nosing around where Cotton was working and got a whiff of the acid. "Cotton," the Chief had said, "I've heard tell every man loves the smell of his own farts, but even someone as ornery as you couldn't be partial to this stench." Cotton hadn't said anything. He'd just ladled on the sulfuric acid, far more than was called for, and that had cleared that damn smart-assed Chief from the room. Cotton had always thought of the Chief as being more management than not anyway, and hadn't been sorry when he had up and quit.

The brimstone would be easy, but what about the fire? He could play it safe, he supposed, and light a match under one of the sprinkler heads. That would soak the room. But that wasn't good enough. That was—common. There had to be something better, a fire with meaning, a punishment that fit the crime of those hot, lusting, sweaty, impassioned bodies.

Cotton had to wipe his face. He'd forgotten himself, almost smashed the scupper to pieces. He took a few deep breaths, tried to finish the work at hand. But his mind kept wandering back to his art project.

Am had told him about how one of the meeting rooms had been turned into an orgy room. These are the kind of people who'd spit on the flag, thought Cotton. Or worse, he considered, shuddering at his brief vision of Old Glory being caught up in some carnal escapades. They were the sorts who just wanted to scratch their itch, and they didn't care who did the scratching. Why, Am had said they had a whole bunch of sex toys on display, stuff that would have even made that Marquis de Sade fellow blush. There were whips, and chains, and clamps, and costumes, and things that buzzed, and hummed, and gyrated.

Electrical things, thought Cotton.

Things that could potentially short out, and spark.

He could make it look as if their lustful contraptions had betrayed them. He could make sure all their gizmos and perverted materials were ruined. He could rain on their sexual parade.

For the first time in his work career, Cotton abandoned a project, deserting the scuppers.

There were more important things to do.

Chapter Nineteen

"I have to go write my story."

Marisa's words were carefully neutral. Her three-hour partnership with Am was still tentative, with about as much trust between them as a shaky deal entered into by union and management.

Am debated his response. A guarded answer probably would have been politic, but he thought it was time their relationship either went beyond that, or finished itself. "All the world is queer but me and thee, dear," he said, "and sometimes I think thee is a little queer."

"What?"

"Supposedly," said Am, "those were the words of a long-married Quaker husband to his wife. It's a quote that tells the human story. Each of us is convinced of our inherent correctness, which means we automatically have doubts about everyone else."

"Am I getting a course in bad psychology?"

"I'd prefer you label it bad philosophy. That's what I majored in back in the Dark Ages."

"The Hotel dick is a philosopher?"

"Enough of one to realize I'm neither a hotel dick, nor a

philosopher. That said, I still want to know how Dr. Kingsbury died. I know it sounds vaingloriously romantic, but
I'm supposed to be the protector of the Hotel."

"A wound to the Hotel's reputation is a wound to you?"
She didn't spare the sarcasm, but Am didn't take offense.
"I suppose so," he said.

"The Hotel's been around for over a century," said
Marisa. "Isn't it presumptuous that you personally feel the
need to protect her honor?"

Am shrugged. "Others have done it before me," he said.
"I guess it's my turn now."

"Maybe your Dark Ages time frame is right," said
Marisa. "That was the age of chivalry, wasn't it?"

Her tone was friendlier, but still perplexed. She couldn't
quite figure Am out. He looked like an aging surfer, but
talked like some kind of monk, or consecrated warrior. In
much the same way she'd heard members of the San Diego
military make pronouncements about God and country, he
spoke of man and Hotel. That shouldn't have made her feel
better about him, but somehow it did.

"I'll be back in a few hours," she said, "but I won't return
empty-handed. I assigned a researcher to do a computer
search on the doctor, so we're going to have a pile of reading matter to get through. I hope your chivalry extends beyond banking hours, Sir Hotel knight."

"Fear not, fair lady," said Am. "My reading glasses await
you."

"Don't forget your magnifying glasses," she said.

"Sooner would I forget my broadsword, lady, nay, my
right arm."

He bowed, managed his performance without a smile.
She shook her head, then left. Their partnership, it ap-

peared, was going to last out the day. Both of them were not a little surprised at that.

Ward Ankeney liked to say that "figures lie, and liars figure." Ward knew better than most. He was the Hotel controller.

In the days before secondhand smoke became an issue, Ward's office had been a smoky den. He polluted with a vast collection of pipes that he called "thinking tools." Even though the state of California had mandated that all offices in workplaces be smoke-free, Ward hadn't given up on his pipes. He sucked on them just as furiously, but now left them unlit.

Ward's display of pipes were hung as proudly as a hunter showing off a 14-point buck. They extended along a rack that took up most of one wall, and were a variety of shapes, sizes and materials. When Ward was particularly confounded, he brought out the largest of his meerschaum pipes, the one with the white bowl that could have held a floral centerpiece. Perhaps not coincidentally, there was a bear's face carved into the bowl. When Ward chewed on that pipe, serious business was at hand. The bear pipe meant do not disturb. Am was glad to see that the bear was apparently hibernating; the controller was chewing rather benignly on one of his smaller pipes.

The pipes were actually the smaller of Ward's office displays. The rest of his walls were taken up with pictures and props from his former vocation. Ward had been an actor, and from his notices, a good one. Then again, no actor has ever been known to frame bad reviews.

"Hi, Am," he said, punching away at a ten-key. "Be with you in just a minute."

Am took the time to look more closely at the office scenery. Despite Ward's investment in frames, most of the pictures, reviews, posters and glossies had yellowed and faded. The thespian mementos had been a part of the office for as long as Am could remember. Curious, he hunted down the most recent review; it was a quarter of a century old.

The hurried clicking of the calculator keys ceased, some more figures put to rest. The Hotel was a sixty-million-dollar-a-year business. It produced more revenue than some Third World countries. And all of those dollars had to be accounted for. It wasn't any wonder that Ward's hands were invariably in constant motion. Even when he wasn't working, Ward always found the need to occupy his fingers in some activity.

Am looked from an old glossy to an expectant controller. The picture showed a much younger Ward in what must have been a Shakespearean production—that, or the accountant had once dressed in wig, jabot, velvet overcoat, pantaloons, and long stockings.

"Accounting and acting," Am said, "seem to me about as complementary as drafting and dancing."

Ward stopped chewing on his pipe to smile. "I probably never would have been an accountant if it weren't for my parents," he said. "They encouraged me to have a major other than dramatic arts. Insisted, I should say. I guess they'd heard too many stories of starving actors."

"I'll bet you're glad you took their advice," said Am.

Ward gave a hesitant nod. "I suppose so," he said, "but sometimes I wonder if my accounting degree didn't make me less hungry as an actor. I knew I could always get a numbers job, even if that wasn't what I wanted. But in

time, especially after the kids came along, it became easier
to settle for that."

Though Ward hadn't been on stage for a very long time,
that wasn't what Am heard in his voice. His aged clippings
suggested he had been a versatile actor, with roles in everything from *Harvey* to *King Lear*. Am continued to examine
some of the pictures on the wall, and Ward did anything
but discourage him, contentedly sucking on his pipe and
giving a running dialogue on the productions.

"Actually made it to off-Broadway in that one," he said.
"It was called *Eternity*, and lasted for one show."

Am moved a step over, far enough for another descrip-
tion. "Pasadena Playhouse," he said. "*Mutiny on the Bounty*.
Played Fletcher Christian. That was my last role, actually.
One critic suggested I was playing Clark Gable more than
Christian. If so, I really missed the mark. I was aiming for
Brando."

The stroll down memory lane took in a few more pictures. When reminiscing about his salad days, Ward's hands
became virtually still. He took a long draw on his unlit
pipe. "Everything seemed so vital back then," he said. "I
never felt so alive."

His words awoke Am to his own mission. Dr. Kingsbury's last living hours had been at the Hotel, and Am
wanted to document as many of them as he could. "Did you
get a chance to pull those charges for me, Ward?" he asked.

"Ah, yes," said the controller, reaching for a packet. "Got
'em all here. What's up?"

Am debated a few responses; the metaphor of life as one
long hotel bill; checking in, and checking out; perusing the
last supper.

"I'm doing a summing-up," said Am.

Chapter Twenty

Executive housekeeper Barb Terry gave Am the same kind of once-over she usually reserved for room inspections, a hard scrutiny that could pick a dust mote off at twenty paces. Barb was usually everybody's grandmother, but at the moment her honest blue eyes looked none too happy. "It's a lot tougher making rooms look bad, Am Caulfield, than it is making them look good."

"This is one case where I hope practice doesn't make perfect," he said.

The situation reminded him of the guest calling room service and saying, "I'd like an order of toast. Burn it until it's neither recognizable nor edible. I'll have orange juice, and make sure most of it is spilled on the tray. Give me half of my eggs runny and uncooked, and the other half burned to a crisp. I'd like my rasher of bacon raw and fatty, and my butter melted. And make sure the juice is delivered hot, and the bacon and eggs are cold."

"Sir," was the response, "we can't possibly create an order like that."

"Why not?" said the man. "That's what you delivered yesterday."

Am had always thought of hotel management as a plate-spinning act. In order to keep those plates rotating atop sticks, to prevent them from falling and crashing, it was necessary to run back and forth and spin the plates. The secret to success is not having too many plates spinning on too many sticks, but the business often conspires against that. All Am wanted to do was work on the Kingsbury case, but before he could do that, there was the plate-spinning to attend to.

The Hotel's professed goal was to provide "unequaled service." Such a pronouncement, Am had always thought, tempted the fates. There had been times when the best of staff intentions had been thwarted by circumstances, but this wasn't one of those times. The inmates were now being offered weapons, and anarchy was being encouraged. Management was preaching neglect and rebellion toward a select group. There were some very confused employees. Cotton Gibbons wasn't one of them. Whereas most children would be perplexed if told—no, directed—to hit a younger sibling, Cotton had gladly followed through on his assignment of disabling the meeting rooms. He had done so without demur, even with apparent gusto.

Am excused himself from Barb, his parting words that she should pass on his approval to her staff for their work.

"I'll do no such thing, Am Caulfield," she said. "Praise them for making a mess rather than for cleaning? Not out of my lips."

She walked away shaking her head. It wasn't the only head that was moving. Cotton was trying to inconspicuously get Am's attention by using a slight come-hither shake of his head. For all of his attempted subterfuge, he was about as subdued as a pitchman. Sighing, Am trudged a few steps away from the front desk. At least Cotton hadn't insisted upon their reciting some kind of secret phrase.

"The Sea Horse Hall smells worse than an outhouse in August," whispered Cotton, "and the Neptune Room . . ."

The maintenance man actually smiled. "Why, who was that Roman guy who was fiddling when his city was burning down?"

"Nero," said Am.

"Yeah," he said. "The Neptune Room looks like Nero was playing 'Turkey in the Straw' just outside."

"It isn't . . ." started Am.

"Barely any damage," said Cotton, "even if it looks like hell."

His satisfaction was evident.

Mr. and Mrs. Lanier, the Swap Meat group leaders, didn't yet know about the sabotage. Most of their convention had arrived earlier on a chartered bus. Since none of the guest rooms had been ready, they had decided to lead their wanton troops on a Black's Beach excursion. It was a good choice. The beach is only two miles north of the Hotel as the crow flies, though the distance is deceptive. Unless the tide is with you, navigating the beach route is impossible, and getting down to the sand anything but easy. Towering over Black's is the Torrey Pines Cliffs. Some beachgoers fancy themselves Spiderman, and like to navigate down the perilous rocks. Though there's a paved road to the beach, it isn't accessible by car. It's a long walk down to Black's, and even a longer walk up. So why trek to this particular beach when there are so many in La Jolla and San Diego that don't require such athleticism? The attraction to Black's is *because* it can't easily be reached. San Diegans with a propensity for not wearing swimming suits have been going there for decades.

The Swap Meat meeting rooms were ruined, their guest rooms were in a state of disarray, and the Hotel staff was primed for incompetence. Am figured they were as prepared for the group as they ever would be.

"So," said T.K. to the other clerks at the desk, "when we check this group in, do we tell them, 'Have a nice day,' or do we say, 'Have a nice lay?' "

Am decided he needed his quiet place.

Chapter Twenty-One

Most of us have our place of refuge. On the job it's not always easy to escape, but in all the hotels Am had worked he had sought and found his "quiet place." Finding such a spot at the Hotel California hadn't been easy, even with its forty acres, and its multitude of settings that looked like backdrops for "Kodak Picture Stops." Am's retreat wasn't along the beach or in one of the ornate gardens; his quiet place probably wouldn't have even been called scenic by most.

He had often wondered what it was about the spot that had captured him. There were certainly other places he could have gone for mere quietude. His refuge was conveniently located, not far off one of the Hotel garden paths. His spot had stayed secluded for several reasons: the PLEASE STAY ON PATH signs (though those were arguably about as effective as most KEEP OFF THE GRASS signs); the barrier of the manufactured streambed that required a decent leap to surmount; and the thin but effective thicket of pampas grass, an invasive plant whose razor edges don't suffer curious fools. Whether out of neglect, or the decision of some forgotten landscaper that the pampas grass should stay, it had long shielded the area behind it from development.

Am's special place wasn't some Shangri-la. It was a small stretch that hinted of a time even before the Hotel. He liked it that his spot wasn't manicured like the rest of the Hotel grounds, was even a little wild. A "natural" San Diego is an arid place, its native plants more akin to desert flora than the vibrant displays of vegetation found in other subtropical locales. Because of San Diego's growing population, it is ever harder to see what San Diego was, with fewer and fewer spots left fallow for the native chaparral and coastal sage communities. Behind the pampas grass curtain were a few indigenous plants: laurel sumac, lemonade berry, ceanothus, a few manzanita, and a scrawny scrub oak. Though there were far more weeds than native plants, there were still stands of black and white sage to be found, as well as coastal sagebrush.

He took in his kingdom while seated on a boulder. The rock had come with the setting, though in a less salubrious spot. Sisyphus-like, Am had rolled it next to the scrub oak. His natural chair and backrest were set atop a slight incline. It had been several weeks since he'd been to his spot, or was that months? He cast a critical gaze around the clearing, unconsciously sniffed like an animal trying to catch an alien scent. Nothing looked wrong, exactly, but something felt different, disturbed. He could discern no difference, though, nothing to indicate that Goldilocks had been there.

Besides, murder was the issue, not trespassing. He had come to his spot not for some bucolic contemplation, but to focus on the hours Kingsbury had stayed at the Hotel. Am blocked out a time chart, divided each hour into fifteen-minute intervals, and started attaching names and events to the times. His task was made easier because of the interview list he had obtained from one of the UNDER organizers.

Thirty-one of their conventioneers had been questioned by Kingsbury in his room, with the interrogations taking up the bulk of his time at the Hotel.

Even though the doctor was dead, Am felt like a voyeur scrutinizing the doctor's charges. Kingsbury's sundry store purchase had been a tube of Preparation H, something Am thought an unlikely clue. Other details interested him more. As he had suspected, the doctor hadn't eaten or imbibed alone, his food and beverage checks attesting to multiple entree and drink orders. Perhaps the servers would be able to offer descriptions of whom Kingsbury had been with. There was also the possibility that the doctor had dined with someone who had picked up the tab. A memo would have to be circulated to all of the restaurant and lounge staff asking for any information on Kingsbury's visits.

When Am finished with his work, he was able to account for much of Kingsbury's time spent at the Hotel. That didn't make Am feel that he was any closer to answers, but he still felt better for having organized his inquiry on paper. His ink trail had only taken him so far, though. There were a lot of people he needed to talk to, and he could think of no better place to start than UNDER's cocktail party later that afternoon. He had already figured out his drink order, a zombie. Thomas Kingsbury would have been amused, if no one else. If Am had his way, more than near-deaths would be discussed at the party.

A mockingbird awakened him from his musing. It was making more chatter than usual for its kind, if such a thing is possible. Was something bothering it? Am heard some movement in the brush. His first assumption was that it was one of the Hotel's half-feral cats. The felines accepted handouts, but usually from a distance. When not hanging around the kitchen doors, they stalked around the foliage of the Hotel. But these sounds were heavy, not cat-like. Someone was approaching his spot.

That had never happened before. Logically, Am knew that he wasn't the only person to know of "his" place. He had found signs of human (or was that Hobbit?) encroachment before—on one occasion there'd been beer cans and on his boulder the chalked-in words "Frodo Lives"—but it was a shock to think that he was about to have a visitor. He had vying, illogical thoughts, was both ready to flee, and to challenge. He felt guilty for being there, as if to be alone in a slightly out-of-the-way spot was somehow unsanctioned; at the same time he was angry that someone dared to trespass into his world.

Am listened to the interloper's progress. The invader knew enough to enter through the slight opening in the pampas grass that didn't demand blood for passage. Tense, Am waited. A head came into view, then a familiar face. It was the last person Am expected, a figure that added to his dilemma. Should I call out? he wondered. Or should I run away before I'm identified?

The Fat Innkeeper suddenly stopped walking. He looked puzzled. There was something about the clearing that wasn't right. Then he noticed Am.

He couldn't hide his look of surprise. Almost, Am thought, the startled expression was comical. The Japanese like to wear facial masks, but when their masks slip off, they truly are revealed.

"Hello," said Am.

"Hello," replied Hiroshi.

Should he lie? Am wondered. Should he say there had

been a report of some Peeping Tom in the bushes? In some
ways he felt like a student on unofficial holiday encountering the truant officer. This was the son of the owner, after
all. He probably expected him to be toiling in some office.
Not that he wasn't working, Am thought defensively. He
was. But how could he explain that?

Similar debates were going on in Hiroshi's own mind.
He was supposed to lead by example. It didn't look right to
be found out sneaking into some bushes. Should he explain? And if he did, would the *gaijin* even be able to understand what he was talking about?

Sometimes people never meet, even those that encounter
each other on a frequent basis. It is often easier to use objects as barriers: a job, a goal, a subject, an agenda; those are
the start and finish of many relationships. On the two occasions Am and Hiroshi had met before, there had been the
sizable matters of a beached whale and the murder to dis-
cuss. Maybe they needed those kinds of things to carry on a
conversation. It is easier to talk about something than it is
to talk to someone. Am felt acutely embarrassed. What was
there to say to this foreigner anyway? But he thought he
owed him some kind of explanation. Sharon said that the
Japanese believed laziness was an inherent American trait.
He didn't want the Fat Innkeeper to think he was shirking
his duties.

"I came here to do some work on Dr. Kingsbury's death,"
said Am. He waved the paperwork, as if to further exoner-
ate him from the unspoken charges.

Hiroshi nodded, and then took a few steps closer. "I came
here," he said, "because it's . . ."

From what he knew of Americans, they always wanted an
explanation, but was this one of those inexplicable things to

them? Japanese distrusted speech, though by his countrymen's standards Hiroshi knew he was considered positively gabby.

"... *shibui*."

In Japan he wouldn't have to explain. His people had been homogeneous for so long. For over a thousand years there'd been virtually no new infusion in the Japanese gene pool. There was a collective sensibility to their nation. He might be able to translate a word to this American, but not a cultural mind-set.

"It makes your mouth pucker," Hiroshi said, "but in a pleasing, pos-i-tive way."

Of the five senses, Am was sure that taste would be the least used by westerners to describe a setting. "Positive," he repeated, then added the alliterative, "pleasing pucker."

This one knows nothing of my country's aesthetics, thought Hiroshi, is ignorant of how we appreciate the quiet and the understated.

Am moved off his rock. He walked over to the lemonade-berry plant, plucked a handful of seeds from it, and put a few in his mouth. "*Shibui*," he said, then offered a few of the seeds to the Fat Innkeeper.

Hiroshi hesitated, then accepted the seeds but didn't immediately follow Am's example of putting them in his mouth.

"The locals call these plants lemonade berry," said Am. "The native peoples supposedly used to swirl them around in water for their tart taste. Don't chew the seeds, though. They might make you sick. You just suck on them a little."

And then you spit them out. With Hiroshi carefully watching him, Am felt self-conscious. Was expectorating some terrible Japanese taboo? Unsure, Am eased most of the seeds out of his mouth into his hand, then as unobtrusively as possible started flicking them into the brush.

" ' 'Twas a brave man that ate the first oyster,' " said Am.

Whether it was curiosity, or Swift's quote that prevailed, the Fat Innkeeper finally decided to experiment on a solitary seed. He sucked on it for a few moments, decided more of a trial was in order, and put the rest of the seeds in his mouth. The taste pleased him. Lemon-like, but quieter. Puckering, but gently so. It was *shibui, shibui* exactly. Maybe this *gaijin* had understood. With some pleasure, with the same spirit in which watermelon seeds are set aflight outdoors, Hiroshi spat out his seeds one by one. Am wasn't about to be denied his own projectiling. He had two seeds left, and he let them fly.

Their ammunition spent, the two men offered grins and nods for one another. Seed-spitting contests, thought Am, the new diplomatic frontier. He motioned for Hiroshi to sit atop the boulder, but to no avail. It is virtually impossible to out-polite the Japanese.

"That place is taken," said the Fat Innkeeper.

"I was about to leave," said Am.

"Your work went well?"

Am wasn't sure if there was any facetiousness in the inquiry. Most American bosses wouldn't take kindly to an underling's retreat into the brush, but Hiroshi seemed genuinely interested.

"I was trying to get an idea of how Dr. Kingsbury spent his time at the Hotel," said Am. "It is good to get . . ."

Should he say, "far from the madding crowd"? Would Hiroshi understand? Sharon had emphasized how very different Japanese and American upbringing was. In America youthful individualism is extolled, whereas in Japan children are taught that success is a group endeavor.

". . . away to think," said Am, compromising his response.

"Yes," said Hiroshi. "This is a good thinking rock, isn't it?"

They both nodded—or was it bowed?—again.

"Did Dr. Kingsbury have a family?" asked Hiroshi.

"No," said Am.

The news apparently bothered Hiroshi. "No one?"

Am shook his head. "His parents are deceased, and he had no siblings. He was married once, but that was a long time ago and there were no children."

"That is not good." The Fat Innkeeper was insistent. "Bad *shiryoo*."

"What?"

"*Shiryoo* means the spirit of someone who has just died. The family takes care of the *shiryoo*. They . . ."

He stretched for the word. ". . . appease it."

"What happens," asked Am, "if the *shiryoo* isn't appeased?"

"We have a word called *gaki*. It is a wandering spirit stuck between the worlds of the living and the dead. It is hungry."

"Hungry?"

"Hungry for someone to care, for someone to set it free."

It was refreshing to hear someone who was Japanese talking about ghosts. The Japanese are usually referenced to automobiles, or electronics, or trade. But some of them, at least, trafficked in spirits.

"There are companies in Japan," said Hiroshi, "which have mass tombs for their workers and families. They don't want them to feel lonely after they die."

That, thought Am, sounded more Japanese. Most Americans would sooner share a social disease than they would a tomb, especially one housing their co-workers.

"I think," said Am, "that's one company benefit you don't have to worry about offering here."

Hiroshi nodded, but it was apparent he wasn't really listening. "It is good you are concerned about this man," he said. "His *shiryoo* should be delivered from the concerns of this world. Unless that is done, there is the threat of *tatari*—curses."

"Do you really think that?" asked Am.

The Fat Innkeeper looked away, embarrassed. "Does it matter?" he asked. "It is traditional to think in such ways, but now traditions are forgotten."

"Maybe that explains our brave new world," said Am. "More wandering spirits and more curses."

Hiroshi didn't smile. "In my country we have *Obon*," he said, "a Festival of the Dead. But it is not what it was. Everyone wants to be a *mobo* or *moga*, a modern boy and girl."

"What about you?"

Hiroshi reddened slightly and looked uncomfortable. It was clearly not pleasurable for him to talk about some matters, but he still apparently felt the need to talk. Am knew from Sharon that the Japanese favored indirect speech, quite in contrast to American "straight talk." One Japanese anthropologist had written a paper on how candid speech disturbed the Japanese, and had concluded with a footnote confessing that even writing about it made him feel uncomfortable.

"Sometimes I wonder if I have become a total stranger,"

he said, "a *mattaku tanin ni natta*—an outsider. I find myself thinking in English because in Japanese it is difficult to imagine the thoughts I have been having. Hideki Yukawa won the Nobel Prize in physics. He said that when he thought about physics, he thought in English. I understand that."

"Did you want to come here?" asked Am.

A slight shrug. "It was necessary. From here I can see better over there."

Neither one of them said anything for a minute or two. Am thought about his words. They were similar to the sentiments expressed by the near-dead. Having almost died had changed their thinking. They said they understood things better now. "Be positive," Kingsbury had said. Words for life, or words for death?

"I have to go look after my dead man," said Am.

"In Japanese, samurai means 'one who serves,'" said Hiroshi.

The translation, thought Am, fit him only too well.

Chapter Twenty-Two

The Hotel limo had picked up Bradford (his real name was Brad, but he had added the "ford" because he thought that was more classy) and his girlfriend Cleopatra (she herself preferred to be called Cleo, but Bradford liked her full name) at the airport. The driver, Bradford thought approvingly, knew his stuff. He'd opened the doors for them, addressed them as "madam" and "sir," and been appropriately obsequious. There had been a complimentary split of champagne iced and waiting for them. Bradford had opened the bottle, looked Cleo romantically in the eye, and had poured. When they clinked glasses, he said, "To us." The words had the proper effect. Her eyes went soft and stupid, and her brain clicked off. She was sure she was in love. That would make matters much easier for him.

Going with him to the Hotel was her declaration of independence. And it was his route to independence. Her old man was the only obstacle between Bradford and money. Mack Harris had made a fortune in his Arizona trucking business. The only thing that mattered to Mack other than money was his daughter. It figured that Mack was the one who had insisted she be named Cleopatra. She was his little princess.

Bradford Beck was similar to Mack in that he also loved money, but he didn't like having to work for it. He had become a stockbroker, not because he had any enthusiasm for the trade, but because the market was something rich people liked to diddle with. When Bradford was at the country club he always had a line of patter that the members liked. He knew how to dress their dress and talk their talk. He wanted in on their fraternity, had assiduously scouted out the moneyed set. He knew their holdings like a sports fanatic knows batting averages. Cleo Harris was the catch he had been looking for. No siblings, no mother, nothing between her and a fortune except for a red-necked, greasy-handed father.

Bradford had done his best to charm her old man. He had been attentive and polite, had pretended interest in his words (what few of them had been thrown his way), and yet the simian had made it clear he didn't approve of Bradford.

Screw him. After they got married, Daddy Warbucks would still want to please his little darling. He'd cough up for a seven-figure house, and that would be for starters. And if Bradford could stomach his spoiled baby for a few years, the payoffs would only get better and better.

"Just you, and me, and the beach, darling," he said. "La Jolla, here we come."

The damn Hotel California wasn't cheap, but in order to make money, you had to spend money. It was Bradford's way of priming the pump. She would see that Daddy wasn't the only one who could protect her, or give her the best. And he could entertain in ways that Daddy couldn't. She'd probably be asking him to marry her. They had all but made their eloping official.

"La Jolla," she whispered, closing her eyes and kissing him.

He closed his eyes and kissed her. He preferred it that way. Bradford didn't have to look at her, could see visions of dollars instead of a slightly overweight bleached blonde. She looked more like a million others than a million dollars, but there were those hidden assets, those wonderful hidden assets.

"The Hotel California," he said. "They were booked up, but I was able to convince a reservationist that it was our special occasion."

Cleo cooed at his masterful manner. He figured the Hotel was perfect. That's where the gentry went. All of Cleo's rich friends had practically grown up there, had escaped Arizona's summer heat by going to the San Diego coast. But not Cleo. Her father had always shipped her off to the East Coast for her summers, had sent her off to his sister for some "womanly influence." Cleo's mother had died when she was young. Wasn't that a shame?

"I hear it's wonderful there," she said.

At the prices they charge, thought Bradford, it better be. But it should be the culminating touch. It would demonstrate his pedigree, his good taste. Cleo was used to the best. She would naturally compare him with Daddy, and he wasn't going to fall short. The stay was already choreographed in his mind—the attentive bellmen, the subservient room-service waiters, the glad-handing maître d', the watchful doorman. He would be a showman, surprise her with goodies and treats, provide her with the best time in her life. He'd give her irresistable romance. And then he'd be rich. God, he'd be rich.

Buoyed by bubbly, the thirteen-mile ride from San Diego's Lindbergh Field (one of the few airports that is actually located downtown and not in some suburb) went quickly. When Cleo caught sight of the Hotel, she couldn't find enough superlatives. Look at the ocean! And the gardens! And the gazebo! Everything so perfect! She could hardly contain her excitement. The last time Cleo had felt like this was when she was a little girl and her daddy had taken her to Disneyland. She leaned over and kissed Bradford. "Thank you," she said. No one else had ever treated her this way. In high school she had only had three dates, two if you didn't count the senior prom, and a friend had set her up for that. Cleo felt grown up now, a lady. And she had her knight in shining armor, her love.

The limo pulled up to the front of the Hotel, glided to a stop in front of the towering palms and the waving flags. The driver was out in a flash, had their doors opened and their luggage on the curb in double time. He said he hoped the ride had been comfortable, and was sure they would enjoy their stay. A bellman, he informed them, would be taking their luggage to the front desk. The driver said all of this in mellifluous and practiced tones, addressing them as if they were royalty. Bradford momentarily debated whether the performance was worth a ten spot or a twenty, and settled for a ten on top and George Washington underneath. He folded the bills so that the driver only knew he was getting Hamilton and a friend, which got them several more bows and expressions of gratitude than if he'd merely handed over the tenner.

Cleo acted as if she had died and gone to heaven. She

kept pulling at Bradford's arm. The old Hotel did have a
lot of charm, he had to admit. He'd heard the Nips had
bought the place a few months back. That had stirred up a
hornet's nest, but they had made a bunch of promises that
they weren't going to tamper with the "Hotel's unique am-
bience." The new ownership had said they were actually
going to improve operations, make the place "run more ef-
ficiently." That sounded just fine to Bradford. He wanted
everything chop-chop, and if the Japs could deliver that,
fine and dandy.

The doorman, dressed in pith helmet and safari outfit,
opened the door to the lobby. "Good day, sir," he said.
"Good day, madam."

Mighty damn fine, thought Bradford.

Cleopatra was chattering about this and that while they
walked through the old lobby. For someone with as much
money as she had been born into, Bradford thought she
acted as if she had been raised in a barn. There were a lot of
attractions, to be sure—flower arrangements big enough to
qualify for their own zip code, crystal chandeliers that
glimmered so much you'd swear the lighting was superflu-
ous, and dramatic tapestries that . . .

Bradford bumped into someone. Automatic words were
uttered at the same time: "Excuse me."

"Jinx," said the woman he had nudged, "owe a drink,"
then she counted to ten and laughed.

"She's got you there," said the man next to her.

Bradford looked puzzled. "Didn't you ever play that
game?" the woman asked.

She asked in such a way that Bradford wished he had.
She was older than he was, about thirty-five, he guessed,
but in fine form. He tried not to stare at the cut of her

blouse, which was very open, but he did take in a few peeks. She had red hair and green eyes, was the kind of woman, he thought, who had a way of beckoning from her lips to her hips.

"Surely you must have played that game, Bradford," said Cleo. "You know, when you say the same thing at the same time as someone else, and you're supposed to say 'Jinx,' and then name your price and count to ten. Whoever counts first wins. Me and Donna used to always be saying the same thing and playing that game. We played for Cokes."

"I play for more than that," said the woman.

"I guess I owe you a drink," said Bradford.

"Doug Walker," said the man, "and the woman you owe a drink is my wife Missy."

"Bradford Beck," he said, "and my girlfriend, Cleopatra Harris."

They shook hands all around. Bradford was certain that Missy grasped his hand with a little more pressing of the flesh than was usual, and held on longer than was customary. Not that he was complaining. Far from it.

"You're lucky my wife didn't hit you up for something more," said Doug with a wink.

"The conversation's young," said Missy. "Who knows, we might cross tongues again."

"We weren't watching where we were going," said Cleo. "I think our eyes were in the stars."

That's it, thought Bradford. Make us look like yokels.

"We'll have to plead guilty to that also," said Doug. "Course they say when you're looking up at the stars, you're at the mercy of the puddles of the road."

Cleo and Doug laughed. He patted her on the shoulder, then rubbed her on the arm.

"Is this your first . . ."

Bradford and Missy said the same thing again. "Jinx," she said, "owe a drink," then outcounted him to ten.

The four of them were hard-pressed to stop laughing. "I think your boyfriend's trying to get my wife drunk," said Doug, patting Cleo's arm again.

"Who says he needs to?" asked Missy.

The laughing started once more. "I better keep my mouth shut," said Bradford. "This could get damn expensive, especially if your taste runs to Napoleon brandy or Cristal champagne."

"I only swallow two kinds of drinks," she said, "a Sloe Screw on the Wall, or a Screaming Orgasm."

Bradford had heard of those drinks, but didn't know of anyone who actually ordered them. For a moment there was silence, then Doug said, "I swear to God it's true. Those are her favorite drinks."

They all laughed again.

"Are you staying here?" asked Cleo.

"We're just about to check in," said Doug.

"So are we," she said.

"Well, I call that happy tidings. We just drove in with another couple, but they're not nearly as fun as the two of you."

He squeezed her arm again. By this time Cleo was used to it, and squeezed him back.

"Shhh," said Doug. "Here they come now. Whatever you do, don't abandon us."

There didn't appear to be much chance of that. Missy was giving Bradford some looks that he thought were promising, very promising.

"Gary and Suzy Corbett," said Doug, "it's time you met Bradford and Cleopatra."

The Corbetts could have been Mr. and Mrs. Claus at about age forty, thought Bradford. Gary had a long beard, still mostly dark, red cheeks, a slight pot belly, and a rubicund nose that could have passed for Rudolph's. Suzy wore granny glasses, had plump cheeks, and wore her hair in a bun. Both of them were oh, so happy. Suzy gave Bradford a big hug, and Gary did the same to Cleo. It was as if they were all old friends. When the six of them walked up laughing to the front desk, it was impossible figuring out who belonged to whom.

"Checking in," said Doug. "The ladies are with me, and I don't know who these men are."

"That's funny," said Missy, "I do."

The laughter started again, even before Missy goosed Bradford.

Margaret Talley was a recent graduate of Mesa College's hotel-motel program. She was a reentry student, had been a homemaker for the twenty years prior to her going back to school. Margaret's world had been that of raising three children. She said that in her two weeks at the Hotel she had gotten a new education on life and human nature. By the sounds of it, those were insights she might have been better without.

"If you'll please register," she said, supplying them with registration cards.

The men did the registering. Usually males are about as proprietary with registration cards as they are with the television remote control.

"This time you don't have to sign us in as Mr. and Mrs. John Smith," said Missy.

"Hard to break old habits," said Doug.

"Get thee to a nunnery," said Gary.

The laughter started again. Margaret didn't ask them, "How many in your party?" She had seen even staid businessmen get their testosterone flowing over that one.

"Two in each room?" she asked.

"Give or take a few," said Doug.

Margaret offered a Mona Lisa smile. Being a veteran of a fortnight in the industry, she was now of the opinion that her schooling should have included a course on "Introduction to the Obnoxious." She tapped into the computer and managed to maintain her smile, though suddenly she was nervous. These were some more of those people, those sex maniacs.

She was glad to see that T.K. had joined her. Margaret figured he was there to help. She didn't know that he had been attracted by the sounds of laughter.

"I'll bet you all want a room with a view," he said. T.K. was rather pleased with himself. Am had thought he was so smart. He hadn't suspected that there might be a third Forster book. But T.K.'s routine didn't go quite as he expected.

"Screw the view," said Missy. "Just make sure it's got a bed."

"Or two," said Gary to some laughter.

"Or three," said Bradford, not wanting to be left out. He wasn't. The laughing redoubled.

Where was the joke? wondered T.K. Comedians are always desperate to get that laugh. They have to know what works, and what doesn't.

"T.K.," said Margaret.

He tried to ignore the new clerk. This apparently wasn't

the E.M. Forster kind of crowd. Maybe he should tell them the story about the guest with the . . .

"T.K.," she said again.

"What?"

"I seem to be having some trouble with the computer."

"You know what hackers say," said Doug, "garbage in, garbage out."

"Not only hackers," said Missy.

They were laughing again. Damn, thought T.K. He wasn't the one getting the laughs. And what was even worse, he still didn't know what they were laughing about.

"T.K.," said Margaret, pointing at the computer.

He looked at the monitor and tried to figure out what was wrong, what the rookie clerk had done. Everything appeared to be okay. "What's the problem?" he asked.

What did she have to do, hit him over the head? "This prompt keeps coming up," she said, emphatically pressing her finger to the group notation of Swap Meat.

"Oh," he said, much relieved. So that's what the laughter was about. Double entendres. These were some more of those mate-swappers.

Bradford had been watching the two Hotel employees. Something was wrong. He could tell the woman was communicating something to the man, and he could guess what it was. He knew how hotels were famous for overbooking. No way were they walking him to another property.

"We have confirmed reservations," Bradford said over-loudly, and with not a little self-importance. He pushed his registration card forward, issued it as a challenge.

Though Bradford was referring to his personal reservation, T.K. assumed he was speaking for the group. "Yes, sir," he said. "We were just making sure the rooms were ready. And they are."

Were they ever. Housekeeping had just finished preparing the rooms from hell. T.K. took Bradford's registration card and called up his reservation on the computer. For some reason the loudmouth wasn't listed as being part of the Swap Meat. That had to be changed. Bradford Beck and Cleopatra (yeah, likely name, he thought) Harris were going to be put where they belonged—in the pervert zone. The only thing that room block was missing was red lights.

"Why, it just so happens," said T.K., with the smallest of leers, "that all of your rooms are next to one another. Even interconnecting, if you choose."

He handed Bradford a key. "You, Mr. Beck, will be the monkey in the middle."

Bradford looked surprised. Those weren't the words he was expecting. Monkey in the middle?

"Say," T.K. announced, "did all of you hear about the psychiatrist who had to examine the patient to determine if he was sexually disturbed?"

To T.K.'s satisfaction, his words got everyone's attention.

"The shrink had a pack of those Rorschach cards, you know, those inkblot things. He held up the first one and asked the patient what he saw.

" 'I see a man and a woman,' the patient said, 'and boy, oh, boy, what they're doing.'

"Then the psychiatrist showed him another card and asked him what he saw, and the guy said, 'I see a man and a woman, and you just can't believe what they're doing.'

"With a sigh, the shrink displayed yet another inkblot, and this time the patient is all but frothing at the mouth. 'I see a man and a woman, and you just can't believe how they're getting it on.'

"The psychiatrist took off his glasses, wearily rubbed his eyes, and then said, 'There's no doubt about it. I'm afraid you are sexually disturbed.'

"'What do you mean *I'm* sexually disturbed?' shrieked the man. 'You're the one showing me all the dirty pictures.'"

Doug and Missy and Gary and Suzy all laughed. Cleo ventured a smile. Bradford was shocked. How could the hired help presume to act in such a way?

"Hey, Brad."

The black man was motioning him closer. Had he just called him by his first name? His real first name? Did the man know him from somewhere? No. Bradford was certain that he didn't. So what the hell was going on? With an all too familiar manner, the impertinent clerk kept signalling for him to approach. Reluctantly, Bradford ventured nearer. T.K. finished madly scribbling on a piece of paper, held it up for everyone to see.

The drawing looked like a big inkblot.

"Hey, Brad. I was kind of wondering if you could tell me what you see in this."

Chapter Twenty-Three

The theme of UNDER's cocktail party was "An Irish Wake." A band was playing the music of the Grateful Dead. Somebody had a sense of humor after all.

The dance floor was full, and the Starfish Room crowded. Am was a man with a mission. He stalked the room and intently stared at name tags, his goal to talk with as many of the thirty-one people Thomas Kingsbury had interviewed as possible. Periodically, he consulted his sheet of names. Approximately every tenth name tag produced a match.

No one had been reluctant to talk. Am had only to mention the name of Thomas Kingsbury and then try and keep up with his note-taking. Many of those he interviewed said they had experienced some form of premonition that Kingsbury was going to die. Several said his aura was off. One woman told Am that she had seen a shadow over him, while a man said he "just knew" something was wrong. None had seen fit to mention those observations to Dr. Kingsbury.

Most remembered their interviews lasting about twenty minutes. The doctor had primarily focused on the physical circumstances of their near-deaths, frequently referring to the voluminous medical forms they had filled out for him. Am presumed those forms had been left in Kingsbury's room and the police were now analyzing them. He wished he could have seen the doctor's notes, wondered what the great skeptic had written down during his interviews. His own notes and observations were rapidly filling his notebook. There is something in human nature that reacts to an expectant pen, that feels obligated to respond at length to a waiting notepad. But Am wasn't only taking down quotes. Scattered through the pages were such commentaries as "Could bore a tree," "Unquestionably certifiable," and "Says it was not the right time for him to die—definitely don't agree."

"Be positive"—Kingsbury's last words. After talking with most of the same people the doctor had, Am wondered at his presumption.

Les Moore ("My real name, swear to God") had seen the doctor at one-thirty on the day he had died. "He was very upbeat, in great humor," Les said. "He had just come back from lunch and I think he had had a couple."

He made a drinking motion.

"That sort of surprised me, since he was supposed to be working. How many people do you know who drink on the job?"

Am took a guilty sip of his zombie. It was his second. The first he had ordered as a silent tribute to Kingsbury; the second drink he justified as being medicinal. Normally, he never drank at the Hotel. Then again, he'd never had to interview the near-dead.

"What do you do for a living, Mr. Moore?"

The fiftyish, bespectacled man said, with some pride, "I'm a CPA."

In the first minute of their conversation Am had written down his observations of "Seemingly normal" and "Very detailed." Two for two, he thought smugly.

"Mr. Moore, you said Dr. Kingsbury asked a number of questions about your near-death experience."

Les nodded. "Three years ago, my family was on vacation at the shore. We've got a place at Bay Head, New Jersey. I consider myself a prudent man, one who doesn't take unnecessary risks. I've been swimming there forever, and never had any problems. I usually swim out to some buoys and back. It was a beautiful July day. Everything was calm."

He remembered a copious amount of details, offered up each once as if they were minor treasures. Am learned the names of the lifeguards that had fished Les out of the ocean, heard how one of them had been attending Colgate, and the other Syracuse, and how one of them actually knew his son (Les Moore, Jr.).

The distilled, very distilled, story was that Les had been brought from the water apparently dead. No heartbeat or pulse could be found. Les said that one part of him could see the lifeguards working on him, while another part of him was "exploring the great beyond."

"I made some notes, actually," said Les. "I thought Dr. Kingsbury would be interested in hearing about my experiences in death. But I didn't really get a chance to share—"

"What kind of things was Dr. Kingsbury interested in?" asked Am.

"The physical. How long before I started breathing again, the possible effects of hypothermia, the methodology of the medical treatment, the drugs administered, my medical history, things like that. He had a checklist, and apparently asked the same questions of everybody. At the time, I didn't think that was very creative of him. Mostly he was just corroborating the information he already had."

"What do you mean?"

"We had to fill out an involved medical history," said Les (he wasn't complaining, as most had about that, but rather seemed to relish the memory), "and sign a medical release allowing Dr. Kingsbury access to our records. I guess I never really expected him to conduct a background search on our near-deaths, but he did. He was apparently very thorough about consulting with our physicians and collecting all of our medical records.

"I suppose that was really the only sensible approach. Anyone doing a scientific inquiry can't rely solely on the memories of the patients. In our short time together, I could see he was very diligent about recording information and confirming details, though, as I told you, I think he gave short shrift to my postmortem. I was prepared to delve into my after-life experiences, tell him about—"

"I'm sure Dr. Kingsbury was pressed for time," said Am, pointedly looking at his watch.

"I offered him my notes," said Les, "but he didn't want them. Perhaps you could use them?"

He gave Am an all-too-hopeful look. "I wouldn't want to deprive—"

"No problem," said Les. "I make copies of everything, just like I advise my clients to do."

I wouldn't doubt it, thought Am. Those who make history usually don't care about the tracks they leave behind, whereas those like Les could probably document every haircut they'd had in the past thirty years. But, Am considered, perhaps he could benefit from the man's excessive chronicling. "You didn't," he asked, "happen to make a copy of Dr. Kingsbury's medical questionnaire, did you?"

"Up in my room!" said Les excitedly. "Along," he added, "with those notes I was telling you about."

Am responded cheerfully to the two-for-one blackmail: "I'd love to see both of them."

Les Moore departed with alacrity. He wanted to tell his story, and really didn't care who was the listener, just so long as it was a warm set of ears. That's the problem, thought Am, with having what you think is a unique experience only to be told by dozens of other people, "Oh, that happened to me." The greatest tale in Les Moore's life didn't seem so fantastic in a setting where everyone else had experienced similar episodes.

Am returned to his name-tag search. To expedite his inspection, he determined that he wouldn't look at faces, only scrutinize the name tags on chests. His technique didn't prove to be a time-saver, however, as he spent too much time imagining the faces above the chests. The names influenced Am's mental pictures. He was a believer that people often grew (or sank) into their names, and that there was a universality of features and characteristics that could be applied to certain first names. Who could trust anyone named Don? And had there ever been a Darlene that didn't like to party? To test that theory (and others), Am conjured up a visage, then, of course, he sneaked a peek; on several faces he was very close; on some he wasn't even in the ballpark. When Am finally encountered a body with no name tag, he had to draw his conclusions not from a name but from the polyester tie, white shirt, and wrinkled blue blazer. What he overlooked was the bulge in the jacket. Am imagined the face, sneaked his look, and then felt very stupid. His mental image wasn't close, though he knew the sneer only too well. Cops aren't big on name tags. They do like guns, however.

"What are you doing, Caulfield?" asked Detective McHugh. "Taking a census of belly buttons?"

No, Am almost said, assholes. But he had survived twenty years in the hotel business by thinking those kinds of thoughts instead of speaking them. "Detective McHugh," he said.

McHugh said nothing, just silently appraised Am. With no confession apparently forthcoming, the detective finally said, "A rather interesting group of people you've been talking with."

Am still didn't say anything.

"In fact, we seem to be talking to the same people. But I guess that's just a coincidence, huh?"

Next time, thought Am, I'll scan the room for faces before I zero in on name tags.

"You're meddling in areas you're not qualified," said McHugh. "This is a homicide investigation."

"Have the autopsy results confirmed that?"

"You can hear the results of the autopsy tomorrow, like the rest of the public."

"Or you can tell me now."

The detective offered a mock laugh and shook his head. "Hear they're holding a séance a little later tonight, Caulfield. Maybe you should just call up the spirit of Dr. Kingsbury and ask him a few questions."

"Is that how SDPD does it?"

McHugh's answer was a hard stare. If looks could kill, thought Am. The detective brushed by him, his footsteps even louder than the ersatz Grateful Dead music.

I wonder, Am thought, if that qualified as a near-death experience.

Chapter Twenty-Four

That bellman, thought Cleo, keeps leering at me. She wasn't sure how insulted she should be. Men didn't usually look at her like that, at least not that she was aware. He wasn't bad-looking, though, that is if you liked the dark, slick-haired types.

Jimmy Mazzelli gave her a wink. She turned away and pretended not to have seen. Bradford was busy talking with their newfound friends, or otherwise he certainly would have disciplined this forward fellow.

She doesn't seem like one of those insatiable-type women, thought Jimmy. She seems normal, even shy. He felt kind of sorry for her, though he didn't know why. "Where you from?" Jimmy asked.

A moment's hesitation: "Scottsdale."

"Oh, a Zonie."

Every summer Southern Californians experience an invasion of "Zonies," Arizonans fleeing the heat. It was mostly a term of endearment, but Cleo decided she didn't like the bellman's familiar tone and turned away from him once again.

He'd offended her. She was kind of cute the way she

turned away. The more he talked with her, the more attractive she became to Jimmy. "What's your name?" he asked.

Why wasn't Bradford walking with them? He was dawdling, was at least a dozen paces behind them. She could hear him laughing. He had never laughed that way around her, at least not that she remembered. "Cleopatra Harris," she said.

"Like the Queen of Egypt, huh?"

She nodded.

"Jimmy Mazzelli, Your Highness," he said, then brought his cart to a stop. "And these are your royal quarters."

He felt a little bad for her sake, he who was regarded as not having a conscience. Jimmy opened the door to the room and motioned for her to precede him. It would have been better if her stiff of a boyfriend were here to see this. She walked ahead, felt an anticipatory thrill. Almost, Cleo wanted to close her eyes. If the room was even half as exquisite as the Hotel . . .

She stopped walking, halted by some unsavory smell. Cleo sniffed uncertainly, afraid to continue forward. Then she shrieked. She had been bumped from behind. That clumsy bellman had run one of the suitcases into her backside. Probably purposely.

"Excuse me," said Jimmy. He hadn't expected her to stop. Hell, he hadn't expected her to be anything like what she was.

Where was Bradford? Breathing through her mouth, Cleo ventured a little farther into the room. She wanted to cry out again, this time at what she saw. The room was . . . awful. Surely there was some mistake.

"Where do you want the bags?" asked Jimmy.

"But the room . . ." she said.

Jimmy looked around. His expression didn't change. "What?"

"It's a mess," she said.

"The maid might have been a little hurried," he explained.

"The maid should be fired," said Cleo.

"What about her family of twelve that she's totally supporting?" asked Jimmy. "What about them?"

Jimmy immediately regretted his lie. Announcing the imaginary brood of children had made Cleopatra uncomfortable. She had feelings.

Cleo opened her mouth to say something, decided silence was best, and closed it. Maybe if she did the same with her eyes, closed them for a second, and . . . No, nothing had changed. Everything was as bad as before. There were sand footprints in the carpeting; there were crumpled newspapers on the floor; there was a pair of panty hose resting over a chair that was on its last legs—literally. She cast a glance at the bed and looked away. The bedspread looked as if puppies had been birthed on it, and a big litter at that.

Cleo felt faint. Even though she was breathing through her mouth, the odor, perhaps the poisonous fumes, were still getting to her.

"I need air," she said.

Jimmy walked over to the sliding glass doors. He gave a mighty heave, but couldn't get the door open. Surprise, surprise, he thought. Jimmy tried again, then apologetically turned to her. "Sometimes they stick," he said. "I'll have to get maintenance up here." As if, he thought, they hadn't been there already.

The glass had a layer of grime, looked as if someone had been cooking bacon for a few years without bothering to clean. Through it, Cleo could barely make out the ocean. The vision taunted like a mirage.

She walked out of the room to the hallway, Jimmy following her. Bradford would deal with this. He had made the reservation. Cleo looked around for him, saw him in the doorway of the next room. Only half of his body was visible. That was probably just as well. The half she could see had a woman's hands embracing his buttocks.

"Bradford!"

He jumped a little, and the hands reluctantly released their hold. As he walked back toward their room, Bradford straightened his tie, then patted down his suit, especially the area around his hindquarters.

"Getting rid of fingerprints?" asked Cleo.

Bradford pretended he didn't know what she was talking about. Jimmy was leaning on his cart, watching the scene with apparent pleasure. The preppie had been busted bigtime. Bradford didn't like being scrutinized, especially by the peons. The staff certainly could use a course on propriety, he thought. They had crossed over that line between friendly and familiar. Hell, they acted as if they were intimates.

He tossed the bellman two dollars. Implicit with the gesture was the unsaid word "Dismissed." Bradford would explain the misunderstanding to Cleo, but in the privacy of their room. Missy was just a bit exuberant—that was all. He motioned for Cleo to go inside the room, but she wasn't about to be herded. Her sudden independence might have bothered Bradford more if he hadn't caught a whiff of something awful from inside the room. What is that smell? he wondered.

Jimmy slowly uncrinkled the dollar bills, made a show of

looking rather forlornly for more, though no one was paying any attention to him. It would have been smarter if he had hightailed it, but he liked watching his Cleopatra. The woman had gumption.

Cleo's eyes were on Bradford. He kept moving his nose around and sniffing. It annoyed Cleo that he wasn't more concerned about what she had seen. "What was going on there?" she asked shrilly.

Bradford kept sniffing. "Nothing," he said. "Missy's just rather high-spirited."

"Is that what you call it?" asked Cleo.

"Yes," said Bradford. "That's what I'd call it."

The smell, he determined, was coming from inside their room. Bradford decided to investigate.

Good time to leave, thought Jimmy. He was out of sight, but not earshot, when he heard a loud "What the hell?"

Cleo hadn't followed Bradford inside. She didn't care about the room anymore. A woman's hands had been clasped around her boyfriend's butt. That was the issue. When he came storming out, she no longer shared his indignation.

"Did you see . . . ?"

She turned from him. His first impulse was to get mad at her. A flirtation was one thing, an assault to the senses quite another. But Bradford remembered that Cleo was a million bucks and then some. His million bucks. "Hey," he said, "we shouldn't be fighting."

At least not before we're married, he thought.

She turned back to him, very quickly, and started crying. He held her. Between sobs, Cleo said, "I'm sorry."

"I'm sorry, too," said Bradford. "I wanted everything to be perfect for you."

He hadn't spent top dollar to get a room that would have put a flophouse to shame. "There's been some mistake," Bradford said, "but don't worry, I'll make things right."

Taking a breath of the outside air, Bradford plunged back inside the room. Tentatively, Cleo followed. She saw him pick up the phone. He knew she was watching, but even if she hadn't been, Bradford still would have looked as if he were ready to chew off the mouthpiece. To his extreme disappointment, he didn't even get the satisfaction of damaging a fellow human's eardrum. The line was dead.

He threw down the phone. He couldn't break what was broken, but it gave him some slight satisfaction anyway. "I don't believe this," he said.

Ohhhhhhh. Ohhhhhhh. Ohhhhhhh. The sound came from next door, along with a pounding on the wall. What was going on, murder? Ohhhhhhh. Ohhhhhhh. Ohhhhhhh. If it was, the woman was taking a long time to die.

Bradford and Cleo looked uncertainly at each other. What should they do?

Ohhhhhhh. Ohhhhhhh. Ohhhhhhh. The screams were faster and louder.

"Oh," said Bradford and Cleo at the same time, but neither said "Jinx" and counted to ten.

"I'm going to go to the front desk and get some satisfaction," said Bradford, immediately regretting his choice of words. He had to speak loudly to be heard. Their neighbor's lovemaking could have passed for a catfight.

Cleo silently nodded. She felt intimidated by the vigorous lovemaking. Bradford was a bit nonplussed himself, though he pretended not to be. Missy's cries followed him to the elevator. The echo stayed in his mind all the way to the lobby. Though he was still angry, his head of steam felt somewhat, well, diverted. At the sight of T.K., his right-eous indignation returned. He was tired of being played for a fool.

"I want to speak to the general manager," demanded Bradford. "No one else will do."

There were other guests at the front desk. They could hear the tenor of his anger. Even the wiseass clerk, thought Bradford, knew better than to say anything back. He merely nodded deferentially, and said, "I'll take you to him."

T.K. walked around the desk and out to the lobby. "This way, please," he said. The two of them didn't have far to go. They stopped in front of a shoe-shine stand.

"Mr. Beck," said T.K., "this is Mr. Toyota, our general manager."

The shoe-shine man nodded and smiled, then motioned Bradford into the chair. Somewhat bewildered, Bradford sat down. He had heard the Japanese were incredibly industri-ous, but wasn't running a hotel and the shoe-shine conces-sion a bit much?

"Mr. Toyota's English isn't the best," said T.K. "But his comprehension is good."

Felipe Valdez had worked as the Hotel's shoe-shine man for over twenty years, and in that time had picked up amaz-ingly little English. But his customers didn't come to him for conversation, they came because he put a shine on shoes that captured a full moon in leather. Felipe started in on Bradford's shoes.

"He likes to shine and listen at the same time," explained T.K.

Probably some new Jap psychology, thought Bradford.

By pretending he's a servant, he actually puts me in his debt.

"Mr. Toyota," said Bradford.

Felipe looked up from the shoe shine. "Toyota," he said, smiling and nodding. They were good cars, he had heard, even though he preferred Chevys.

"Toyota," said Bradford, trying to pronounce it as the man had.

The shoe-shine/general manager nodded.

"I'll leave you two," said T.K.

Bradford talked and Felipe shined, occasionally nodding. Bradford told him about the insolent front desk clerk, and the horrid condition of his room. Felipe might not know English, but he did know anguish.

"Sorry," he said to the man in his chair.

The word made Bradford feel better. At least the manager cared. Bradford spoke on. Would Mr. Toyota see to another room assignment? Perhaps upgrade them to a suite for the indignities they had suffered? Or, at the least, would he have their room cleaned at light speed?

"Okay," said Felipe.

"Okay," said Bradford.

Felipe helped him down from his chair. He smiled and said, "Five dollars." He knew that much English at least.

"Five dollars?" asked Bradford.

"Five dollars," said Felipe.

Smart, Bradford thought. The Japanese, more than anyone, knew time was money. The general manager could listen to problems, shine some shoes, and still make extra cash. Was that a new way of doing things? It seemed a little strange, though. You come with a complaint, someone shines your shoes, and then you pay money. It was definitely different.

"Five dollars," announced Bradford and Felipe at the same time.

As if programmed, Bradford said, "Jinx, you owe me a suite, one, two, three, four, five, six, seven, eight, nine, ten."

"No ten," said Felipe. "Five dollars."

Bradford gave him the five bucks, and the funny-looking Jap thanked him loudly. Shaking his hand, Bradford wondered what, if anything, Toyota was going to do for him. But he had said "Okay," hadn't he?

As Bradford walked away, he couldn't help but admire the shine the man had put on his shoes. His loafers looked better than new.

Chapter Twenty-Five

It was the strangest prayer Am had ever heard, if indeed it was a prayer. In the good old days a prayer usually started with some invocation to God, and ended with an "amen." These, apparently, were not the good old days.

Brother Howard (he didn't call himself the reverend, or father, or rabbi, or some of the more familiar religious titles) had offered his own unique liturgy. It was an invocation of sorts, although he never used the word "God." Brother Howard relied upon euphemisms, referring to the Good Guide, the High Host, and the Supreme Conscience, to name but a few. Contextually, it was difficult figuring out if Brother Howard's God was the embodiment of enlightened mankind, or a deity. The ambiguity bothered Am. Purported holy men who can't say "God," he thought, revealed quite a spiritual stutter.

The theme of Brother Howard's speech centered on listening to the dead. It wasn't exactly the séance that Detective McHugh had presaged, but it was close enough.

Brother Howard didn't need the prophets to back up his observations. He called upon a patchwork philosophy, managed to draw in everything from the Tibetan *Book of the*

Dead to the kind of quotes you find in *Reader's Digest*. The world had but to open their ears, said Brother Howard, to hear the voices of the dead. These voices, apparently, were that much more accessible if you bought Brother Howard's videotapes, audiotapes, and books.

He didn't wear a clerical collar but a black turtleneck, and sported an ankh instead of a cross. He was modern times, believed in an earring instead of a hair shirt. The mote in his eyes was the result of bright-blue contact lenses. He had a turquoise bracelet, and a large turquoise ring. Maybe that's why he made so many "Great Spirit" references. Brother Howard was about forty-five, and knew the crowd's preferences better than a Bible-thumper knows chapter and verse. He was of average height, and average weight, and he knew the averages. His hair was dark, save for a silver streak that ran from front to back. Am figured in the dark it probably glowed.

"T.S. Eliot," said Brother Howard, "wrote these words:

What the dead had no speech for,
     when living,
They can tell you, being dead: the
     communication
Of the dead is tongued with fire beyond
     the language of the living.

Eliot also wrote, remembered Am, "In the rooms the women come and go, talking of Michelangelo." Given a choice, he would have preferred conversing about Michelangelo.

"Why is it," asked Brother Howard, "that the bards hear what we cannot? Let me read again: 'The communication of the dead is tongued with fire beyond the language of the living.' "

He allowed for a literary moment, a silence to let everyone contemplate the words. "I don't need to tell many of you who are here about the great outer reach (Brother Howard also preferred euphemisms for death). But I can teach you to listen, and hear what is being said. Listen now."

Brother Howard let an even longer silence build. "Did you hear anything?" he asked.

No one replied.

"Do you know how to listen?" he asked.

Again, no one said anything.

"Do you want to learn how to hear the dead?"

This time the crowd responded. Many yelled. There was head-bobbing fever. Everyone, except Am, was enthusiastic. He thought it was a rare person that listened to the living, so why did everyone imagine the dead would so capture their attention?

Brother Howard offered some "attuning" exercises. The dead apparently made themselves known in a number of ways. They didn't exhibit themselves like poltergeists, he said, didn't rattle or shake things, or fly around the room. The dead existed in another plane. They didn't speak, at least not like the living, but anyone could develop an "inner ear" to sense their presence.

And if you believe in Tinkerbell, thought Am, just clap your hands together.

The UNDER attendees tried following Brother Howard's advice. They closed their eyes and were instructed to "release their spirits and open themselves." While everyone around him was trying to do just that, Am found himself thinking about the Fat Innkeeper. Hiroshi had talked about spirits, had even suggested you had to listen to them, and in some cases appease them. He wished he could close his eyes, and do as Detective McHugh had suggested, just ask Thomas Kingsbury some questions. But if the dead were talking, Am couldn't hear what they were saying. There were only the echoes of Dr. Kingsbury's last words, and those weren't any help at all.

Brother Howard's listening session came to a close. An UNDER dinner banquet awaited. For those interested, he said, communing with the dead would continue after dinner. Brother Howard also mentioned he was available for private consultations, and, of course, his "exploration and listening guides" could be had in the dealer's room. Words from the grave apparently didn't come cheap. The dead were a much bigger business than Am had ever imagined.

In any enterprise, there are the sincere, and those who attempt to exploit the sincere. Brother Howard spoke the New Age message well, but there was something about him that indicated the language was a new one to him. But if he was a wolf, thought Am, at least he knew to wear natural fibers.

A familiar face passed by and awakened Am from his musing. "Clara," he called. "Clara."

She chose not to hear him, tried to lose herself in the crowd. Am pursued her, finally caught up, and then blocked her path.

"Oh," she said. "Hello, Am."

He shook his head. "Clara, you know better."

Clara Appel tried to pretend she didn't know what he was talking about. For years, she had been persona non grata at the Hotel. To look at her, you would have thought

she was an honored guest. Clara's clothing was always immaculate, her makeup impeccable. She was in her late
fifties, to all appearances a well-heeled La Jollan. Once, she
had been just that. But she'd been divorced a dozen years,
and the settlement she had received was now spent. You can
take the woman out of La Jolla, but not the La Jollan out of
the woman. Clara had never been able to adjust to her new
circumstances. The Hotel had always been her playground,
her place to spa and dine. Even though she was destitute
(she spent the year going from friend's house to friend's
house, though never acknowledging her financial straits),
Clara didn't see any reason to give up the Hotel. She just
"adopted" groups. Clara had participated in countless conventions, had sipped the choicest liqueurs at hosted bars,
had dined on the finest banquet food, all at the expense of
the group and/or Hotel. It was hard not feeling sorry for
Clara. She didn't attend the gatherings merely for the free
eats and drinks. Clara was convinced that she would meet
her future husband at a group function. In her fantasy, they
would live happily ever after—in La Jolla, of course.

"Let me walk you out, Clara."

"That's kind of you, Am."

"Breeding" and appearances were important to Clara. If
she was ever reduced to a shopping-cart existence, Clara
would probably put a Mercedes medallion on the grille of
the cart.

The Hotel had tried to dissuade Clara's frequent appearances, using tactics that ranged from psychological to con-
frontational. Everyone from the police to counselors had
been brought in. Clara had been threatened and cajoled,
had spent time in both jail and county mental health, but
her brief incarcerations didn't seem to bother her. She al-

ways returned to the Hotel. One manager had even tried bribing her, had offered Clara complimentary lunches on a periodic basis if only she wouldn't keep crashing functions, but she couldn't be bought off.

When asked to leave, Clara never resisted, but that didn't stop her from coming back the next day. Though the banquet staff would never admit it, many of them turned a blind eye to Clara's presence. It was easier to ignore her, to treat her like the other conventioneers. She was a chameleon that fit into every group function, and was especially good at weddings. Am wondered how many times she had ended up in wedding albums, with the puzzled bride and groom both at a loss to figure out who the mystery woman was. "But I thought she was your Aunt Doris . . . ?"

"Did you enjoy the talk tonight, Clara?"

She offered Am a slight, regretful smile, and shook her head. "I am afraid I did not, Am."

That surprised him. Clara invariably expressed delight at all the gatherings she attended. It didn't really matter what the event was. Clara had sat through more presentations than most figurehead royalty, had listened and happily mingled with gatherings of butchers, and bakers, and candlestick makers.

"Why didn't you like it?"

"I didn't care," she said, with patrician dignity, "for Brother Howard."

Am nodded agreeably. Brother Howard certainly didn't offer old-time religion. "His message was a little bit different," he said.

"His words didn't bother me," said Clara firmly. "It was the man himself."

Her vehemence was unusual. Clara's conversations always

tended toward the pleasant. She was invariably polite (even on the one occasion when the police had handcuffed her and led her off the Hotel grounds for trespassing, vagrancy, and violating a restraining order, as well as a few other charges that Melvin Carrelis had insisted upon).

"He's definitely not your usual man of the cloth," said Am, fishing for more.

Clara didn't respond. They continued walking, were almost to the lobby when she spoke again. "Not long after I separated from my husband," she said, "I went to visit my mother, who was very sick at the time. She had emphysema. She was not very accepting of her . . . situation.

"Perhaps," Clara said with a small smile, "it runs in the family."

Crazy, thought Am, like a fox.

"My mother," she continued, "started doing things very unlike her. She had always prided herself on being very proper, but her illness changed that. She started looking desperately for a magic cure, made a point of visiting everyone who claimed they were a healer. Brother Howard belonged to that unsavory ilk, even if he didn't go by that name at the time.

"I accompanied her to his . . . spectacles. The sessions were called 'The Healing Within.' He offered a very slick snake-oil show. God had given him the power to teach others how to heal themselves, he said. He strutted around holding the Bible like he was the author. Apparently, he was on some healing circuit, went around the country offering his courses. That was smart of him. By being a rolling stone, he never stayed long enough for the funerals. My mother signed up for his three weeks of lessons. Some took to his healing very well. The deaf heard, and the crippled walked, that is if seeing is believing. But what I witnessed most was Reverend Gardenia doing very well by himself."

"Gardenia?"

"Not a name easy to forget. Sometimes he was even referred to as the 'Gardenia of Eden.' "

That, thought Am, was reason enough to distrust him.

"At the end of the course the Reverend Mr. Gardenia pronounced my mother on the road to recovery. That good news cost her around five thousand dollars. She was dead within a month of paying that out."

Clara thought for a moment, then offered another of her soft smiles. "I prefer his current racket," she said. "Now he preys on the dead. Better them than the dying."

Michael the doorman opened one of the lobby doors for them. With his deep bass he wished them a good evening. Clara didn't usually exit or enter through the central portals of the Hotel. She knew the Hotel grounds better than most employees, was well-acquainted with all the back doors.

"Thank you for seeing me out, Am," she said.

"I'm sorry I had to get in the way of your dinner plans, Clara." He reached for his wallet, pulled out a ten-dollar bill, and tried to give it to her.

"Don't be silly," she said, her pride preventing her from accepting the money.

Am tried to think of some words that would make the money acceptable to her, but couldn't come up with any. Next banquet, he decided, he'd make sure the staff turned a blind eye to her presence. Clara always seemed to know which functions offered prime rib, apparently her favorite meal. He'd make sure she got a heaping portion.

Chapter Twenty-Six

"What the hell is the matter with this place?"

Cleo had not bothered to respond to Bradford's first dozen pronouncements, but she was getting tired of hearing the same rhetorical question over and over. "A watched pot never boils," she said.

"Watch me boil," muttered Bradford.

He was waiting for some, any, satisfaction. That funny-looking Japanese manager Toyota had told him everything would be "okay," but not a damn thing had changed. He and Cleo had waited around for an hour now. Most of that time they'd had to listen to Missy's lovemaking. The woman put a steam whistle to shame. You'd think she would have been worn out, but no sooner was her scream-ing done when a party started up in her room, a party, by the sound of it, that was loads of fun.

Not that they hadn't been invited. Doug and Missy had yelled for them to come on over, but Cleopatra was still sulking. Bradford had tried to make it right for her, to smooth things over. He'd flagged down that damn leering bellman, asked him to get them a bottle of bubbly. The bellman had returned with the champagne a short time later, had even set everything up nicely. Bradford had thought their luck was changing. But then that bellman had asked that damnable question to Cleopatra. "How old are you?" Bradford had told him she was twenty-six, but the bellman insisted upon seeing identification. You'd think Cleopatra would have had the sense to have had a fake ID, but no. She was three months shy of being twenty-one, reason enough for that prick bellman to take away the champagne. What galled Bradford most was that he had already paid for the champagne and given the man his tip.

"I'm going to the bar," said Bradford, "to get us another bottle of champagne."

"Are you sure you're not going to stop by the party?" asked Cleo.

"No, I'm not going to stop by the party."

He tried to keep the edge out of his voice. Things were definitely not going as planned. By this time he had expected them to be well on their way to making wedding plans—without any talk of a prenuptial agreement, of course.

"I want to make everything better," he said, striking a note somewhere between ingratiating and wheedling. "I had this idea of how everything was going to be, and I'm sorry it hasn't happened that way. What I figure is that we can wet our whistles, and then get something to eat. Maybe by the time we return, some magic elves will have transformed this room. If not, we can check out and find somewhere else to go."

Cleo's face softened. He did care. "Hurry back," she said.

Anyone working in the hospitality industry knows *the look*. It isn't something that can be confused for anything else. *The look* is the picture of an employee who has the need to scream, but is restrained by circumstance or surroundings. When encountering *the look*, Am knew it was advisable to run the other way, because if you didn't, the odds were you'd soon be wearing that exact same face.

Ted Fellows, the Hotel's sous-chef, had *the look*. He was standing in the middle of the kitchen doing nothing. In any kitchen, the most conspicuous pose is immobility. All meals for the Hotel's four restaurants and fourteen meeting rooms came out of the same kitchen. No one ever just stood around in the kitchen. Workers were shirking their duties if they weren't doing three things at once.

"Am," said Ted, waking up from his catatonic state.

"Have to run, Ted," said Am without looking at him. "Security matter."

"Am . . ."

Though he slowed down, Am still refused to look at the sous-chef directly. "Is it a safety or security matter, Ted?"

"It's a matter I know you can help with, Am."

That was the problem with Am's having been the assistant general manager of the Hotel for so long. No one really took his security position seriously. Was it right for him to intervene? The Japanese way was not to assign blame, but instead to fix the problem. In that, he shared a kindred philosophy.

Am stared at Ted's nose. That gave him the appearance of looking at him without having to endure *the look*. "Ted, you have a food-and-beverage director. You have an assistant food-and-beverage director. You have a catering manager. You have a banquet director. And most of all, you have a chef."

As if on cue, the chef appeared. Marcel Charvet considered himself the rightful heir to Escoffier. He had lived half of his sixty years in America, and most of those in California, but he was as French as the guillotine. And about as friendly. Marcel's English wasn't great, but his shouting was. Whenever he was short the word, he wasn't short the volume—or the spit. Marcel didn't talk so much as spray.

"Ze catering give us ze wrong information," he shouted, moving close to give Am a shower. "I am not Christ. I cannot feed ze crowds with just a few fishes and breads."

It was unusual for Marcel not to claim godhood. Am looked to Ted for an explanation.

"There's a wedding dinner going on now," said Ted. "Catering says they gave us a prospectus . . ."

"Zay lie," said Marcel.

"But we could never find it. We knew from the master schedule that the dinner was for two hundred, so this morning Marcel called over for details . . ."

"And zay tell me two hundred chicken cordon bleus."

Marcel said it with all the certainty of the French. Ted quietly offered the other side: "Catering says they specified two hundred chicken forestières."

"Zay lie," repeated the infallible Marcel.

Finger-pointing between departments was a way of life. More politicking goes on in the average hotel than goes on in Cook County. But wasn't chicken chicken?

"What's the difference?" asked Am.

"Most of the wedding party is Jewish," said Ted.

Am remembered what Mark Twain had once written: "The difference between the right word and the nearly right word is the same as that between lightning and the lightning bug." For some reason Twain seemed to be reverberating in his subconscious. There was another quote that was somehow appropriate, but Am couldn't come up with it.

"I guess the chicken cordon bleu wouldn't work then," said Am.

The dish was made with ham and cheese, which was not in keeping with Jewish dietary laws. Ted shook his head.

"What explanation have we given?"

"I told them that the cordon bleu was meant for another party, and that we would be getting their chicken up to them shortly."

"We zhould have just zed zat catering screwed up."

Am ignored Marcel, save to wipe his face a little. Ted had offered a good lie, one that could be worked upon and gilded. Some complimentary wine while they waited, and another round of bread. But that didn't explain the standstill in the kitchen. Everyone should have been double-humping it to get the revised chicken out.

"Why? . . ." started Am.

"I am not Christ," said Marcel, in a second rare confession. "I cannot feed ze crowds—"

Am waved him to silence. He had already heard the fishes-and-loaves analogy.

"We don't have nearly enough chicken, Am. What we have could take care of fifty or sixty."

"And . . ."

The long "And" was Marcel. "Catering has not apologized," the chef said. "Zay make ze mistake and zay expect us to make everyzing right. If zay want to get us more chicken, thatz fine by me."

"Can we recycle the chicken cordon bleu," asked Am, "and make it into chicken forestière?"

Ted shot another glance at Marcel. "I threw all ze

chicken away," said Marcel. He looked rather proud of what he had done. "To try and serve ze food again is against ze health codes, no?"

Marcel always thought his culinary laws exceeded any state or federal mandates, and had the same respect for health inspectors that he did for week-old fish. He would have thrown the chicken into the trash out of pique, nothing else.

"It's too late for our purveyors to bring us more chicken," said Ted, "which leaves the option of the local supermarkets, but I imagine a lot of those birds are going to be frozen. We can defrost them in the microwaves, but still, I'd say it would be the better part of two hours before we could get the entrees out."

Appetizers, Am thought. On the house. But then more bad news.

"Mr. Kaufman is the bride's father," said Ted. "He's already furious. He's ready to challenge Vesuvius now. I'd hate to see him in two hours."

"And what am I supposed to do about that?" Am snapped.

Ted shook his head. He didn't know. He just hoped that Am had some answer, some miracle. Even the best-run restaurants run out of selections. Most kitchens use large blackboards to keep a running score of unavailable items. The universal restaurant distress code is employed, the out-of-stock ingredient identified by the telling numerical identification of 86.

Am looked over to the blackboard. Sure enough: "86 Chicken" was now chalked in, the barn doors firmly closed after the animals escaped. Or at least the chickens.

Though he knew he should be uttering a prayer to Saint

Julian, all Am could think about was the origins of "86." The terminology came out of taverns, the end result of those who had swilled too much eighty-six-proof rum. The drunks were eighty-sixed. Funny how terms evolve, thought Am, even when mankind doesn't.

"The Colonel," he announced.

"The Colonel?" asked Ted.

"Have your crew make the biggest and best batch of forestière sauce they've ever created. Ladle it on the Colonel's birds, bathe the chicken enough to obscure its origins."

Ted was nodding. There were two fast-food chicken outlets nearby that were about to do a great business.

"I am going to promise Mr. Kaufman his chicken very shortly," Am said. "Don't make me a liar."

Ted yelled some order, then ran out. Marcel went around spitting, "Who is zis Colonel?" His idea of fast food was a three-course dinner.

Am straightened his tie. Early in their careers hotel managers learn how to march smiling into the Valley of Death. Am was grateful for having learned the art of mollifying guests by tutoring under one of the great practitioners. Gary Tolliver had been a GM who always approached unhappy guests with a concerned face, always heard them out with a constant assortment of clucks and sympathetic noises. His overt distress was so great and touching that guests always went away happy. Am never knew anyone else who approached Gary's knack. Guests always remembered him for his caring ways. They didn't respond to Gary because he gave them the world, because in most cases he never even brought up the subject of an adjustment. And it wasn't that Gary readily resolved their complaint. Often, he did nothing. It was just that Gary listened, and sympathized, so well.

No one needed to introduce Am to Mr. Kaufman; perhaps no one dared. He was standing outside of the Spinnaker Room wearing a tux. His arms were folded, and he was glaring at anyone who appeared to be employed by the Hotel.

Now how was it that Gary did it?

"Mr. Kaufman? Am Caulfield. It's my pleasure to make your acquaintance."

Why was it that guests had always taken up Gary's hand so readily? And why was it that Mr. Kaufman ignored Am's outstretched hand?

Mr. Kaufman started his long harangue. Am knew better than to interrupt, figuring the man needed to relieve himself of his anger; and besides, if he talked long enough, the chicken might be delivered before he finished. In the absence of roasted chicken, Mr. Kaufman accepted roasted employee. Am felt well-done after about five minutes.

"It was an affront." (To his credit, Kaufman never repeated his descriptive words—prior to "affront" had been the words insult, travesty, miscarriage, perversion, and Am's favorite: "A scenario that would have made clowns weep.") "My mother, she's almost ninety, wanted to know why they started serving the food, then took it away. I told her it wasn't hot enough. She's Orthodox. God forbid that I should tell her you tried to serve us ham. That was an outrage. That was offensive. I wonder if it wasn't done purposely, wonder if it was meant as an anti-Semitic deed."

He stopped talking, gave Am his first opportunity to answer. "I can assure you, Mr. Kaufman," Am said, "that there was absolutely no anti-Semitic message in what occurred. It was one of those very sorry misunderstandings. Please believe me when I tell you it was just a mistake, and please accept my apology on behalf of the Hotel."

Kaufman looked as if he still had his doubts. Am worked on those. "And as recompense for your inconvenience, I'd like to offer your party some complimentary wine."

Kaufman showed signs of weakening. "And," Am added, "maybe in the few minutes it takes to bring out the chicken, we can also scare up some appetizers for you."

"What kind of appetizers?" he asked.

Am thought for a moment. The popular items were made in bulk every day. "How about some shrimp or crab cocktail? Or maybe some lobster parfait?"

Maybe Gary was successful because he just made sympathetic noises. Am, on the other hand, tried to communicate with words. In this case, apparently ill-chosen words. Kaufman's red face showed him the error of his ways. But what had he said?

"Why don't you offer poison while you are at it?" he hissed. "Have you been listening to me at all? Many of our guests are Jewish. Does that mean anything to you?"

Am suddenly understood. What he had offered were shellfish selections, about as in keeping with kosher dietary standards as the three little pigs.

Am spoke from his heart, even if his speech sounded like a squeal: "Mr. Kaufman, it's not that we are anti-Semitic . . ."

His words hung in the air, made everyone walking by in the hallway pause to listen.

". . . it's just that we are incompetent."

Support for Am's assertion came from an unexpected source. Bradford Beck was walking by, overpriced champagne in hand.

"Truer words were never spoken," said Bradford. "This place reeks of incompetence."

Am gratefully accepted the endorsement. "Thank you," he said.

Chapter Twenty-Seven

The swingers had been entirely too understanding, Am thought. They hadn't checked out en masse, hadn't said conditions in the Hotel were unacceptable to them. They were disappointed that their meeting rooms were out of service, and went so far as to say that the Hotel guest rooms needed refurbishing, but that wasn't enough to deter them from their "love-in."

Any other group, thought Am, would have walked out. It was just their luck to have a patient gathering of perverts. Why couldn't they act like other conventioneers and be totally unreasonable, threatening, and uncompromising?

The good news was that the swingers seemed to be keeping to themselves, content to stay within the boundaries of their second- and third-floor room blocks. Employees (self-described as "sex sentries") were positioned around their rooms to make sure it stayed that way.

Am remembered what Harry Truman had said: "If I hadn't been President of the United States, I probably would have ended up a piano player in a bawdy house." Despite the fact that his repertoire only included "Chopsticks," Am felt that he had ended up in Truman's other career.

His walkie-talkie sounded. "Am, this is Central," said Fred. "There is a Ms. Donnelly waiting for you at the front desk. That's a *D*—David, *0*,—Ogden . . ."

"Understood," responded Am.

"Ten-four," said Fred, the disappointment in his voice palpable.

Marisa hadn't arrived empty-handed. She was carrying two full briefcases, and had an assortment of papers wedged under her arms. She didn't object when Am volunteered to lighten her load.

"The lives and times of Dr. Thomas Kingsbury," she said.

"I was sort of hoping for an abridged version," said Am. He had only assumed the burden of half the paperwork, and that was still weighty enough. He wondered if his feeling weak was the result of the day, or of his low blood sugar. He was hungry enough to eat anything—except chicken.

"Have you eaten dinner?" he asked.

"I haven't even eaten breakfast," she said.

"Then let's look at a menu before we look at these papers."

He took her to Poseidon's Grill, the darkest of the Hotel's four restaurants, and the least ostentatious. There was a booth available for them, which was just as Am wanted. All of the booths were partitioned off, allowing very private spaces. Am and Marisa sank into the dark burgundy leather, and were immediately comfortable. The Grill didn't have the ocean view of the other restaurants, and wasn't nearly as trendy. The food was familiar, and when ordering, diners weren't required to try and pronounce unfamiliar words. Beer could be ordered from the tap, most of the brands American. The biggest choice of the evening was whether to call for rare, medium, or well-done. There are times, thought Am, when it is a pleasure not to have to think.

He looked at Marisa as she scanned the menu. She appeared different in candlelight; that, or maybe he was viewing her with new eyes. This was the closest thing resembling a dinner date he had had with anyone since Sharon. He was finally beginning to accept that he and Sharon were now just friends, but his heart was slower on the uptake than his brain. He remembered how he and Sharon had been brought together by three deaths and their resolve to figure out what had happened. Reminiscing about their courtship was like trying to remember a white-water rafting trip, the two of them navigating treacherous currents and reacting to forces greater than they were.

Was that his initial attraction to the hotel business? Had he been seduced by the sheer energy of hotels? At the Hotel he knew that on any given day over five hundred rooms could be checking out, and another five hundred checking in. But the business wasn't rooms, it was people, humanity in many guises and agendas. The challenges were always immense. Maybe he was an adrenaline junkie, needing greater and greater stimuli to kick him over the edge. It was strange, and maybe sick, that women seemed to come into his life only when somebody died. Or was that the only time he let himself be vulnerable?

Marisa looked up from her menu, saw him gazing at her, read what was in his glance, and didn't immediately close the shutters.

"Is this the time we tell each other our carefully edited biographies?" she asked.

"No," said Am, acknowledging the sudden presence of their server, "this is the time we order."

She said she rarely ate red meat, and then ordered a rare New York steak with bourbon-glazed onions. He wasn't sure whether her pun was deliberate, but smiled anyway and wondered why it was that women always announced what they rarely did. He had the sixteen-ounce T-bone, and didn't bother to tell her that he, also, didn't often eat red meat. But then he didn't eat much tofu either.

When the server had left, they looked at each other again. Leisurely, fully. Though Am was famished, Marisa's presence provided him a form of sustenance. Inside him something was stirring, something that had been missing, something indefinable except in its loss. It was nice to know that certain feelings weren't forever lost to him. They had just been misplaced.

"Say something, philosopher," she said.

At least, Marisa thought, she knew that much about him.

" 'There is more to life,' " he said, " 'than increasing its speed.' Mahatma Gandhi."

"Do you agree with that?"

"Wholeheartedly. Unfortunately, I seldom practice what I believe, or do so with about the frequency that I surf, which isn't very often these days."

"Why?"

"I have a demanding mistress. Or I'm getting older. Or maybe I'm not as certain of what I believe as I should be, and it's easier getting caught up in other currents."

"You sound like a confused philosopher."

"I told you I wasn't a philosopher. I'm just someone acquainted with many philosophies."

"You also told me you weren't really a house dick."

"I didn't want you to think of me as a type."

"A type?"

"I don't spend my time watching cop shows. I don't even own a handgun."

"I do," she said.

Marisa could see his surprise. "Guess you'll have to reevaluate my type, won't you?" she asked.

"No," he said, "I'll just have to reevaluate whether I should ever argue with you."

Their salads were brought out, and their waiter asked them if they'd like pepper. Both nodded. Marisa wasn't satisfied with just a few cranks of the pepper mill. She put the server through the mill—literally.

"Would you like some salad with your pepper?" asked Am.

"When I was a little girl, my father called me a Mexichaun," she said. "He told me I was half Leprechaun and half Mexican. That translates to being half Mexican and half Irish. I guess it shouldn't be a surprise that I like my food spicy."

"Thank you," she finally told the waiter, whose face was a little red from his exertions.

Marisa Donnelly, mused Am. The name fit her roots. Southern California continues the melting-pot tradition of the country. "Mexichaun," he said aloud. The word seemed to apply. She was exotic, had the dark hair, and the green eyes, and the olive complexion. And there was something fey about her, something otherworldly, or at least it seemed that way looking at her. "Does that mean you're ready to reveal some hidden treasure?"

"You'll have to catch me first," she said.

There was a look between them, and some mutual short-ness of breath, and two minds wondering what was really there between them. "Are Mexichauns hard to catch?" he asked.

"Extremely," she said. "But I hear not impossible."

She had been caught before, but not held, and to hear her hints, she had never been able to give her treasure up com-pletely. They offered bits and pieces of themselves, confirm-ing to each other that, yes, they were that person the other saw. Marisa learned about Am's on-again, off-again love af-fair with the Hotel. The looming presence of the Other Woman didn't bother her. To be fully human, she said, was to indenture yourself to something other than flesh. In her own case, she thought that words mattered, that certain stories should be pursued like the Holy Grail.

They discussed their days. Am was torn about whether he should tell her about the swingers; in the end he did. He made her promise it was "off the record," but her pledge didn't call for her not to laugh. Wayward whales, swingers, the near-dead, the actual dead, "fowl"-ups, the meetings be-tween East and West, and pretenders to the throne prompted her to comment, "This is a very strange king-dom."

Am liked her phraseology. "Strange kingdom" summed up the Hotel California very nicely. And what was he, the knight-errant? Or just plain errant? No, he remembered, he was the samurai.

Chapter Twenty-Eight

Perhaps the oddest thing about their dinner was that even in the midst of the pheromones and fantasies neither of them forget about what had brought them together—the death of Dr. Thomas Kingsbury.

Even before dessert (a very decadent mud pie), they were sorting through the pile of papers that Marisa had brought with her. Flashlights supplied by the maître d' helped illuminate the documents that made up Thomas Kingsbury's life. It must have looked odd to the other diners, almost like a scene from a campground, with lights playing out from behind their booth much like the illumination offered from a shrouding tent. To Am and Marisa, that was almost how it felt. They were enclosed, together in their task. By mutual consent, they put aside the doctor's scientific papers, most having to do with blood diseases ("Even Dracula," said Marisa, "wouldn't want to read these"), and concentrated on the newspaper and magazine articles. Dr. Kingsbury invariably made for good copy, always exposing one fraud or another. He loved putting the spotlight on cons and bunco artists, and was quoted as saying that "in the light and heat of the sun, slugs shrivel quickly."

The names changed, but many of the stories were the same: healers who claimed to have cures for everything from lung cancer to AIDS—all at a price, of course. Am was reading yet another of those pieces, the modern medicine man supposedly touched by God, but at the same time touching up his terminal patients for as much mammon as possible, when he suddenly recognized the familiar name of the Reverend Mr. Gardenia. Kingsbury had enrolled in one of Gardenia's "healing within" classes, and then documented how the weak and sick had been preyed upon. Through the media, the doctor publicly challenged all of Gardenia's purported cures. The reverend had tried to counter the arguments of his detractor, had even produced some true believers who stood up and said they had been made well by his course and their faith in God, but Kingsbury had been relentless and loud, and in the end had prevailed. The workshops had closed down, and the Reverend Mr. Gardenia had disappeared. Until the reemergence of Brother Howard, that is.

"Right about now," said Am, "Brother Howard is teaching others how to listen to the dead. For a price."

"I'm curious about both the dead and the price," she said.

Am called for their check, was told by the waiter "Right away," but it didn't work out that way.

"I want to see the manager."

How many times had Am heard that sentence, and that tone of voice, that unique combination of imperious, demanding, aggrieved, and whiny? It promised an earful. It promised an ax to grind—no, more than that, an ax to be wielded, and planted in the backside of the hapless manager.

The voice carried, as all such voices do. It advertised a

threat. Conversations around the restaurant stopped, everyone tuning into the event. Forks were lowered, heads were turned, and the sacrificial lamb was produced. Scott Bockius was an all-around nice guy. Like any good maître d', he remembered names, knew some nice little jokes, and was passably good at singing "Happy Birthday to You," which he probably did half a dozen times a night. Judging from what he was facing, "Bridge Over Troubled Waters" was the song he should have been boning up for.

The complainer was holding his napkin like a gauntlet, and appeared as if he wanted to use it to slap a face and issue a challenge. His posture was rigid, his jaw somewhere up in his mouth. There wasn't foam around his lips, but you looked to be sure. He was around forty, had dark, well-groomed hair, and was immaculately dressed in a black double-breasted suit with a floral, neatly pressed handkerchief resting in his pocket. He was good-looking, if you could ignore the supercilious hauteur and attitude that he carried in his eyes and bearing, the one that said, I-am-more-than-a-mere-mortal-look-upon-me-and-know-that. Am had a one-word translation: prick.

Scott looked like a beaten dog even before they started talking. "Good evening, sir," he said. "I'm Scott Bockius—"

"You are," said the man loudly, "the manager of this"—a sorrowful shake of the head—"place?"

Scott was the bird caught up by the mesmerizing stare of the snake. The man's eyes had that feel and power to them. Scott shook his head in synchronized movement with his summoner, then realized he was contradicting himself.

"Yes, sir . . ."

"I am Dr. Joseph," the man said, announcing the name like a thespian broadcasting to the balcony, as if the name should mean something.

The name did mean something, at least to Am. He tried to remember.

"I have had," said Dr. Joseph, "the worst dining experience of my life. Would you care to hear about my landmark meal?"

Scott was already wiping his brow. "Perhaps we can talk in my office . . ."

Dr. Joseph wasn't about to be sequestered. "We will talk here. If I were to move, I would probably regurgitate what tried to pass as a Caesar salad, and what was purported to be London broil. That would be a relief to my stomach, but I doubt it would sit well with your other patrons. It would be, however, a fitting tribute to the meal."

"I am sorry . . ." started Scott.

"What was sorry," interrupted Dr. Joseph, "was what was served."

He announced his litany of complaints. The salad was hot, and the soup was cold. His meat was supposed to be rare, and it was closer to well-done. Masticating on tough leather, he said, would have been an enjoyable experience next to trying to grind down what was served. As for his date, he would probably have to use his professional expertise to have her stomach pumped. Her fish might have been fresh, as advertised, but only at the turn of the last century. To put their meal in medical terms, Joseph said, was to pronounce gastronomical malpractice.

While he ranted, Am tried to see beyond the words being offered. For having been served such a purportedly awful meal, the doctor's plate was amazingly clean. It was also apparent that his date wasn't enjoying his tirade. She was an attractive blond woman, perhaps thirty, who appeared ready to crawl under the table, and not because of ptomaine.

Long before Dr. Joseph finished his unfavorable culinary review, Scott was ready to wave the white flag. Those who have made careers in the hospitality industry generally have done so because they enjoy being in a profession that pleases. It is a rare business where you are a constant recipient of smiles and thank yous, with guests genuinely happy to pay you for pleasure. No one in the hospitality industry is fool enough to think that the guests are always right, but their training is to try and make it right for the guest. The only out that Scott could furnish was to comp the meal, which he was more than ready to do.

"Excuse me," said Am to Marisa, sliding out from their booth. He walked up to Scott, put a hand on his shoulder, and said, "I'll take over." The maître d' was happy to let him. He shot Am a grateful look, then quickly stepped aside and walked away.

Am offered a friendly smile to Dr. Joseph and his date. "I'm Mr. Caulfield," he said, "and I'm with the Hotel. I'm sorry that you didn't like the meal. I've made notes of your complaints, and we will endeavor to improve upon our shortcomings."

He didn't offer anything else, just stood there. The doctor looked at him expectantly. Am offered a blank stare in return.

Dr. Joseph finally produced a pen. "I didn't catch your name," he said.

I wonder if he's a psychiatrist, thought Am. The pen was a good touch, almost as intimidating to a hotel employee as a gun. Even when they were absolutely in the right, staff knew that condemning letters had a way of clinging and damning an employee's career.

"Mr. Caulfield," said Am, then exaggeratedly spelled it: "C-A-U-L-F-I-E-L-D."

When a hotel employee doesn't offer you a first name, serious enmity has been declared.

"And your position?"

"Administration," said Am.

The playing field between guest and staff is not an even one, nor should it be. To work in the hospitality industry is to declare yourself a professional servant. But in this instance Am knew better than to offer a first name or a title. He was facing a man who at best would patronize him, but would more likely try to grind him into the restaurant's carpeting.

Neither man said anything. Am stood there, and the doctor pretended to elaborate on his notes. His scribbles lasted half a minute. When he finished, he looked back at Am. To speak first would be a tactical error. Both men knew that, but Dr. Joseph spoke anyway: "Our meal was inedible."

"I apologize that it wasn't to your satisfaction," said Am.

"It goes without saying," he announced loudly, "that I'm not paying for such a travesty."

"No," said Am quietly, "I don't think it does."

Joseph stared at him. The script was not going as expected. He was used to bellowing and getting his way, with apologies at that.

"Do you know who I am?" asked the doctor loudly, leaving lots of room for the echoes: I am powerful; I can make your life miserable; I can have your job or your head, as I see fit; I know the owner and we're best friends.

"Yes," said Am, "I do." There was no insolence in his tone or words, but there were echoes there also: You are a bully; you are spoiled; you are self-appointed royalty without any sense of noblesse oblige; you are a con artist.

To the entire room, it was showdown at O.K. Corral. The men locked eyes. Neither offered a retreat. In the end it was Joseph who turned away and looked at his date. "Let's go," he said.

"There is the matter of your bill," said Am.

The doctor turned to him angrily. "There is an implied contract," he said loudly, "that the customer has to be satisfied with the product and service rendered. We were not. I have no intention of paying one penny."

"There is more than an implied contract," said Am, "there are laws, in fact, which state the customer must demonstrate that he or she has sufficient means to pay."

Joseph didn't need to feign his outrage. "I make more in a week," he said, "than you do in a year."

His assertion, Am thought, was probably only too true. "That wasn't the question," said Am. "I asked you whether you could demonstrate whether you have the means to pay. If you don't, then I can only assume your intent was to defraud an innkeeper, and we will be forced to press charges."

Everything was out on the table, with the exception of the doctor's wallet. It was a tough poker game, with the last bet already called. With a loud sigh, as if this were the most ridiculous thing he had ever suffered, the doctor raised his hand toward his jacket pocket, then, abruptly, he lowered it again. Turning to his date, Dr. Joseph said, "Show them the money, dear."

The woman's face expressed shock. "I didn't . . ." she

started, then tried again: "You invited me . . ." Finally, in tears, she said, "I don't want to go to jail."

"No one's going to jail," said the doctor. Unconsciously, both of them turned to Am, who said nothing to allay their fears.

"Perhaps we can talk in a quieter spot," said Dr. Joseph, his speaking voice suddenly soft.

"I would prefer you remain seated, sir," said Am, his words deferential, but at the same time all but accusing the man of being ready to run off and skip out on his bill.

"I must have forgotten my wallet."

Am looked away and coughed. Short of shouting "Liar!," it was the most effective way of announcing "bullshit" to the entire restaurant.

"I can be back in less than an hour with the money." Dr. Joseph didn't try to hide the pleading in his voice.

"I think," said Am, "that the police should be involved in this affair."

His date started crying again. Am considered her tearful countenance, sighed, and then appeared to relent. "All right," he said.

Some of the doctor's confidence returned. He stood up, motioned for his date to do the same. The game, his all-too-erect back seemed to be saying, had been played to a draw.

"But," said Am, "we will need collateral."

Annoyed, Joseph said, "What do you mean?"

"We have to make sure that you will return to pay your debt," said Am, leaning over and examining their dinner bill. With drinks, their check came to seventy-five dollars. "Adding in a twenty-dollar tip," Am said, "no, I'm sure you're a generous man, including a twenty-five dollar tip, you owe us a hundred dollars. We will need something of at least that value to secure your return."

The doctor opened his mouth, and then closed it. He patted down his body, then stared at his date. "No way," she said, then added bitterly, "you'd probably just leave me here to rot, or have me do dishes until your debt was paid off."

"I was thinking of your jewelry," he said.

"Use your own damn jewelry," she said.

She was familiar enough with him to know that around his neck were several strands of gold. He reached up to his collar, loosened his tie, then managed to pull off the chains. The design was serpentine. Am wasn't surprised.

"They're worth several hundred dollars," he said, handing them over.

Am weighed them in his hand like a suspicious pawnbroker. To his mind, they didn't quite tilt the scales of justice. "And your watch," he said, sticking out his hand.

Aware that the eyes of every patron in the restaurant were on him, Dr. Joseph tried to remove his watch. It took him several efforts. "I hope you're satisfied," he said, handing it over.

Even though Am appeared eminently so, he didn't comment. "I'll give you a receipt for these items," he said. "They will be safely stored in the security safe for a period of . . ."

"Stuff your receipt," said the doctor.

Am nodded, then leaned close to him and whispered something. Everyone strained to hear, but the words remained between Am and the doctor, though their effect on Joseph was unmistakable. He was a man inflated by his own pompousness, but now he was leaking every which way. His escape from the restaurant was like the last gasp of a balloon let loose; roundabout, erratic, and frenzied. His date tried to follow him, then gave up. After two false starts, and literally bumping off one table, he found the exit, and was gone. With his absence, everyone in Poseidon's Grill started talking. As Am returned to his own table, he was the recipient of furtive, and not so furtive, glances.

"All right," said Marisa. "What did you say to him?"

"Whatever do you mean?"

"Don't play cute."

Am picked up a spoon, looked at it, milking the scene for all it was worth. He saw Marisa start, as if she had just remembered something, but she didn't say anything, merely waited for his explanation.

"I'm not so brave," said Am. "I had some insider information which I was willing to gamble on. The local restaurant association recently circulated a flier on our Dr. Joseph. His girlfriend, former girlfriend, that is, wrote a quite damning letter about him. She said that whenever he went out to restaurants he made a point of never paying. According to her, this behavior first surfaced when they went out for dinner a year ago and he realized that he had forgotten his wallet. Rather than explain the situation to the manager, he decided to complain about the meal. Getting everything comped gave him a rush. She said that after that evening, whenever they went out to eat, the doctor always made it a point of leaving his wallet at home so as to 'improve his performance.' He said the meal always tasted that much better to him knowing it cost nothing. She apologized for going along with all of his deceits, but claimed that she thought it was just a passing, if sadistic, phase of his. Part of the reason for her leaving him, she said, was that he became more and more of a bully over time, brow-beating servers and staff—and her.

"When I asked him for his watch, I was thinking about all those powerless servers and staff he had bullied. Many people don't last in the hospitality business because they don't like having to be a willing punching bag for the obnoxious. I pushed the moment, went against my training, because I wanted him to know how it felt."

"How did you know she didn't have money?" asked Marisa.

"I didn't," said Am. "I noticed her purse was rather tiny, but I was holding my breath when he tried to pass the paying off to her."

"You still haven't told me what you whispered to him," said Marisa.

"I told him his game was over. I told him if he ever complained in a restaurant in this town again we would be serving up his ass as the special of the day."

"Spoken like a true lawman."

Am tipped an imaginary ten-gallon hat to her. Marisa didn't curtsy. She was rather proud that she didn't even know how to curtsy. Instead, she pushed a table tent over his way. Am picked it up. PRIME TIME IN BRINE TIME, it said. The promotions had been going on for the past year. The Hotel had revamped and expanded its Brine Time Lounge. It was now a forum for featured comedians, singers, and performers, for entertainers that had at least nostalgic appeal, the kind that still appeared on cable channels, or late-late night television, their routines the opening acts in Las Vegas or Atlantic City, or as headliners in such venues as the Hotel. According to the table tent, for a limited time (two weeks), world-renowned Skylar was appearing at the

Brine Time. There was a picture of him, dark, brooding, and mysterious, which was all the more incredible because the man was staring at a spoon.

"You were posing a minute ago," said Marisa, "and your pose reminded me of the promotional material."

Am shrugged. He hadn't been trying to imitate Skylar, didn't even know enough about him to imitate him. From what he remembered, Skylar was a magician of sorts.

"I was also reminded," she said, "of the enmity between Thomas Kingsbury and Skylar."

She fished out several articles, handed them over to Am, who scanned the headlines. As Tommy Gunn the Magician, Kingsbury had done more than entertain. Sometimes he had revealed the unthinkable—showed what really was up his sleeves. He didn't like his fellow "practitioners of the art" giving themselves exotic airs, putting themselves on mysterious pedestals. Tommy Gunn loved what he called honest magicians, those who performed sleight of hand, who could conjure through illusion or practiced method. What he couldn't abide were those who claimed their powers came from sources other than the tangible or explanatory. He had taken on Skylar years ago, when the so-called "mentalist" was at the height of his fame and attracting an almost cult-like following. Skylar said he used the "potency" of his mind to perform his feats, but Doubting Tom went on record to declare that the only way Skylar was using his mind was for self-promotion.

The headlines reminded Am about the public feuding and triggered a few memories. He remembered how Tommy Gunn, dressed very much like Skylar, had demonstrated how he could bend keys and cause a timepiece to stop. Skylar said he did these things with the power of his mind; Tommy Gunn was of a mind to show differently. He demonstrated how friction could quickly and inconspicuously be applied to metal, how flesh could easily bend steel, and even stop time. ("This is one Timex," he announced, "that took my licking and now isn't ticking.") He called Skylar a fraud, with the resulting lawsuit dragging on for a year or two until it was finally dropped.

"Thomas Kingsbury," said Am, "would have used a bullhorn to tell the emperor he wasn't wearing any clothes."

"Yes," said Marisa.

Am carefully examined the table tent, then looked at his watch. "Mr. Skylar still has another show to do tonight," he said. "I sense we'll be paying him a late night visit."

"Did you divine that," she asked, "or are you just guessing?"

He held up a spoon, looked deep within it. Marisa rolled her eyes, and then positioned a spoon and a knife in crosslike form as if she were warding off some evil. They laughed at their ridiculous posturing, didn't care that they were still being watched by the other diners.

The maître d' approached their table. "No check for you tonight, Am," he said. "I put your tab on management and promotion."

"Thanks, Scott."

"No," he said, "thank you." Then he lowered his voice so guests couldn't hear: "You got to tell me, Am. What did you say to make that jerk disappear so quickly and quietly?"

"A magician," said Am, "never reveals his secrets."

That is, he thought, almost never.

Chapter Twenty-Nine

Halfway back to his room, Bradford heard the music of a mariachi band in the courtyard. Maybe that was the ticket, he thought. Serenade Cleo with some music. That ought to put her back in good form.

He approached the wandering minstrels. All that their outfits were lacking, he sniffed, was neon. There were four of them, and they were going from table to table. Ten dollars bought you two renditions of bad Herb Alpert. There weren't too many takers.

"You guys do room service?" asked Bradford.

Their leader was the fattest guy in the group, a Mexican with a Pancho Villa mustache and a cerveza belly. His English was definitely north of the border: "It's not out of the question," he said, starting up the negotiations.

Bradford pulled out a twenty, but Pancho didn't reach for it, didn't even blink. He added another ten, but the leader still wasn't biting. Bradford started slowly to put the money away.

"For fifty we'll give you ten minutes," said Pancho. "You and your lady come out to the balcony, and we'll sing up to you. It's a guaranteed success, man."

Bradford didn't want to be telling the help about the problem with their sliding glass doors. "Forty," he said, "and I'll want you playing in the room. We'll get the true effect that way."

Pancho acted as if he were thinking about it, and finally shrugged. "Okay," he said. "But we'll have to mute the horns. Your neighbors might complain."

"You don't know our neighbors," said Bradford.

"What's your names, and what's the room number?"

Bradford told him, and was promised a visit within the next fifteen minutes. He handed the man a twenty, and promised the other twenty after their performance. "I want something romantic," he said.

"No problem," said Pancho.

There was something about that Cleopatra, thought Jimmy Mazzelli, something special. She didn't belong among those swingers, and she certainly didn't belong with that stuffed-shirt boyfriend of hers. He was probably the one leading her astray. Something should be done about it. Something had to be done.

Nobility wasn't usually Jimmy's strong point. The bellman was a hustler, always in search of a quick buck. Perhaps instinctively, he sensed that Bradford was a fellow hustler, and maybe that brought out his competitive juices, but for whatever the reason, this was one time Jimmy wasn't acting solely on the basis of money. There was a damsel in distress, and he was the one who was going to help her.

Jimmy had foiled the first champagne delivery by insisting upon seeing Cleo's identification. He had figured she was under twenty-one, was trying to be older than her years. He had known that wouldn't stop her boyfriend from getting another bottle, but it had bought Jimmy enough time to figure out a new scheme. It was the kind of plan he probably should have run through Am, or maybe even legal, but he didn't have time. He was a man with a mission. Jimmy waited with two of the sex sentries, had joined them in watching what was going on. You needed a flow-chart to figure out who had gone where, and who was with whom. No one, Jimmy was glad to see, had gone into Cleo's room, that is, until her peacock preppie reappeared with champagne and two glasses.

He's probably trying to get her drunk, Jimmy thought, and then make her do things she otherwise wouldn't. That made him mad, made him want to act, but he knew that he had to give them a few minutes. He played out the scenario in his mind. By now the jerk had probably opened the bub-bly. Jimmy couldn't act until she'd had at least a glass. Then was the time to strike.

At regular intervals, doors opened and closed. The only common denominator between all the swingers seemed to be their libido. They looked and acted very differently, were of various shapes, sizes, and ages. Some wore costumes, leather outfits being the most common. Feathers were dis-played, many of them creatively situated. There was makeup that would have looked out of place anywhere ex-cept at a Halloween party, and exhibitionists who wore nothing at all. Still, there were more business suits than birthday suits, and a lot of conservative dresses, even if some men were wearing those dresses, and some women the suits. Clothes-swapping seemed to be going along with mate-swapping.

"Geez," said one of the sex sentries, a college student majoring in anthropology and getting to play Margaret Mead firsthand, "it's like we should be beating drums."

"They don't need the encouragement," said Jimmy.

He looked at his watch. It was time. Jimmy left his post and walked to the hallway, but he wasn't the first to make it there. Ray Ortiz and his boys were scanning room numbers and evidently looking for a gig. Their mariachi outfits put most of the swinger costumes to shame. They were wearing large black sombreros with red tassels, and had on black-and-gold vests that were embroidered with Aztec designs. Their black leather boots were shined to a fine finish (it was a tradition of theirs to have Felipe the shoe-shine man give them a once-over), and they wore billowy white shirts with ruffles. Mariachis with an Elvis flair. Jimmy knew only too well that Ray's group couldn't play for shit, but they always did look like a million dollars.

"Hey, Ray."

"What do you say, Jimmy?"

The two had a long-standing business relationship. Jimmy got a five-buck kickback from Ray every time he sold some moon-eyed couple on the idea of a little mariachi serenade. The usual arrangement was for Ray and his band to walk out to the beach and perform, directing their tunes upward to some balcony like troubadors of old. Jimmy would provide the band with the first names of the couple, and then Ray and the boys would belt out some string and brass tunes about a-mor-e, weaving the names into their songs and making them a twosome for the ages. That always made Dick and Jane, or Barry and Linda, very happy. The tradition (as explained by Jimmy to the couple) was for the woman to reward the minstrels by throwing down money and roses from the balcony (Jimmy also got a kickback from the Hotel florist).

On several occasions more than money and roses had rained down on the musicians, with garters, negligees and other intimate apparel being among the fallout. It wasn't as if Tom Jones were performing, but love ballads always seemed to release the feminine passions. Ah, love, thought Jimmy. It made the world go round and made him some good coin.

"Which room you playing?" asked Jimmy.

Ray consulted his sheet. "Two-twelve," he said. "Bradford and Cleopatra. Tough names to remember, let alone work with."

"I got something else for you to work with," said Jimmy.

Those damn mariachis should have been along by now, thought Bradford. He had spent the time cleaning up the room. So much for Japanese efficiency. No one had yet come to fix up the place, and he was tired of walking around in a sty.

Cleopatra had already had one glass of champagne, and it seemed to be having the desired effect. She was encouraging him to sit down with her, "and relax." He had told her there would be time enough for "relaxing" soon, but that a surprise was coming. Cleopatra loved surprises. She kept asking him what it was, but he wouldn't tell her.

There was a knock at the door. "The cavalry," he said to Cleopatra, then told her to sit tight. As expected, Pancho Villa and his troops were there.

Cleopatra was beside herself. This was all too romantic. Bradford accepted her excited hug as his just desserts. They sat on a sofa and waited for their song. There was some competing music coming from the party next door, but it wasn't as loud as the partygoers. Bradford was glad they'd be sending some happy sounds of their own back. Take that, he thought. The musicians took their places. The room was intimate, the lighting low (with a solitary twenty-five-watt bulb for the entire room, it couldn't be any other way). An unseen signal passed among the band.

Ray Ortiz had never thought he would end up running a mariachi band for his livelihood. In his younger days, he had played around with several rock bands, had always prided himself on being an outlaw singer, a cutting-edge player. That was before the wife and kids. Desperate for a job, he had filled in as a mariachi. It was the longest temp job in history. He'd been playing the mariachi standards for over a decade, what he called Mariachi Muzak. People liked to hear the same songs, and that's what they gave them. To be able to do something different, to deviate from the same old routine, excited Ray. He started the song. He hadn't sung it for twenty years or more, but remembered the words. Or most of them. Jose Feliciano had been one of his favorites.

The expectant smile on Cleopatra's face stayed frozen in place. The song wasn't quite what she had expected. It wasn't lyrical, or soft, or lulling. And the worst sin of all— it wasn't romantic. But then again, "Light My Fire" will never be considered one of the twentieth century's great contributions to romance songs.

Ray wasn't crooning, he was howling. If he was supposed to be emulating a dog in heat, he was doing a good job. He moved closer to Cleopatra, started gyrating his rolls of flesh in her face. He looked like Elvis in his last days.

Bradford's mouth was open. This spectacle was not what he had paid for. This was obscene.

The mariachis were gamely trying to belt out the song, but they were a group that was hard-pressed to handle tunes they'd played a thousand times before. They weren't about to give up, though. It wasn't over until the fat man signaled, and Ray didn't look as if he were anywhere near doing that. He was into it, really singing, asking for his fire to be lit. Asking over and over, as if imploring the gods.

Bradford wished he had a fire extinguisher. He would have loved to have sprayed it on the caterwauling tub of lard. Who did he think he was, Chubby Checker? He tried to shout for silence, but the man was making too much noise to hear him. Bradford was tempted to kick him right in his jiggling stomach, but restrained the urge. There were four of them, but every second the music continued made those odds less and less daunting.

The song ended moments before the brawl would have occurred. Bradford didn't trust himself to move. Cleo weakly clapped. There were others who were more appreciative. Applause could be heard from next door, along with ribald yelling.

In a voice meant to freeze, wither, frostbite, and kill, Bradford asked, "What was that?"

" 'Light My Fire,' " said Ray. "The Doors did it, and Jose Feliciano, and—"

"That is not what I meant," he said. "What you just did was not mariachi music." Just what it was, Bradford's voice insinuated, was a bit lower than dog doo.

Artistic pride surfaced. "I don't like to limit our art form, man. We take lots of request."

"Silence being the most frequent of them, I'm sure."

Jimmy was right, thought Ray. This guy was a jerk. He looked at his watch and said, "If that's what you want to hear for the next five minutes . . ."

They weren't going to get away that easily, Bradford decided. He had paid for them, and they were going to play. He would even choose for them. "You will play 'La Bamba,'" he demanded.

Ray looked at his fellow troupers, then shook his head. "We don't know that one."

"You don't . . ." started Bradford, then realized the man was putting him on, trying to get him mad.

"How about 'Guantanamera'?"

"Don't know that one either."

"Guantanamera" is the ultimate staple of Mexican mariachi. Not hearing it performed during any given set would be a modern miracle. But Bradford wasn't going to lose face and insist.

With heavy sarcasm, he asked, "Do you know any songs besides 'Light My Fire'?"

"Yeah."

"Well, then by all means, grace us with one of them."

The band had known all along what their second song was going to be. They had more than a passing familiarity with it. That's what happens when you need cash and you're willing to perform at bachelor parties. They really didn't have the right instruments, but they played anyway. Loudly.

It took a few seconds for Bradford to name that tune. Gypsy Rose Lee probably could have named it in one note. Among universally recognized songs, it has few peers. The mariachis played "Stripper." When played correctly, there is an almost comic element to the tune, an exaggerated musical bump and grind. For once, the band caught that moment, the mariachis hitting just the right inflection and rhythm.

The door flung open. Ray had left it open for Jimmy, but

it wasn't the bellman who walked inside. It was Missy. When she entered she was fully clothed. That wasn't the way she left.

As the mariachis played, Missy shimmied and shook and disrobed. She performed directly in front of Bradford, popping buttons to the notes, shaking her dark hair in his face, offering him zippers and clasps and her person. He sat there unmoving, but very watchful. The band played on with increasingly more exuberant notes. This was better than having panty hose thrown down on them from the balcony, much better. Their playing, and Missy, brought the party from next door into the room, a raucous, clapping crowd. The room was soon overflowing with swingers. Cleo turned to ask Bradford to do something, and saw his mesmerized face. Salome had never had such a rapt onlooker.

Missy was down to her briefs. A slight pull and her bra was off, a little tug and her undies were on her finger. Velcro, thought Bradford, but that wasn't all he thought. His intense gaze didn't go unnoticed. Standing in front of him, Missy twirled her bra around one finger, and her underwear around the other. The majorette act ended when she deposited her underclothing on top of Bradford's head, covering his eyes.

Everyone except Cleo laughed. Bradford removed his undergarment blindfold, and looked around at the laughing crowd. How did all these people get in my room? he thought.

"You owe us twenty bucks, man," said Ray.

Bradford was too confused to argue. A naked Missy was helping herself to a glass of champagne. She had, he observed, worked up a slight sweat. He handed the twenty to

Ray, who didn't even try and hit him for a tip. Jimmy had already given him an extra twenty-five bucks.

Where was Cleopatra? Bradford looked around and saw her talking to that damn bellman. She was crying. Naturally. And now she was following the bellman out of the room.

"Hey!"

She didn't hear him. The mariachis weren't playing, but everyone was talking. Who had invited the circus to his room? It was like a Fellini movie was happening in front of him. No, worse. He had to fight through the crowd. Bradford wished he were wearing blinders. Were those three people really . . . ?

"Cleopatra!"

This time she did hear him. The bellman positioned himself between them. "Please don't interfere, Mr. Beck," he said. "It was my sad duty to already have to make one citizen's arrest."

"You what?"

Jimmy tried to sound official. That was something new to him. "I warned both of you about the consequences of underage drinking. Cleo confessed that she drank a glass of champagne. So I was forced to arrest her."

Bradford looked around. What was next? Carrie Nation and a bunch of ax-wielders storming into the room? "You've got to be kidding."

Jimmy looked his sanctimonious best. "No, sir, I am not."

"Get out of the way and let her go."

Bradford's cultured voice, that same voice he had worked on for so long, was gone. So was the country-club tan, replaced by a red, angry face. Brad Beck wanted to hit somebody.

"Mr. Beck," said Jimmy, "please don't force me to involve you in this. I don't think the courts would look kindly upon your contributing to the delinquency of a minor. Cleo and I both thought it best that she, and she alone, pay the consequences."

Brad took a deep breath. Damn it! This bellman with the New York accent was talking like a big-city shyster. And worse, he was making sense. Couldn't they revoke his broker's license if he was convicted of a felony?

When in doubt, thought Bradford, speak in a universal language. "Can't we be reasonable here?" he asked, reaching for his wallet.

It pained Jimmy to tell him that they couldn't be reasonable; it pained him very much when he saw the amount of the bribe being offered. Almost, he succumbed. But he couldn't, not with Cleo standing there. Jimmy wondered whether he was going soft in the head.

Bradford was wondering the same thing. This wasn't happening, was it? His intended very rich wife was being led away, all but handcuffed. He should do something. What was that line about a fair maiden never being won by a faint heart? Maybe he shouldn't be hasty, though. If he popped the bellman, they could easily prove assault. And besides, it was Cleo they wanted, not him. Bradford turned to her, offered his best sorrowful face, which looked truly pained. Her fortune—his fortune—kept proving elusive. "Don't say anything to them, dear, until you talk to a lawyer."

It wasn't what she expected. Cleo was hoping for a little more John Wayne. With tears in her eyes, she nodded.

Jimmy started to lead her off. She was going to jail. What would Daddy think? It was all so tragic. They had only walked about a dozen paces when Cleo turned around. Her intention was to yell "I love you" to Bradford, but she never delivered those words. She saw him being led away also— by that naked woman back into their room.

Chapter Thirty

Brother Howard's appointments were being handled by a woman who identified herself as "Arielle, his assistant." She wore Birkenstocks, and her hair was braided with turquoise beads. The obligatory crystal dangled in front of her tie-dyed shirt. Though she spoke New Age, she was only too familiar with the words VISA, MasterCard, and American Express. The Brother was in session, she said, but could see them next. Their initial thirty-minute consultation would be two hundred dollars. Am silently handed over his plastic, resisting the impulse to tell Arielle that they just wanted to talk to the dead, not have someone killed, but when Arielle called in for a credit-card approval Am couldn't contain himself any longer: "That's not really necessary," he said. "A lot of dead people can vouch for me."

"And apparently a few of the living," she said, noting the approval code number. With a smile, Arielle directed them to an anteroom, and wished them "peace." It was almost enough, Am thought, to make him nostalgic for "Have a nice day."

The waiting room was just off a suite. Marisa put her ear to the door to see if she could hear anything, but Am didn't make her eavesdropping easy. He paced the room, only stopping periodically to examine his credit-card voucher.

"You think you could turn this in as a newspaper expense?" he asked.

"You think you could turn it in as a hotel expense?" she asked back, pointedly repositioning her ear.

Am started pacing again. "I can try," he said. "I can put it in as a miscellaneous security expenditure. Maybe accounting won't notice."

"If it doesn't fly," she said, "I'll go halvsies."

"Two hundred dollars," said Am. "How can he justify those prices? It's not like there's a Dead People's Union. And the Teamsters aren't involved in transporting us to 'the other realm.' At least I don't think they are."

"It *is* a long-distance call," said Marisa. She could hear voices in the other room, but couldn't distinguish any words. Reluctantly, she gave up, choosing to surrender in a comfortable chair. Am sat down next to her.

"Ever been to a séance?" she asked.

"No," he said. "Why solicit spirits when you don't have to? We already have the Hotel ghost."

"Ghost?"

"His name's Stan, not that we're on a first-name basis."

"Are you putting me on?"

He shook his head. "Most of the staff swear by him, and some of them swear at him, especially the women. Stan likes to show off for ladies. He turns lights on and off, and opens doors. We've had these official-looking paranormal experts come out and do studies, and they always go away reporting 'unusual activity.' Psychics and receptives are always saying they feel Stan's presence."

"Maybe we should ask Brother Howard to get us in touch with Stan."

"Dr. Kingsbury," said Am, "is haunting me much more than Stan."

"We'll have to do something about that," she said.

Am liked Marisa's ambiguous tone. He had wondered if that special feeling between them would extend beyond their time in the restaurant. Sometimes the magic is ephemeral, its life short-lived and dreamlike. Relationships, he thought, were about as easy to explain as ghosts, and potentially as frightening.

"What are you smiling about?" she asked.

"Ghosts of the past," he said.

They talked about the present instead, skating for the most part around anything personal, content to converse in anecdotes and job-related stories. Their jobs were similar, Am insisted, in that both of them were in the communications business. Half his time, he said, was spent acquainting staff with "situations."

He told her about what wasn't advertised on hotel VACANCY signs, how over ten thousand lawsuits were filed each year against U.S. hotels claiming negligent security, and how behind those lawsuits were over ten thousand sad stories, and ruined vacations, and even destroyed lives. She heard in his words the unsaid conviction of "Not at my Hotel," and once again thought of him as the Old West sheriff, even though he was quick to say that he was "no house dick, just a temporarily displaced hotel manager."

His disclaimer notwithstanding, he told her about the crime-prevention program he had started at the Hotel, how he tried to educate both guests and staff on safety, and how difficult it was to tread that thin line between making the inn secure without making it into a stalag. But what he couldn't teach, he said, was common sense. When guests physically went on vacation, their minds followed. They walked around waving rolls of money, and thought nothing of wearing ten pounds of jewelry. They answered the door without verifying who was there, and were careless with their keys. Criminals never need invitations, he averred, but too many guests offered them anyway.

"The kids that used to call identifying themselves as being from the utility company and asking if your refrigerator was running have grown up," said Am. "The punch line is no longer, 'Well, you better catch it before it runs out your door.' It's often a gun."

He explained how intruders often used house phones to call guest rooms, identifying themselves as being from the "front desk" or "maintenance," and stating that there was a problem in the room requiring their attention. The best locks didn't help, he said, when guests willingly let their assailants inside.

Guests weren't the only ones scammed. In going through old complaint files Am had found a number of similarly written letters from the same area in Canada. The letters detailed regretful dining experiences at the Hotel restaurants, with vivid descriptions of waiters spilling wine, busboys dropping mustard, and wayward nails in chairs snagging and ruining clothes. They asked for, and ultimately received, compensation. Their requests weren't for an amount to make anyone suspicious. The claims were all for fifty dollars or less, but they added up. On impulse, Am decided to check on the receipts tendered just to confirm the establishments were legitimate. Someone's home computer had apparently been very busy cranking out forms.

None of the dry cleaners, tailors, or clothiers had been, or were, in existence. That prompted Am to establish a new policy requiring restaurant personnel to deal with the problem immediately, eliminating after-the-fact payments.

He began to have a second sense for what rang true and what didn't. He described one scam that had bothered him more than most because it had appealed to the better instincts of the trade, and in its deceit justified cynicism. A nineteen-year-old man had written requesting a complimentary stay, saying he had "a rare and dangerous cancer called Ewing's Sarcoma." The note said "My debilitating surgery and chemotherapy don't allow me to work, and have left me with no funds." His parents, it went on, "had honeymooned at the Hotel, and I hope the magic and wonderful memories it brought to their marriage might pass into my own life, as the survival rate for my type of tumor is less than 35 percent."

Am decided there were too many violins in the letter. He phoned the San Diego Hotel Motel Association with his suspicions, and learned that another hotel had called in describing the very same letter. A subsequent investigation revealed that identical letters had been sent to thirty San Diego hotels, nine of which had agreed to provide complimentary stays before learning that the letter was just a ploy for free room nights. Am wasn't sure whether he was prouder that he had recognized the scam, or that nine hotels had cared enough about another human's plight to want to help without asking too many questions.

"That's the problem with scams," said Am. "It makes good people suspicious. It stops you from doing the right thing, makes it that much easier for you to say no without even thinking because we've all been trained to be distrust-ful.

"I think that was a part of Thomas Kingsbury's anger. He didn't hate the 'ghouls' so much as what they did to the human spirit. As he saw it, they plundered the dying and soured the living, distracting everyone involved from the life-and-death issues at hand."

Am's righteous indignation was cut short by the opening of a door. Brother Howard stepped forward and bowed. "Welcome," he said. "Please join me inside."

He held out his arm for them to enter the parlor. There was a table inside, but no crystal ball. On the table were some books, videotapes, and audiotapes. All of them had Brother Howard's picture on the cover, as well as gold stars with the prices.

Brother Howard motioned for them to sit. He sat down and appeared to offer a silent prayer, his holy head resting atop the fingertips of his pressed hands. When he finished with his meditative moment he smiled, then reached out with his hands to both Am and Marisa and made the announcement, "Let us join in a circle."

Holding Marisa's hand was fine by Am, but he didn't much like being in the clasp of Brother Howard. Was he in the grip of a murderer? He was supposed to take the lead in this interview—Marisa had had first crack at the mental-ist—but he found it difficult to ask questions of a man he was holding hands with.

"Marisa Donnelly and Am Caulfield," said Brother Howard, "both of you have expressed interest in gaining ac-cess to another realm. I can enable your passage, can direct you on the way, but in the end each of you will have to make your own journey.

"To hear the dead is not an easy thing. Most of us cannot even hear ourselves. We need to attune our listening, need to get comfortable with our own beings, and come to terms with all of our senses before we can attempt to venture beyond.

"Our first exercise will be for you to listen for your heartbeat. It requires total silence and concentration. Why is it that we can hear and feel our hearts after vigorous exercise, but not at other times? It is there all along, but usually silent, waiting to be discovered like so many other things. Picture in your mind this tireless engine in your chest, this constant clock which we have tuned out of our senses."

Brother Howard closed his eyes and stopped talking. Am watched him to see if he was peeking. As far as he could see, he wasn't. Marisa followed Brother Howard's example. She actually seemed to be trying to listen to her heart. Am thought she was going a little far. The silence, and the handholding, continued. For want of anything else to do, Am started listening for his heart. His breathing became lighter and slower. Several times he felt on the verge of picking up that elusive beat, but always it escaped him. His thoughts started to float, his consciousness a series of run-on sentences . . .

. . . how long have we been listening probably five minutes that's about thirty bucks of silence and they say talk is cheap they ought to price out silence can't hear my heart but if i could it would be about a dime a beat should have brought along a stethoscope and pulled it out but what he really wants is to get a bead on our wallets just wait until he describes the length and treatment of his snake oil that's one pitch that's going to get cut short with my own questions wonder how he'll respond to the name of doctor kingsbury maybe i should bring his name up casually and ask brother gardenia reverend howard to listen to what he has to say and oh by the way doc just how am i supposed to be positive in a world with so many of these bloodsuckers . . .

"Am," said a voice. "Am."

Brother Howard gently shook Am's arm. He hadn't been asleep, Am told himself, not exactly, but he had drifted. Red-faced, he returned.

"Good," said Brother Howard. "Very good."

Am turned a little redder. In all the world, this was the last person from which he wanted to hear praise.

"You see how Am let loose of his conscious mind," said the Brother. "That is often necessary. We need to open ourselves up."

The star pupil glowered a little. At least they weren't holding hands anymore, he thought.

Brother Howard turned to Marisa. "Did you attune to the beat of your heart?" he asked.

It was her turn to look embarrassed. "Yes," she said quietly.

Had she really? Am wondered. He wished he could have heard her heart, wanted to know how it sounded, and pounded.

"What about you, Am? Did you find your heart?"

No, he wanted to say, I think I lost it. But he simply shook his head. That didn't discourage Brother Howard. He said that what they had done was merely an exercise, one of many to build their awareness.

"I don't have special hearing aids," he said, "that will provide you the ability to hear the dead, but I do have a program"—he tapped the table and brought their attention to his tapes and books—"that has allowed many to succeed in that quest."

"Are you sure this ability can be taught?" asked Am.

"There is no question about it," he said.

"How is it," asked Am, "that you succeeded in bridging this rather enormous gap, when others have not?"

"I am by no means the first to have done so," said Brother Howard. "Mine is a God-given ability, not unlike those who can see auras, or those who have second sight."

"And you just woke up one day and heard the dead?"

"Not quite so simple as that. I think for most of my life I sensed the fragments of communication around me that were not of this world, but I was never quite sure of what I was hearing. Over time I was able to distinguish the messages, and learned how to better tune into them."

"Do you carry on conversations with the dead?"

"I wouldn't call them conversations. I prefer the term 'dialogues.' "

" 'How's the weather?' Or, 'What's up?' Those kinds of dialogues?"

Brother Howard looked disappointed. "Nothing like that," he said. "Human words fail in describing the nuances of communication, especially with the dead. The dialogues are meanings and meetings beyond our terminology."

"Can you call up any of the dead you want? Abraham Lincoln? Robert Frost? Napoleon? Martin Luther King?"

"My techniques are not those of a séance," said Brother Howard. "You will find the 'who' is not important. It is the 'there.' "

"Not the destination, the journey."

"Exactly."

"You didn't answer the question, though," said Am. "Are

you able to communicate with a particular person who has died?"

Proudly, firmly: "I am."

"That's impressive," said Am, "considering how many billions of people have died. Is there an A T and T over there?"

"Are you trifling with me, Mr. Caulfield?"

"No," said Am, "I'm just trying to understand."

Brother Howard stared at him for several seconds. "There is no telephone system," he said. "There is an awareness far beyond this earthly plane. It is the reality of 'I think, therefore I am.' The dead aren't in hiding. They've merely eclipsed their bodies."

"The main reason we're here," said Am, "is that we want to talk with someone who recently died. Is it possible for you to be our intermediary and help us communicate with him?"

It was apparent, despite Brother Howard's seeming reluctance, that he had been asked this question before. "This was supposed to be a training session . . ."

"Methinks thou doth protest too much" was what Am wanted to say, but instead he said, "If we have to pay extra, we quite understand."

"Money is not the issue," said Brother Howard, but in the end it naturally proved to be just that. They agreed on an additional hundred dollars.

"With whom would you like me to communicate?" asked Brother Howard, "and what is it you would like to know?"

"Dr. Thomas Kingsbury," said Am, "and who murdered him."

Brother Howard didn't react to either the name or the request. He asked for them not to move or talk, even to keep their breathing quiet, then he closed his eyes and grew still. It was three or four minutes before his eyes opened again. He took a deep breath, sighed slightly, and shook his head.

"Sometimes it happens this way," he said. "The dead do not always speak. I could not find the one you wished."

Am noticed he didn't say the name aloud. "Are you sure you got his right name?" he asked.

"Thomas Kingsbury," said Brother Howard. "Dr. Thomas Kingsbury."

Am nodded. "Well, since he's not available, I guess we'll have to ask you some of the same questions. Do you prefer that we call you the Reverend Mr. Gardenia, or Brother Howard?"

He didn't respond to the baiting, merely said, "Brother Howard is my legal name."

"But you were the Reverend Mr. Gardenia?"

He shrugged, then said, "Since neither of you are here to learn, I think it is time this session came to a close."

"But we are here to learn," said Marisa. "Mr. Caulfield is head of Hotel security. And I'm with the *Union-Tribune*."

"I have nothing to say."

"Did the two of you talk while he was here?" Am asked.

"Why are you asking these questions? The newspapers reported that he died of natural causes."

"Never believe what you read." This from Marisa.

Brother Howard's vow of silence didn't last. "I was in the dealer's room," he said. "We have a booth there where we sell our material. Business was very good. There was a line of customers and suddenly there was this commotion. A man was pushing to the front of the line.

" 'Brother Howard,' he said loudly. Mockingly. 'It's so

good to see you again.' I knew at once who he was. My persecutor was there in front of me. He pretended to be very solicitous, interested in my teachings. He made quite the scene looking at my wares and acting as if they fascinated him. Then he brought out his notebook and made an entry as to when I would be speaking. 'I'll be there, *Brother Howard*,' he said, 'oh, you can be sure I'll be there.' His voice told me clearly that he would be there to crucify me, to announce what he perceived as my misdeeds of the past."

"And that's not how you view your past?" asked Am.

"I tried to help the very sick," he said. "Do you condemn doctors for making a living doing the exact same thing?"

"You promised cures."

"I offered hope. I can show you hundreds of testimonials . . ."

"And now you listen to the dead?"

Self-righteously: "Yes, I do."

"But you couldn't hear Dr. Kingsbury?"

"It might be that his spirit still lingers around here," said Brother Howard, "and hasn't passed over yet."

One of the Fat Innkeeper's *shiryoos*, thought Am.

"Or maybe," reflected Brother Howard, "he just didn't want to talk with me."

If that was the case, thought Am, he really couldn't blame Kingsbury.

Chapter Thirty-One

Skylar's presentation (in his contract he forbade it to be called an "act" or "performance") was just ending when they arrived. The grand finale was a bunch of forks and spoons turned into Dali-like flatware. The crowd clapped enthusiastically, and Skylar, dressed in black, frowned at them, bowed very formally, and then walked off the stage.

Getting backstage was easy, but getting to see Skylar was not. His manager provided interference, claimed that Skylar was always exhausted after his "demonstrations of the mind" and never talked to anyone. Marisa acted disappointed, said she was a "big fan," and, "Oh, isn't it a shame that I won't be able to interview him." The manager perked up at her words, asked a few questions, then verified her journalistic credentials. He was suddenly willing to help, and went to talk with Skylar. It was apparent that reporters were no longer clamoring to interview the mentalist, but Am didn't think that was what got them inside. While they were waiting a door opened, and an enormously large brown eye stared at them—or rather, stared at Marisa. Why, wondered Am, hadn't the mentalist just conjured a picture of her up in his mind from inside the room? The door opened in about the time it took Skylar to get his eyeful.

"Open Sesame," said Am.

Skylar kissed Marisa's hand and managed to ignore Am completely. He led Marisa to a chair, offered her a drink, and said he was so pleased they could have this time to chat.

"I do not allow photos," he said to Am, not bothering to look at him but assuming he was the photographer. "Do not set up your cameras. My manager gives out publicity shots. Talk to him if you're interested."

Am made no move to leave, instead found a chair. Skylar looked momentarily disappointed, then turned his attention back to Marisa. He was a handsome man, had been born and raised in Lebanon, had the good looks of a prince straight out of *One Thousand and One Arabian Nights*. Skylar had the reputation of being a ladies' man. He did have a certain charisma, Am had to admit, a personality that demanded attention. His eyes could have qualified for lakes. He had straight white teeth, and a mocha complexion set off by very black hair. Too black, Am thought, looking a little closer. Yes, it was dyed. And those enormous dark eyes of his had eyeliner around them. Making those discoveries made Am feel a little better.

He wondered if Marisa had noticed those things. It didn't look like it. The two of them were laughing together over something, Skylar's hand lightly touching her arm. He said something, and then squeezed her shoulder. Am was sure Skylar's voice had been worked on as much as his hair; it was deep, full-throated, and had a mysterious echo to it, as if it emerged from a great cavern. He kept offering Marisa his white teeth. Probably capped, thought Am.

"When did you discover your gift?" asked Marisa.

"I will present you with my book," he said. "It will tell you how I came from a family renowned throughout our country for our powers."

Why was it, Am wondered, that everyone they talked with seemed to have an autobiography on hand? Wasn't it enough to have a business card anymore?

"I'd rather hear it from you," said Marisa. "It's so much nicer hearing things firsthand."

She giggled. She actually giggled. The woman knew how to flirt. Here she was, intelligent and motivated and self-directed to write important words, and she knew how to flirt. To Am's way of thinking, that didn't seem right. To Skylar's, it was just fine.

"I will tell you anything," he said. "Anything."

She was as good at asking questions, thought Am, as she was at stroking Skylar's immense ego. He watched her rope him in. A man who was out for answers would have tossed the lasso and fought like hell to bring him down. She didn't work that way. Skylar was roped, caught, and tied up and he didn't even know it.

"You have fans around the world," she said.

"Everywhere," he agreed.

"They must have been as disappointed as I was when that awful man said those lies about you. What kind of a world is it when someone has to try and tear down a being of your stature just to make himself look good?"

"He's dead!" said Skylar. The words were offered in glee, then slightly reconsidered. "I knew he would die," he said.

Am wondered if Marisa was as short of breath as he was. "You did?" she asked.

"Yes. When he made up his . . . stories . . . three years ago, I sued him. And I foresaw . . ."

He touched his index fingers to his temples.

". . . that he was going to die a tragic death because of what he had done."

"What do you mean?" asked Marisa.

His large, dark eyes were hooded, cloaked by his eyelids. "Kismet," he said.

"Kismet," repeated Marisa.

"Allah punished him for his lies. And he did it right in front of me."

Am couldn't resist. "Right in front of you," he said.

"Yes," said Skylar dramatically. "The man died in this Hotel last night. And he thought he could laugh at me. I like that old saying: He who laughs last, laughs best."

"I can't imagine anyone ever laughing at you," said Marisa.

She missed her calling, thought Am. She should have been an actress. And then a nagging doubt: She wasn't performing with *him*, was she?

"Just the night before last," he said, "he had the nerve to challenge me in front of a crowd. I was on stage, halfway through my demonstration, when he presented himself. I knew who he was right away. I wanted to call security and have him thrown out. But I could not interrupt my mental exhibition.

"Standing beneath me, he called up a greeting, acted as if we were old friends. In a loud, mocking voice he said that he'd be having a few magic shows of his own before the week was through. Then he looked at his watch, shook it a few times as if it wasn't working, and said he must be going, that he had a date with a deceitful destiny, or some such nonsense."

"What an awful man," said Marisa.

"He now tells his lies in hell. He had no idea what trouble his evil would bring him, and couldn't know that by attacking me he wrote his own epitaph. My enemies all die horrible and mysterious deaths."

"Dr. Kingsbury wasn't the first of your enemies to die in a suspicious manner?" asked Am.

Skylar smiled, as if remembering fond memories. Any potential answer was interrupted by a knock at the door. Skylar let a room-service waiter enter. On his tray was a pot of coffee. The server was surprised that Skylar had company.

"I can get more cups, sir," he said.

"That is not necessary," said Skylar in a magnanimous voice. "I have extras."

The waiter nodded and left. "Will you have some coffee?" Skylar asked Marisa.

"Thank you," she said.

"It is a special Turkish blend," he said. "I have it served to me after my last nightly demonstration everywhere I go. Some people say they can't sleep if they drink coffee. I find I can't if I don't drink it. Cream? Sugar?"

She shook her head. "That is how I like it," said Skylar. "Leaded, as I hear some people say. Or in this case, superleaded."

He handed Marisa her cup, and then poured himself one. They both sipped appreciatively.

"Excuse me," said Am, then pantomimed his own cup.

Skylar sighed, then poured. "With cream and sugar, if you don't mind," added Am.

The mentalist did, but provided them anyway. Skylar

was sipping, and looking into Marisa's eyes, when Am spoke again. "And a spoon, please."

Skylar didn't disguise the malevolence in his look. He was not a man who liked to be interrupted. To challenge him, he had said, was dangerous.

He handed over a spoon. Am thanked him, and started to stir, then noticed the metal was twisted, bent in half.

On Skylar's profile, Am noticed, was the smallest of smiles.

Chapter Thirty-Two

"So," said Cleo, "what you're really saying is that I haven't been arrested."

Jimmy nodded. "I kinda thought you just needed to get away for a little while and think about what you're doing to yourself."

They were sitting in the employee's cafeteria drinking coffee. Cleopatra's eyes looked as if they had a permanent puffiness to them. She kept sniffling, and Jimmy kept offering her napkins.

"But we just came here for a getaway," she said. Then, emphatically: "It was supposed to be romantic."

"Romantic to me," said Jimmy, "is walking along the beach at sunset hand in hand with my special lady. Romantic to me is dancing by moonlight. Romantic to me is finding a special view and sharing it with a special someone."

He gave her a clueing look. She could be that special someone. Not that Jimmy had ever done any of those romantic things he had described. Up until now he had never even thought about doing them. Most of his relationships had been short-lived. For some reason the women he had dated hadn't liked staying up all night getting the sporting scores from around the country.

"All of that sounds nice to me," admitted Cleo.

"I know a special view," he said. Mount Soledad, he was thinking. From there you could see half the world, but most people just went up there to make out.

She reached over and patted his hand. "You've been very special to me," she said. "But I'm in a relationship."

"One relationship I could understand," said Jimmy, "but multiple . . ." He shook his head.

"What do you mean?"

"You know."

"No, I don't know."

Jimmy looked at her. She really didn't. It was worse than he had thought. "Your boyfriend's trying to get you involved with a bunch of swingers."

"Swingers?"

"Adam and Eve and Dawn and Steve. Mate-swappers."

With total incredulity, she said, "You're wrong."

"I wish I was. They call themselves the Swap Meat."

"Bradford is not a—a—swinger," she said. "He has been as upset about everything as I have."

"He didn't look too upset back in the room."

Like most low blows, it worked. A thoughtful look came over Cleo's face. She remembered their initial meeting with the other couple. Could it have been planned? Did that other man actually think that she . . . ? How disgusting. How absolutely repugnant. Cleo stopped accepting napkins. She was mad.

"I don't believe any of this," she said.

Words invariably uttered, Jimmy knew, by those who did believe.

Chapter Thirty-Three

They sat discussing murder in the Lobby Lounge. Bars that are located directly off hotel lobbies traffic mostly in the captive-audience market and the spontaneous-purchase category, with guests either waiting to get into their rooms, or wanting to get a drink without having to bother going very far. It was a better place than most to be discussing murder. The Lobby Lounge was very tropical, with lots of green foliage, running water, and fountains. Maybe there was too much water. Marisa had excused herself three times to go to the bathroom. On her most recent outing she had explained, not a little embarrassed, that "the running water keeps giving me less than subliminal messages."

It was almost midnight. The lounge wasn't very crowded, but it wasn't a place to hide either. It was a spot to see, and be seen, with only floral barriers between the loungers and the lobby. Am was drinking a mineral water. One cup of Skylar's Turkish coffee had been enough electroshock therapy for the night. He'd tried to return the mentalist's favor, had left him a somewhat unbent spoon.

The cocktail server interrupted Am's thoughts. "Would you like another?" she asked.

"Uh, no, thanks," Am said, his smile covering up for his having been startled.

It was slow, so she wasn't in any rush to leave. Am looked at her name tag, confirming the first name he wasn't sure off. Tracy, it said, and in smaller letters, Mission Viejo, California. She'd been at the Hotel for less than a year. Am remembered they had talked one time about her graduate studies at San Diego State.

"Did you have a good night?" he asked.

"The good thing is my shift is almost over," she said. "I have a date with a hot bath."

"I think I have that same date."

"Will your friend want a refill?"

Marisa was drinking cranberry juice. A diuretic, as if she needed one. Her glass was still half-full. Am was afraid the sight of a full glass might immediately send her back to the bathroom.

"No, thanks," he said. "I'll close out the bill whenever you're ready."

"Thought you might say that," she said. Tracy presented the bill on a little tray with two peppermints.

"Enjoy your bath," he told her.

"You, too," she said.

He looked at the bill, and not for the first time was glad he didn't have to pay the Hotel prices. Because he was entertaining someone from the Fourth Estate, he would charge this to advertising and promotion. The Hotel policy afforded the servers only an eight-percent gratuity on such accounts, so Am added a few dollars of his own. He placed the bills atop the bar charge. Just a few hours back, he remembered, he had been examining Dr. Kingsbury's bar charges.

Come to think of it, one of the doctor's tabs had come from the Lobby Lounge.

Tracy was talking with the bartender, and Am had to use all but semaphore flags to get her attention. She casually made her way back to him. "What do you need?" she asked. "Bubble bath?"

He fished through a pile of papers, came up with a recent picture of Dr. Thomas Kingsbury. "Wonder if either you or Dave recognize this man."

Tracy didn't need to show the picture to the bartender. "He came in here late the other night," she said. "Was sitting right about where you're sitting."

"Was he alone?"

"No. He was joined by a woman."

"What did she look like?"

"Platinum blond. Good-looking. She was at least twenty years younger than he was. Not his daughter, though."

They never were. "Did you hear any of their conversation?"

"No. They wanted to be alone."

"How would you describe their mood?"

"Happy. He was rather jovial. He ordered several shots of Goldschlager Schnapps."

"I'm not familiar with that drink."

"The yuppies like it. It's damned expensive, and for a reason. There's actual flakes of gold in the bottle."

"No!"

"I'll show you."

Tracy went back to the bar just as Marisa returned to the table. In the time it took to explain his inquiry Tracy reappeared with the bottle. She also had two full shot glasses.

"Dave signed these to the management folio as an educational tasting," Tracy said.

Am raised an eyebrow, then gave a dubious wave of thanks to Dave. He hated to think how many red flags would be raised if his own day at the Hotel were tracked through receipts. It would be tough enough to explain everything, and he was alive. Poor Kingsbury wasn't.

Marisa shook the bottle and held it up. Golden flakes rained down through the amber liquid.

"It reminds me of Christmas,'" said Marisa.

"Christmas?"

"The day after Thanksgiving we'd always bring out our Christmas boxes. I couldn't wait to play with the snow domes."

"Snow domes?"

Marisa excitedly demonstrated with her hands. "You know," she said, "the glass domes you shake and then the snow falls down."

Ah, he thought. His family had called them water globes, but like Marisa's, they had also brought them out for the holidays. The winter scenes were as close as he ever got to snow growing up in San Diego. Am looked at the bottle. She was right; when it was stirred up it reminded him of the globes, save that these were golden flakes, not snowflakes, and they didn't fall on carolers, and chalets, and ice skaters; they were supposed to fall down upon open throats, not open sleighs.

They thanked Tracy, handed her back the bottle of Goldschlager, then raised their own shot glasses. The gold flakes had settled at the bottom, but when they clicked glasses the gold rose and dispersed. They downed the contents in a gulp. The schnapps kicked in from the gullet on down.

"Phew," said Marisa. "That's what I call a real gold rush."

Am felt the same way. The liquor packed a punch. He looked at his glass, and noticed some gold flakes clinging to its side.

" 'Saint-seducing gold,' " he said, quoting from Shakespeare, but remembering neither the play nor the scene.

A few gold flakes also clung to Marisa's glass. "I suppose these are dregs we should drink," she said.

A strange idea came to Am. He considered explaining, but it was too late. Besides, the idea was far-fetched.

"Let's leave them," he said. "The drink's too rich for my blood anyway."

Chapter Thirty-Four

They waited for the valet to bring Marisa's car to the front of the Hotel. Am always thought the Hotel was particularly beguiling at night. Beyond the entryway, soft lights illuminated the gardens, the coastal clouds adding a fairy-tale mist. The Hotel always dressed up for the evening, her antique lines accentuated by the shadows. She was an ageless storybook setting, a place where once-upon-a-times began. The gentle ocean breeze circulated pleasant promises, the scents of jasmine, gardenia, and roses making wonderful chemistry with the brine. Swaying palm trees lined the road, gently dancing to some airy tune and the rhythm of the sounding ocean.

"I enjoyed myself tonight," Marisa said, "even though I'm leaving with more questions than when I arrived."

They had dissected the motive for someone's wanting to murder Dr. Kingsbury. There were reasons aplenty, revenge heading the list. Besides Skylar and Brother Howard, there were countless others that the doctor had exposed. Fear could have also contributed to his murder. Brother Howard, in particular, must have been feeling vulnerable. He had already been driven out of one business by Kingsbury, and just as he was starting another, the doctor had turned up. Adding gasoline to the fire was a game that Kingsbury evidently relished. He had confronted both Skylar and Brother Howard in front of crowds, had acted as if he were ready to duel with them again. Were there others the doctor had challenged?

"I enjoyed myself, too," said Am.

"We shouldn't have, though, should we?" she asked. "I mean, here we are looking into the death of a man."

"You needn't feel guilty," said Am. "And you don't have to take my word, you can take Kingsbury's: 'Be positive.'"

She smiled, raised her face up to his. "Yes, that's right, isn't it?"

Her smile, and upturned face, remained looking at him for a long moment. Was that an invitation, or was she just being friendly? Should he kiss her? Hadn't they just agreed there was nothing to be guilty about?

A screech of tires interrupted the moment. The headlights of Marisa's red Mazda Miata spotlighted Am's uncertainty. The car came to a sudden halt, and the valet jumped out and opened the door. They walked over to the car. Am had already validated her parking, but there was the matter of a tip. The valet gratefully accepted her money, but still stood sentry, waiting to close the door behind her.

"I'll tuck her in," said Am.

"Yes, sir," said the valet, and took off at a run. There were others waiting for their cars.

They both laughed a little, and then laughed a little more, neither knowing what to say, or how to end their evening. "I'll call you," she said. "The autopsy results are supposed to be announced sometime tomorrow, which means I'm going to be busy writing a story."

"And I'll be following up on a few leads," said Am. He almost told her about his idea again, but held off.

"Thanks for everything," she said, extending her hand.

He started to shake it, then brought her hand up to his lips and kissed it instead. Marisa got into her car without saying anything, barely acknowledged him with a wave as she closed the door and drove off. Am couldn't help but wonder if he had misread the situation, if he had put his personal interpretation on professional friendliness.

Her car had to do a loop to get out. He was still standing at the curb when she passed by. Her return message to him wasn't in Morse code, and wasn't hard to interpret. The headlights of the Miata opened and closed, gave as blatant a wink as was automotively possible. And then the roadster sped off.

Am wasn't sure how long it took him to notice he was being summoned, but the voice on the walkie-talkie sounded absolutely peevish by the time he responded.

"This is Am," he said.

Flanders had the graveyard dispatch. He had started him on his workday, sending him off to see Takei over sixteen hours ago. Am wondered if his day would ever end.

"About time," said Flanders. "I'm not interrupting anything, am I?"

His last words were hopeful. The Hotel grapevine, which circulated any personal information faster than light, was obviously in good working order.

"What do you have?" asked Am.

"Call came in at twenty-three hundred and . . ." There was a pause while Flanders tried to figure out military time. He soon gave up. "At ten minutes before midnight." Am had to endure the rattling of papers over the walkie-talkie.

Flanders was the least officious of all the dispatchers, just one of the reasons he worked graveyard. There are some people who are made for the vampire shift, who know they don't fit in with people who circulate during the light of day. Flanders was one of those.

"We got us a code . . ." Some more shuffling of papers. " . . . a code green in the Crown Jewel Suite."

Code green, thought Am. Green was, he remembered, a suspected break-in of a guest room. When Chief Horton had made up the color codes, his logic had been that burglars usually took "the green."

"If I were you, Am," said Flanders, "I'd go up armed."

Alarmed, Am asked, "Armed?"

"Lady's none too pleased," Flanders said.

He should lecture Flanders about dispatch protocol, order him to switch to the alternate channel and pointedly, graphically, even, describe how many goddamn hours he'd been at the Hotel and how he didn't need any of his crap. But Am was too tired to expend that kind of energy, and this wasn't something he could delegate. You don't send an underling to Lady Death.

"Okay," he said.

"Ten-four," said Flanders. The words sounded like "tent floor." Flanders was chewing on something, probably another jelly doughnut.

Lady Death was surprised to see him. It was usually the other way around. She was waiting outside her room, and looked as if she were afraid to go inside. Am reintroduced himself, and announced his position at the Hotel. Angela said she had figured Am for some other Hotel capacity, something he was pleased to hear, but the rest of what she had to say wasn't so pleasant.

"I arrived back at the Hotel just minutes ago," she said. "And found, . . . well . . . you'll see."

He entered the room and she followed, quite clearly wanting him to lead the way. "In the next room," she said. "On the bed."

Am walked into the room and saw that someone had come in after turndown and left more than good-night mints on the pillows. The bedspread had been pulled back, the white sheets apparently a better backdrop for the blood-like lettering that had been left: R.I.P. Beneath the large red letters were torn-out pictures of Angela Holliday and the word DEAD.

"I assume they found my books," she said, "and ripped out my picture, and that particular word, from the book covers."

For once, "dead" didn't seem to be Lady Death's favorite word. It only took Am moments to confirm her suspicion. Several dozen of her books lay strewn on the floor, their covers torn apart.

"Did you notice anything else of yours missing or disturbed?" he asked.

"I don't know. I didn't hang around after seeing that message. I ran from the room and found a house phone. I doubt whether my call to the front desk made much sense."

"You did the right thing," said Am.

He turned on some more lights, then stopped at the bar and picked up a comfortable cudgel, a bottle of wine, before starting his exploration. Am methodically made his way through the suite. With each step he became more and more convinced that the suite had been designed for paranoia. There were too many places for a potential assailant to be hiding. His search took in bathrooms, walk-in closets, cabinets, sofas, beds, armoires, and hidden corners. In the suite's second bathroom Am discovered the "blood" on the sheets—two empty bottles of red fingernail polish. The bottles had been tossed at the mirror above the sink, causing the glass to crack in several places. Someone had seven years of bad luck coming.

Angela entered the bathroom behind Am, gasped as she saw the damage. Through the cracked reflection he watched as she raised her hand up to her mouth. Her pale features were now preternaturally so. In another circumstance, with another person, Am might have thought she had seen the dead.

"The fingernail polish yours?" he asked.

She moved closer, examined the labels without touching them. "They're my brand," she said. Angela searched through her cosmetics bag, and confirmed they had been taken from there. As far as she could determine, nothing else was missing.

He continued examining the suite. There were no more surprises, nothing else out of the ordinary. Am was thorough, even went so far as to open the Steinway baby grand piano, but found only a little dust. He made a mental note for housekeeping.

His inside search concluded, Am turned the balcony lights on and went outside. No one was lurking behind the planters, or hiding under the patio furniture. There was only the ocean, calling from seven floors below. He looked for signs of forced entry, but didn't see any. Then he checked the two entry doors to the suite, which didn't appear to have been tampered with either.

"Was the door locked when you returned?" he asked.

"Yes."

"And are all your own keys accounted for?"

"I was only given one," she said, "and I still have it."

Takei had promised him they'd be getting electronic locks by next spring. There had been relatively few problems with the automatic dead bolts currently in use at the Hotel, but there was the constant concern of outstanding keys. Security was good about rekeying rooms with unaccounted-for keys, and keeping an accurate key inventory, but they weren't perfect. Human error couldn't be ignored either, with guests often not shutting their doors completely, and housekeepers forgetting to lock all the windows and sliding glass doors. Since the Crown Jewel Suite had two entry doors, it was only too possible that one could have inadvertently been left open. Thieves were opportunists. But Am reminded himself that this wasn't a case of a thief calling, but a terrorist.

"Have you received any other threats?" Am asked.

"One," she said in a small voice. "Just yesterday. I was doing a radio show. After we finished I was told I had a call. I identified myself, and this voice said, 'Speaker for the dead? Dead will be your first language very soon.' And then he hung up."

"He?"

"Yes. The voice was muffled but it was male."

"Do you have any enemies?"

"None that I know of."

Am called the Rover on his walkie-talkie, told him to come to the Crown Jewel Suite to rekey the room, then turned back to Lady Death. "Would you prefer sleeping in another room tonight?" he asked. "I can assure you total anonymity. No one will know where you are."

She ran a hand through her platinum-blond hair, sighed, then shook her head. "I don't know," she said. "It's hard for me to think clearly."

"Why don't we sit down?" Am suggested.

The suite offered too many choices of where to sit. Angela hesitated, and then steered him over to the bar area. "Can I get you anything to drink?" she asked.

"No, thank you."

"It was such a long day," she said. "All I wanted to do was get some sleep. Now I'm afraid to sleep."

She walked behind the bar, found a glass, and started looking through the bottles.

"How'd your signing go?"

"I have writer's cramp."

"Isn't that good?"

She nodded. "But if it's going to be like this for the next three months, I think I'll be referring to my publishing contract as a pact with the devil."

Lady Death poured from a familiar bottle. Am took a closer look. "Goldschlager," he said.

"Yes. Funny, first time I tried this was a few days ago. I had never even heard of it. But I enjoyed it so much I had room service bring me up a bottle."

In a courtroom, lawyers don't like to ask questions of witnesses when they're not already sure of the answer. "How'd you happen to try it?" Am asked, knowing that Dr. Kingsbury had been seen drinking with a younger blond woman.

"Tom Kingsbury," she said sadly. Angela looked at the drink as if she should be questioning its heritage, sighed, then took another sip. "I was . . . unprepared for his death," she said. "He was so vital."

Anyone else would have said they were upset to hear about his death, but that sentiment wouldn't have gone with the philosophy Lady Death preached.

"How did you happen to know him?"

"I met him for the first—and last—time the night I arrived. I had filled out one of his questionnaires and he wanted to speak to me, but with our schedules it was tough finding a time good for both of us. We arranged to meet the night before the conference began. I had a late flight in, but he said that was okay, because he was a night owl."

"What kind of questions did he ask you?"

Lady Death didn't appear comfortable with the inquiry. "Why do you want to know?"

"Tomorrow," said Am, "we suspect the coroner will be announcing that Dr. Kingsbury did not die a natural death."

She didn't immediately react. When she did, it wasn't as Am would have expected. "I should have known," she said.

"Why?"

"He wasn't a man on his last legs. Far from it. I got the distinct feeling he was less interested in my out-of-body experiences than in my body itself."

Lady Death shifted slightly on the barstool. She had on a black jumpsuit that closely followed the lines of her trim figure. If the doctor's academic interest had waned, Am could certainly understand why.

"What made you think that?"

"Looks, comments. You don't need to be a mind reader to see the obvious. He asked me the appropriate medical questions, but I think he would have much preferred playing doctor to being interviewer."

Norma with the Bette Davis voice had alluded to the same thing. The doctor appeared to be an incorrigible flirt—or worse.

"What medical questions did he ask you?"

"Specifics about my near-death."

Just as he had done with his other UNDER interviews. Am gave her an inquiring look, asked Angela in his glance to elaborate. "I can see you haven't read my book yet," she said.

As if there had been time. "A real death has taken precedence," he said.

"Without any of the medical jargon," she said, "I fell and struck my head. It was a severe blow. I was in a coma, and the prognosis was that I was going to die. The doctors were right in that—I did die. Dr. Kingsbury wanted to know about the particulars, and I gave them to him."

Am asked her to remember as much as she could of their conversation. She said they hadn't been together all that long, no more than ninety minutes. The doctor had spent some of the time "filling in his blanks," some of the time "eyeing her speculatively," and the rest "just talking and drinking." She remembered that he had "at least" four shots of Goldschlager to her two. The drinks had loosened him up for some freer talk.

"He got on his soapbox and played the skeptic," she said, "claimed that death was the end of the human organism, save for some residual recycling. He knows better now."

When Am finished with his questions, Lady Death had a few of her own. They talked for a while, each getting more comfortable with the other. Am told her about the investigation and couldn't help but sound pessimistic. There were so many trails, he said.

Lady Death tried to appear unconcerned, but she didn't quite pull it off. "Do you think there's a connection," she asked, "between the threat left for me and Thomas's killer?"

Am reached out a comforting hand, lightly placed it on her shoulder, and offered some reassuring words. Kingsbury had enough of his own enemies, he said. It was likely she had just riled up the indignation of some zealot. He told her that people who threatened rarely followed through, and that it was the quiet ones you had to watch out for. Am didn't know if that was really true, but she seemed to appreciate his words. She put her hand atop his, placed him in a position where he couldn't easily remove his hand from her shoulder.

"This is all new to me," she said. "The speeches, and radio, and television, and the fancy hotel rooms, and the lines of people waiting to talk with me. New and somewhat disconcerting."

Not to mention the new death threats, thought Am.

"I miss home already."

"Where's home?"

"A little town in Colorado. Paonia. Right now I just want to click my heels together and say, 'There's no place like home. There's no place like home.'"

She was wearing black pumps, managed to ease them off her feet and let them drop to the thick carpeting. Her toes worked their way under Am's pant leg and moved along his calf.

"It will be difficult for me to stay in this room by myself tonight," she said.

Am considered her words. He wasn't sure if her toes were

actually warm, or whether it was his skin that burned wherever they moved.

"We can move you to that other room . . ." he said.

"I don't want that bother," she said, still massaging his calf.

"I think I could use that drink now," Am said.

She took her time removing her digits, withdrew her fingers first, then her toes. While she was pouring his drink, Am called the Rover on his walkie-talkie and asked him to return to the Crown Jewel Suite. It would be his second visit in less than half an hour; he had already rekeyed the locks to the room. Angela slid Am's glass of Goldschlager over to him, and finished pouring another of her own.

"What was that last page all about?" she asked.

"I'm going to assign you a private sentry tonight," said Am. "He'll be posted on your doorstep."

It wasn't the solution she had proposed, and he wasn't sure if it was the one he wanted to offer, but it was the right thing to do. Angela raised her glass, albeit a little slowly, and Am did the same thing. Before they touched glasses, Am asked, "Did Dr. Kingsbury offer any toasts the night he was with you?"

Lady Death thought a moment. "Yes," she said. "He repeated the same one several times. 'All that glitters is not gold.' "

Chapter Thirty-Five

"I appreciate your walking me to my room," said Cleo, "but it's really not necessary."

"It's my pleasure," said Jimmy.

She was glad he was insisting, but didn't want him to know it. Cleo felt a little guilty for leading Jimmy on. She expected to leave him at her doorstep, say good night, and never see him again. The thought didn't appeal to her, but she had arrived at the Hotel with another man, someone until that very afternoon she had considered her dream man. That vision was slightly tarnished, but Cleo still wasn't willing to believe that Bradford was part of the swinger's group. There were some nagging questions, though. Why hadn't he volunteered to go with her to the police station when he thought she was being arrested? And why hadn't he insisted they check out if, as he said, their accommodations were so unacceptable?

Jimmy said little as they walked, but he, too, had questions. Why was that yuppie even with Cleo? She wasn't his type. He had carried the bags for thousands of Bradfords before, the kind of guys who lived for appearances, whose women were always stick-thin and ate only yogurt and fruit, and drank spring water. Jimmy preferred a woman with a little meat, and a little spunk—like Cleo.

They arrived at room 212. There wasn't any noise coming from inside, the mariachis, and the party, apparently long departed.

"Thank you for everything," she told Jimmy.

"I'll wait out here to make sure everything is okay," he said. He wasn't going to be dismissed that easily.

She liked his answer. Cleo wasn't sure what she wanted to see inside, she only knew that she had to go through the door and look. The room was dark and unkempt. Nothing had changed on that front. Cleo stumbled forward trying to see. Was that a figure in the bed, or just a lumpy bedspread? "Bradford," she called, walking closer. She called out his name a second time, then patted the bedspread, confirming its rumpled state, and Bradford's absence. Where was he?

Cleo looked around for a note, but didn't find one. What she did find was Missy's Velcro underwear, a calling card she could have done without.

"You okay?" Jimmy's voice came from the door.

"Yes," she said. "I'll be along in a minute."

Cleo stood in the middle of the room considering her options. Maybe Bradford was looking for her, had gotten over his shock of seeing her being escorted away and was now raising Cain at the front desk trying to find out where she was. When she reappeared at the doorway she wasn't carrying suitcases as Jimmy had hoped, but she did have a thoughtful expression on her face.

"Do you have a pass key?" she asked Jimmy.

"I can get one in two shakes of a lamb's tail," he said.

It wasn't a lamb's tail she was thinking about. Jimmy ran

off to get the key. In his absence, Cleo started walking around the second floor, her movements tracked by the sex sentries. She reminded them of a robin, walking forward, pausing with a slightly cocked head, then continuing along. Jimmy proved almost as fast as his boast, arriving back at her side breathless. In the past, only the promise of a big payoff had made him move quickly. It had to be love.

Cleo didn't notice, or chose not to, his breathless state. "You say the Hotel segregated the swingers in certain sections?" she asked.

"Second and third floors," panted Jimmy. "Most of the rooms are connecting. You might have noticed the staff we have posted to make sure they don't try wandering off and . . ."

"Let's go to the third floor," said Cleo.

Jimmy led the way. There were several parties on the third floor, or maybe it was one party spread along half a dozen of the connecting rooms. The noise was loud in several rooms, but Cleo kept walking forward, oblivious to the laughter and shouting, listening for something.

"If all the people attending this orgy were laid from end to end," said Jimmy, pausing for effect, "I wouldn't be a bit surprised."

Cleo didn't look amused. Quite rightly so, he thought. No woman he was interested in should have been amused at such a remark.

As they moved away from the party rooms, other noises became apparent. Someone's smoke alarm was sounding, thought Jimmy. No, it was the fire alarm. But it wasn't that either.

"Ohhhhhhhh. Ohhhhhhhhh. Ohhhhhhhhh. Ohhhhhhhh, Gawddddddd."

"Open that door," said Cleo.

Jimmy would have opened it anyway. Someone was in pain. Someone needed help. He followed Cleo inside. And there, she saw what she had to see. Bradford and Missy didn't notice them. They were busy.

"I'll need some help with my luggage," Cleo said to Jimmy.

Chapter Thirty-Six

The insistent flashing red light of Am's message machine wouldn't let him pass by. He was thankful to see that there was only one message. Still, why did he always feel that pushing the machine's "play" button was like playing the slots, with the end result usually bad news? Don't be the Hotel, he prayed.

"Am, this is Sharon. It's about midnight. Maybe I should call the Hotel. No, I guess not. If you get in, call me. And if you're asleep, sweet dreams."

He looked at his watch, saw that it was a little past one o'clock. It was unusual for Sharon to call this late. Hell, it was unusual for her even to be calling. He dialed her number. She picked up on the third ring.

"*Hajimemashite,*" said Am, doing his best to sound Japanese, and give Sharon cardiac arrest.

"That means 'Nice to meet you,'" she said.

Wrong greeting, thought Am. But at least she sounded a lot more awake.

"I think the Japanese are better at relationships than we are," she said.

"We?" asked Am.

"Americans," she said, then after a long pause: "Us."

He wondered what was coming. Sharon was usually direct, but tonight she was rambling. "*Giri* takes place over *ninjoo*," she said. "Duty over feeling. They always think of the *ie*, the household, or social organization. The *ie* is a basis, a framework, where they know their positions, and roles, and obligations. You know what makes a Japanese person more guilty than anything else? It's when they fail to behave as expected."

In an intuitive flash, Am asked, "And what makes you feel guilty?"

There was a long silence. "I went on a date tonight," she said.

It hurt, but not as much as it would have five hours earlier. She'd been ending their relationship for months now, or at least trying to change it.

"The Japanese don't trust love," she said. "I think I'm the same way. Romantic love is *mono tarinai*—lacking something. It doesn't have the concrete foundations of the family, and business, and the outside world. That's why Japanese don't understand western romance. They think it's unreasonable for two people to believe they can get so much out of a relationship. Love is not enough for them."

"Did your date tonight have those same passionless views?"

"We have many of the same goals."

He felt compelled to play devil's advocate. "Are goals enough?"

She didn't answer, at least not directly. "Is it so wrong to try and look down the road ten or twenty years? Relationships, like businesses, need to take that long view. By some accounts, half of Japanese marriages are *omiai*, arranged.

Their divorce rate is far lower than ours. The marriage prospects are discussed and considered among the family. It isn't just a man and a woman entering the marriage, but families, and extended families, and even society."

"You keep forgetting you're not Japanese," Am reminded her. "Was your date?"

"No."

"So you went on one date and decided you needed to plan the rest of your life?"

"No," she said, "I went on one date and decided it was time to get on with my life. What's between us isn't settled. It needs to be."

"Got a silver stake?" asked Am. "When you're killing love, or the undead, you have to pierce the heart."

"I know," she said.

She did know. Am decided to make it easier on both of them. "I went on a date tonight, too," he said. "You'd probably be happy to know it started as business, but that's not how it ended, at least I don't think it did."

The news was a relief to her. She wanted to know details, which meant Am had to tell her about his day, a telling which took quite a while. Sharon had advice for him, as usual, revealing background about the Fat Innkeeper he didn't know. When she finished, there was the silence of the hour.

"You weren't good for me, Am Caulfield," she said. "There were too many nights you kept me up like this."

"I was good for you." Even as he said it, Am knew he was speaking in the past tense.

"I'd go to work the next day and be tired."

"It was a good tired."

"You're a hopeless romantic. You're a dreamer."

"Don't knock it until you've tried it."

"I tried it," she said wistfully.

Another silence between them. Their words were said, and passing under a bridge, flowing, flowing, to wherever the spirits of lost love go.

"Tell me a Japanese folktale," she said.

He considered excerpting from the *Tales of Genji*, revealing to her that the Japanese could wax romantic themselves, but that wouldn't be a folktale, and the time for that was already past.

"In northwestern Japan," he said softly, "the snow sometimes reaches a depth of ten feet or more. Half the year the landscape is covered with snow.

"She arrived with the first snowstorm. The young man, a bachelor, heard a noise outside the door, and opened it up to find her. She was naked, but not shivering, her hair long, her skin very white. The young man helped the beautiful woman inside. Within a week they were married.

"Their love was deep and full. The snow wife asked him not to talk about how she had come to him, made him swear that he would not. To please her, he made that promise. The snow fell, and they were happy.

"As spring approached, and the weather grew warmer, the snow wife became thinner and thinner, her complexion ever more wan and pale.

"The man threw a party just before summer. All of his friends were there. Everyone was drinking sake and being boisterous. When his friends asked him how he had met his beautiful bride he told of their first meeting. Then he called for his wife to come out, but she did not answer, and when he went to the kitchen he found only his wife's kimono lying in a pool of water."

Sharon was quiet for the better part of a minute. "I wonder if she would have lived through the summer," she finally said.

"Some love is only meant for certain seasons," said Am.

"Thank you."

He pretended to be Bogey. "We'll always have Paris," he said. "Or was that Tokyo?"

She laughed, said "Sayonara," then ended their connection.

Chapter Thirty-Seven

His clock radio gave him the option of being awakened to "alarm" or "music." Am chose a more drastic alternative, waking to a local news station that believed in broadcasting its call letters with Klaxon intensity every five minutes (even more frequently during Arbitron rating periods). Between the call letters and commercials were the usual international stories of war, famine, and devastation, followed by more call letters and commercials, then the invariable local news of congested freeways, city budget problems, the Padres losing, and pleasant weather, save for morning and afternoon clouds. The news was delivered in "happy format," which was as satisfying as a chocolate-coated suppository. Am managed not to move through two reveille charges of call letters, was just beginning to rouse himself when the broadcasting team announced their teasers before yet another break.

First happy voice: "In national news, the President will be going on a peacekeeping mission to the Middle East."

Second voice, slightly happier: "In local news, surprising autopsy results at La Jolla Strand."

Third and final voice, happiest and with more inflection

than all: "And in sports, it went to twelve innings at the Murph" (the "Murph" was short for San Diego's Jack Murphy Stadium, but Am had already heard the Padres had lost).

The autopsy. Am reached for the radio and turned up the volume just in time for an additional blaring dose of call letters. It must be sweeps week, he thought, then reconsidered. If that were the case, there would have been a teaser on local massage parlors, or, he thought guiltily, an announcement about a week-long series on swingers.

He had to wait five minutes for the story he wanted, which gave him too much time to worry. There would be press all over the Hotel's grounds, with the kind of stories that might panic the guests. The media would probably try and resurrect other calamities that had occurred in the Hotel's past, or—worse—might dig up some buried stories. When you have 712 rooms, there are a lot of closets for skeletons.

"Surprise autopsy results," said the announcer. "Sea World pathologists . . ."

Sea World, thought Am. What do they have to do with Thomas Kingsbury?

". . . announced today that the beached gray whale that turned up in front of the Hotel California on the La Jolla Strand died from having ingested some drift net. Our own Brian Fisher has more on the story."

Am had heard the story before, but this time it touched him personally. He knew how the monofilament drift-net lines used by the modern fishing industry could stretch ten, twenty, even hundreds of miles, how these lines often broke off and became traveling death, trapping fish in their wake. The lines were deadly ghosts, drifting and killing, drifting and killing. The smaller pieces weren't any less deadly. Sea turtles mistook them for jellyfish snacks, and ended up with their intestines twisted inside out. Sea lions ended up with sometimes slow-acting garrotes around their necks; as they grew, the net tightened and constricted, cutting deep into the flesh, leaving open wounds with the end result of strangulation. Even giants weren't impervious to the nets. What the lines couldn't capture they could invade, ultimately tangling and entwining innards and making the kill. The uncontrolled drift lines were man's great black magic, immortal, without mercy, created to rove and kill.

Am turned off the radio. There was no word yet on the other autopsy, a headache yet deferred. He had wanted to get to work early, but decided there was another priority. He looked through his album collection, mentally acknowledging that he was still a dinosaur for having one. These days it's hard to find record stores. LPs are endangered species, kept precariously alive by a few fossils.

He found the album, took off the record sleeve, and wiped some dust off the vinyl. Then he played the whale songs, and added a few cries of his own.

Chapter Thirty-Eight

Annette's radio had never worked as long as Am had owned her. Her relative silence, which usually lasted as long as they were in sight of the ocean, was one of the best things about her. One of his friend's young sons enthusiastically called her a "big horse." She was a horse of a different color for sure.

Annette drove contentedly along the coast, humming her "life's a beach" chorus. When Am arrived at the Hotel he pulled into Outer Mongolia, sliding in next to a silver Infiniti that was being parked at the same time. Most employee vehicles knew the potholes of Tijuana only too well, with fully half the staff carpooling from south of the border every day. The average employee's car was witness to a score of dings, and was a hundred thousand miles removed from the dealer's showroom. You didn't often see luxury cars in employee parking, which made Am notice the Infiniti, and especially its driver.

He was surprised Hiroshi didn't have the valets bringing his car to and from the Hotel. Am remembered how his former GM had never deigned to walk out to the parking lot. He always made a point of marching over to the valet stand

and turning on the stopwatch mode on his watch, a motion that struck fear in the hearts of the parking staff. If his car was there within five minutes, the valets were safe. Anything over that time, and there was major trouble. It was refreshing to see an owner parking his own car. If that was the Japanese way, it wasn't all bad.

The Fat Innkeeper had not yet noticed Am, but he had noticed Annette, was walking around her making little noises.

"Good morning," said Am. Even though he had listened to the entire whale album, it was still a little before 8 AM.

"Good morning," said Hiroshi, slightly bowing. There was an excited look to his eyes. He pointed to Annette and asked "1950?"

"1951," said Am.

"Beautiful."

"Thank you." Am was convinced Annette heard all the compliments directed her way, and responded vainly.

"May I see under the hood?" Hiroshi asked so politely, and looked so shy, you would have thought he was asking to look under a woman's skirt.

Am opened the hood. Compared to modern cars, there wasn't much to see. The engine, a flat-head 3.9 liter V-8, was remarkable in its simplicity. His neighbor Jimbo claimed the car was incredibly easy to work on, but then he didn't have to pay for the parts. The Fat Innkeeper traced his fingers along the engine, gently touching here and there. He had a big smile on his face. "Beautiful," he said again.

"Would you like to see inside of the car?"

"Yes," he said. "Very much."

There's a lot of room in a 1951 Ford wood-paneled

wagon. Hiroshi explored most of its inches. Then he sat behind the wheel, looking as happy as a kid navigating a
bumper car.

"I'd tell you to take her for a spin," said Am, "but getting used to the gears takes a little bit of doing. Maybe
later we can go for a ride."

"Today?"

Hiroshi's eager response surprised Am. He obviously
didn't know that the American translation of "maybe later"
was "when hell freezes over."

"That's fine," said Am. "How about this afternoon?"

"What time?"

"Is three o'clock good for you?"

"I will be here," Hiroshi said.

Reluctantly, the Fat Innkeeper took his leave of Annette
and joined Am. They fell into step, walking along one of
the garden paths toward the Hotel.

"America was a wonderful place in the nineteen fifties,"
said Hiroshi, his nostalgic tone surprising Am. It wasn't as
if he had lived in America during those times. Hell,
thought Am, the man hadn't even been born then.

"It ruled the world," Hiroshi said. "All nations fell in re-
spectful step behind it. And it offered such abundance, such
wonderful ostentation. Like your car."

Hiroshi's English was very good. Most of Am's American
friends wouldn't have even attempted the word ostentation.
But he wasn't sure he liked the Fat Innkeeper's speech. It
sounded like a national postmortem. The country still had a
heartbeat, didn't it?

"America was great then," said Hiroshi. "It was the hope
of the world. It was the flagship."

And now there was a new rising sun. Am decided to

argue. It was, after all, the American way. "Maybe the United States is just navigating a new course," he said. "Ostentation had its time. So did goldfish swallowing and panty raids. Another era has arrived. Now we have to try and reinvent our greatness."

"Goldfish swallowing and panty raids?"

Sushi before anyone in America knew the word, innocence before being jaded. Was the thought translatable? Were white picket fences, main-street parades, and coffee shops with homemade pie? Or were those just nostalgic images, and no longer the heartbeat of the land? The new America was a place where salsa now outsold ketchup, a place of change.

"No one ever told us puberty was difficult," explained Am.

Hiroshi might have understood, or he might have just been acting polite. He offered a considerate nod. They walked along in silence. Am was about to excuse himself and cut over to the security hut when the Fat Innkeeper asked him: "How is Dr. Kingsbury?"

Am wasn't sure if Hiroshi's question sounded funny because his English was inadequate, or whether there was a cultural interpretation involved. The Japanese treat death very differently from Americans, in particular if a family member has died. Their ancestor worship often confuses westerners, who sometimes hear them referring to the dead as if they were still among the living.

"Dr. Kingsbury was a very committed man who was not afraid of stepping on toes," said Am. "I've already found several people who would have welcomed his death."

Go ahead, Am thought. Be the messenger and give him more bad news. "The autopsy results should be released this morning, and his murder announced. You might consider keeping a low profile. The media is sure to be around."

The Fat Innkeeper didn't seem to be as concerned with the media as with Dr. Kingsbury. "It is a shame he died here"—he searched for the word—"incomplete."

Am interrupted. "A *shiryoo*."

Hiroshi shook his head slightly. "Worse," he said. "A *muenbotoke*, a wandering spirit. It is that sad existence between life and death. I think that is where Dr. Kingsbury is now. He is disconnected from his household."

Was there some autobiography in his remark? Sharon had discussed Hiroshi's relations with his own family. The oceans weren't the only expanse between him and his kin. If she was right, in many ways the younger Yamada was in exile.

Am considered the new word. *Muenbotoke*. Westerners often call Japanese "the devil's language." American youngsters (some of them) learn 26 letters; Japanese children (all of them) learn a minimum of 1850 characters. The Japanese language itself has fewer sounds than any other major language, which requires its speakers to ascribe numerous meanings to its sounds, and the listeners to understand all the nuances. Mastering the language was difficult enough. A westerner who is proficient in the devil's language always surprises, even frightens, the Japanese, but their language is often thought to be a lesser hurdle to understand than their culture. Most Japanese are convinced that their culture can never be interpreted by a westerner. A *gaijin* will always be just that—an outsider.

"There is a waiter on the Hotel staff named Adnan," said Am. "He's from the Middle East. Adnan says he drives slowly in America because he doesn't want to die here. He wants to die back home, where he says people know how to show that they care."

"Adnan drives slowly in America," mused Hiroshi, then thought a little more about what Am had said. "Is that why you work so hard investigating the death of Dr. Kingsbury? To show that the Hotel cares?"

Was that the point of his story? The Japanese were always analyzing even casual conversations, searching for meanings. No wonder talking was scary to them. "Something like that," said Am.

"Listen to his spirit," said Hiroshi. Had he taken a course from Brother Howard? "Don't be afraid to use your *dai rokkan*—your sixth sense."

"I have problems enough with my five senses," Am said.

He regretted his petulant tone of voice, but the Fat Innkeeper didn't seem to notice. "I go this way," said Am.

Hiroshi paused to bow. "I will see you at three o'clock."

Am returned his bow, and then they parted paths, the Japanese man continuing west, and Am going east.

Chapter Thirty-Nine

For the second morning in a row Am was greeted with the message that Mr. Takei wanted to see him immediately. At least Flanders wasn't on Control. The information was passed on by Jan Calvin, a dispatch who resembled the "old" Aunt Jemima, the one who was fatter than her successor, and didn't have a modern 'do. The same sort of corporate thinking had replaced a gray Betty Crocker with a younger brunette. It was only a matter of time before the government entered into the lipo and hair-coloring act and started offering a youthful George Washington on the dollar bill without his white wig. Probably without his fake choppers, too.

"What's up?" asked Am.

Jan much preferred giving out her homemade cookies than bad news. "Another pretender," she said.

"No," said Am. "No. No."

"I've already sent Officer Wilson to Mr. Takei's office," she said. "Carlos Calderon is also there."

Carlos was a reservationist. "Why Carlos?" asked Am.

"The new wannabe general manager doesn't speak English very well," said Jan. "Carlos is translating."

Great, thought Am. The HRD imposter was running out of gullible Americans. Now he was recruiting Mexicans. *Mierda*. Translate that.

"Anything else?" He hoped they were at least up to the *B*s on an alphabetical Hotel trouble list. Botulism and bubonic plague came to mind.

"Ward Ankeney called," she said. "He had a question about a charge you submitted."

So soon? One of the last things Am had done the night before was submit an expense form for his session with Brother Howard. He had tucked the chit in the middle of other paperwork, hoping against hope it might just be processed. Red-flagged first thing. Why was it that the Hotel was invariably efficient when it went against his interests?

"He wants you to see him whenever it's convenient for you."

So he can give me a face-to-face no, thought Am, instead of one over the telephone. Am picked up his walkie-talkie, gave Jan a weak imitation of a Roman salute, then went outside and commandeered a utility vehicle. There are some mornings you feel every pothole in the road was carved with your name on it. Am found more than a few of those. Halfway to the administrative offices the vehicle died. He abandoned the cart, kicked it, and walked the rest of the way.

Diana Wade was the only person in the administrative offices. She smiled at Am, said that "this boss was easier to evict than the last," and that he was being interviewed in the Board Room.

"What do you mean, 'interviewed'?" asked Am.

"Mr. Takei's decided to go into the detective business," she said.

He hurried over to the Board Room, regretting that he couldn't speak Japanese better. In particular, Am wanted to know how to say "shit."

Takei had probably seen some American films where the suspects were interrogated under strobe lights. The Board Room was a meeting planner's dream, had lights designed to key on speakers, or spotlight whatever necessary. Takei had the lights on the kid. He was eighteen or nineteen, and looked scared. He was sweating a lot (the bright lights weren't helping), and declaring what must have been his innocence in high-pitched Spanish. Takei wasn't buying any of it. He was pacing around smoking a cigarette, had his own personal black cloud hanging over his head. Carlos was translating and looking like he felt sorry for the kid. Security Officer Wilson, a Camp Pendleton Marine who worked a few shifts a week to supplement his pay, was eyeing the suspect disdainfully. The kid wasn't putting up a fight, and he was giving out a lot more than name, rank, and serial number.

"Wilson," said Am.

The flattop Marine squared his shoulders. "Yes, sir."

That was one good thing about the Marines. They taught you how to kill politely. "Why don't you go write up a report and leave it on my desk."

"Yes, sir."

Takei wasn't as easily dismissed. It was clear he was not pleased to see Am, but that wasn't anything new. He ignored him, continuing his pacing. "Ask him," said Takei, "if he could make a selection of this man out of a police assemblage of characters."

When Takei was excited, his accent was more pronounced and his English more circuitous. Carlos had trouble following what he was saying. "Excuse me?" he said.

"Pardon?" asked Takei.

"He wants to know," said Am, "if the kid could pick out the man who hired him in a police lineup."

As if the police would organize a bogus personnel-director lineup. Am's disgusted tone was easily translatable in any language, but Carlos was wisely only interpreting the words. Am thought about what was going into the equation. A Japanese mind had produced an English inquiry that was disdainfully simplified by an American (make that Californian) and then handed over to a first-generation American Latino who delivered it to a Mexican. The result was more high-pitched protestations. Carlos duly notated the response. He had been keeping notes. Am picked up his notepad, saw that it was half-full.

"Have they delivered the sand-filled rubber hoses yet?" he asked Takei.

"What? I don't understand."

Am shook his head, turned back to Carlos. "Did the fake HRD identify himself as Fletcher again?"

The boy looked up into the lights, acknowledged a familiar name. "Señor Fletcher?"

That answered that. "And did Señor Fletcher speak Spanish?"

"Well enough," said Carlos, "to make José here think he was going to be chief executive officer. *Jefe.*"

"*Jefe,*" repeated the boy.

"The phony personnel guy brought a Spanish-American dictionary with him, Am," said Carlos. "He told José that they needed a new boss who spoke Spanish very well be-

cause most of the staff was Mexican and they couldn't understand what the Japanese wanted them to do."

"Might be something to that," said Am with a loud sigh.

Cultural understanding doesn't happen overnight. Sometimes not even over years. Am had known Ana, one of the
Hotel maids, for over a decade. She had invited him to her
son's high school graduation party in National City, and he
had been the only gringo there. Everyone else at the fiesta
was given tortillas, but Ana gave Am white bread, had
made a special point of buying it just for him because she
knew he was coming to the party. Though Am would have
much preferred the tortillas, he ate the white bread as if it
were manna from heaven, and in so doing had probably per-
petuated yet another stereotype. It was the first white bread
he had eaten in years.

"Okay, Carlos," said Am. "Why don't you take the kid to
human resources and have him fill out another application."

Carlos nodded, started translating to the bewildered
young man. Takei suddenly awakened, turned to Am.
"What are you doing?" he asked.

"Trying to do my job, part of which is acting on safety
violations. Mr. Takei, it goes against fire regulations to be
smoking in an enclosed space within the grounds of the
Hotel. I'll have to ask you to extinguish your cigarette."

Takei's eyes bulged out. They were red and furious. For a
second Am thought he was going to swallow his cigarette.
He didn't, but he did act in a manner decidedly un-Japanese.
He broke his cigarette in two, dropped the pieces on the
conference table, and loudly announced, *"Kusou!"* Then he
turned around and angrily marched out of the room.

Sometimes answers come to you unbidden. Guess I now
know how to say "shit" in Japanese, thought Am.

Chapter Forty

Ward Ankeney was chewing on one of his small pipes and whistling at the same time. At least someone was in a good mood.

Am sat down in a chair, offered a greeting, then innocently asked, "You had a question about an expense report of mine, Ward?"

The controller took the unlit pipe out of his mouth, nodded, then started hunting through a pile of paperwork for Am's receipt. "You turned in a voucher that seemed pretty ambiguous, Am," he said. "If I didn't ask you about it, then you-know-who would undoubtedly come down on me for not asking."

At one time Ward had been the final word on all financial and accounting questions. Although by title he was still controller, now he reported to Kiichi Matsuda, the chief financial officer. Ever since the Japanese had taken over, there had been a hierarchical musical chairs of managers and staff throughout the Hotel. At least Yamada Enterprises hadn't just assumed control of the property and then fired most of the staff, an all-too-common occurrence during American takeovers.

Ward handed Am the expense report in question. For several seconds Am pretended to look at the paper as if he couldn't understand what was wrong with it, then decided to give up that ruse.

"It's like this, Ward," he said, then told him the story.

The controller listened with interest. During the course of the telling he picked up a slightly larger pipe and started chewing on it. Ward did very little in the way of interrupting, just made a few notes on a yellow pad of paper, but probably did that just to give one of his hands something to do. When Am finished, Ward played with the pad for a few moments.

"I don't know, Am. Writing down 'security expense' and then submitting a credit-card receipt looks pretty lame. Majordomo Matsuda likes more substantiation than that."

"Like what, Ward? A message from one of his ancestors? The more I try and substantiate the charge, the weirder it's going to look."

The controller didn't say anything, just looked over the expense report and credit-card voucher. The slip said "B.H. Enterprises."

"You didn't hear it from me, Am, but let's assume on your expense report this 'B.H. Enterprises' was listed as a consultant. The new ownership seems pretty keen on hiring every consultant in town. And without fudging too much, you could say you received advice on a security matter. Given that kind of notation, I'd probably be able to approve payment without asking you anything."

Ward dropped the expense report on the desk and looked the other way. Am got the idea, retrieved the report and tucked it away. As far as Ward was concerned, he had never seen Am's initial submission.

They talked a little bit about Brother Howard, which resulted in one of Ward's stage stories. "Houdini was famous
for exposing phony mediums and spiritualists," he said. "I
played his character in the stage version of *The Great Houdini*. There were lots of wonderful props that made it look
like I was doing fantastic escapes. The audience applauded
loudest when I was shucking off ropes and weights. I think
they thought I was shedding them for real.

"Before Houdini died, he confided in several special
friends that he was going to announce his presence during a
séance through a message only they would know. Though
his friends attended numerous séances, and though the
spirit of Houdini was supposedly materialized in those sessions, his special message from beyond the grave was never
announced. Death was the one escape Harry couldn't pull
off."

One of Am's few personal effects in the security hut was a
picture of Houdini being lowered into water. The escape
artist was weighted down by anchors and heavy metal, with
chains wrapped around his entire body. The picture was an
inspiration to Am, who always liked to think that there was
always an escape, some solution to be found.

There was no picture of Houdini on Ward's walls that
Am could see, no review of the play. Maybe the reviews
hadn't been very good for that production, or, more likely,
there just wasn't enough space on the walls for all of Ward's
trouper memories. The controller started in on another
Houdini anecdote. While Am listened, he once again
scanned the mementos of Ward's life, his stage effects (and
affects) on the office walls. For some reason, Am kept coming back to one picture, Ward's *Mutiny on the Bounty* glossy.
What was there about it that troubled him? Captain Bligh

was being confronted by Fletcher Christian. They were on the deck of a ship looking very dramatic. Christian, played by Ward, looked self-righteous, the justice of his cause reason enough for him to go against all of his training. Like in most such photos, it was clear Fletcher Christian was wearing too much makeup . . .

". . . the decision wasn't easy for young Erich Weiss," said Ward. "His father was a strict rabbi, and couldn't easily give his blessing upon his son's dreams to be a magician . . ."

"It all stops now, Ward," interrupted Am.

Larry Young hadn't been the only GM applicant who had commented on the HRD's strong hand gesturing, the body language of a thespian. But what made Am certain of his thoughts was the name: Mr. Fletcher. Ward had returned to his last role, that of Fletcher Christian. He had identified himself as "Mr. Fletcher" to all the young men, and for whatever reason, he had led a mutiny.

Ward gave Am his best puzzled look. "What are you talking about, Am?"

"You know," he said.

The controller averted his eyes, turned back to his pipe and started examining it. Apparently it wasn't the right pipe. He replaced it in the rack and reached for the largest of his meerschaum pipes—the Bear. Serious business was at hand.

"What I don't understand," Am said, "is why you set up those boys. Most of them were nice enough kids. Telling them they had the general manager's job was cruel."

Ward ran his finger along the Bear's head. He didn't argue, didn't say anything. His face was amazingly neutral, hinted at nothing. It must have been easy for Ward to fool the young men, and to give off different appearances each time. He was no stranger to painting his face, probably always kept his make-up bag handy for the next role.

Fine actors don't need words. Ward announced his guilt silently. He went through the ritual of preparing a smoke, of declaring his defiance. For years he had abided by the no-smoking rule, but this was a final declaration of rebellion. He put a certain pomp and circumstance into the filling of his pipe. There is something very ritualistic, almost ecclesiastical, about the measuring, and placing, and filling of the bowl, the movement of the tobacco chalice up and toward opened lips. Only one thing was out of place in the production. Ward's hands were active in a way unusual to them. They were shaking.

Pipe smokers usually don't inhale their tobacco, but maybe this was a time and place Ward thought his inner soul needed a baptism of smoke. He took in a long measure of his bowl, then blew the smoke high in the air.

"I did it to get back at Takei," he said. "I wanted everyone to laugh at him."

"Why?"

"You want the long answer or the short answer?"

"The right answer."

"I wanted to humble Takei like he's humbled me. I wanted him to know how it felt to have youths, callow youths, come in and say they were ready to take over his position confident they could do his job. The young men were there to show Takei that he is only a title, not a true ruler."

Am shook his head. The explanation wasn't good enough. "You jacked around a lot of people, Ward, me among them."

"That wasn't my intent, Am."

There was pathos in his voice, plenty of it, but a trained actor can produce that in his sleep. Am asked the same question again: "Why?"

The pattern had been established. Ward sucked on his pipe, then words and smoke came out. Am needed to know the smoke wasn't being blown up his ass.

"A few months ago the front desk was shorthanded," he said. "They needed a PBX operator. Takei marched into this office and said he wanted someone at the switchboard for a few hours. Then he pointed to me, acted as if I was the most expendable person in the accounting office, and said, 'You.'"

Smokey sigh. "I suppose it was his way of showing that he was the boss. I had been vocal about some of the changes going on, even challenged Takei on some of his new policies. He has Mr. Matsuda cowed, so I figured it was my job to stand up to him. Controllers are usually a pretty autonomous lot, so he made sure mine was a public humiliation. I've kicked myself a few thousand times for not saying anything that day. I just got up and went out to the switchboard."

Ward blew off, and out, some more smoke. "Why didn't I say anything, Am? I've asked myself that over and over. And I still can't find any answers I like."

Am knew the answers. Most people do, can count them every day when the alarm clock goes off. "I hear your oldest is in veterinary school," Am said. "That must be damned expensive."

"That was one of the echoes in my mind," Ward said. "That's what I kept telling myself, but who ever has enough money? It wasn't my finances that silenced me. Takei made me feel old. Useless. Not financially bankrupt, but morally.

He stripped away my illusion of being poor but proud, showed me to be middle-class and weak. I had to prove to myself I wasn't as enfeebled as he thought, that I still had some bite."

"Next time embezzle," Am suggested.

"That would have been too easy," he said with a little smile. "Too cheap."

Final act, Am thought, with Ward at his meerschaum pipe, me in my usual saddle on the horns of a dilemma looking for Solomon-like wisdom. The new ownership had certainly caused enough ulcers and bewilderment among the staff. One of the most common phrases to be heard was "The Japanese don't understand." The sentence was finished with a host of laments, including, "how we do things," and "why we do it that way," and "tradition." The Hotel California was a special place with a lot of special people, and the sentiment was that the Japanese were trying to fit the property and its characters into a pre-cut pattern. You don't, or shouldn't, do that with a unique design. "It's not broke," was the staff sentiment, "so why fix it?" Ward had dared to say that out loud, but apparently it hadn't translated well into Japanese. Like so many others, he was made to feel expendable, that all his years there didn't add up to very much.

Ward blew a smoke ring. Am watched the tight circle expand. It moved across the room, widened as it drifted. Then it hit a wall and dispersed to blue-gray heaven. The show continued, Am's jury remaining out for three more smoke rings.

"I want your letter of resignation, Ward," Am finally said. "Don't give any reasons, just make it effective two weeks from the date of receipt."

Ward closed his eyes, collapsed his shoulders a little more, and nodded. It was the verdict he had expected.

"But don't date it," Am said.

The patient suddenly had a pulse again, even if he seemed to stop breathing at Am's words. "I'm going to hold on to your letter of resignation," Am said. "And I don't need to tell you that I better never see . . ."

"You won't, Am."

"And one more thing, Ward."

The controller looked up expectantly. "Put out that damn pipe before you set off the water sprinklers."

It was his morning, Am thought, for having to discipline rebellious smokers. For putting out fires.

As Am was leaving the office, Ward called out to him. Once a ham, always a ham. The man hadn't forgotten how to close a scene.

" 'Reputation, reputation, reputation! O! I have lost my reputation. I have lost the immortal part of myself, and what remains is bestial.' "

After an appropriate spell of silence, Ward announced, "*King Lear.*"

You don't overstay your scene. You exit, stage right. And that's what Am did.

Chapter Forty-One

It felt good to solve a mystery, even if it wasn't the case Am was actively working on, and even though he had more stumbled on the answer than not. At least his "real" investigation wasn't going to be hindered anymore by young men announcing themselves as general manager, and he wouldn't have to deal with the subsequent eruptions of Mount Fuji-Takei.

There were two piles on Am's desk: one was the paperwork and the deferred duties of his job, and the other was the information he had gathered on the Kingsbury case. The job pile was higher, but not by much. It needed to grow some more.

The problem with any kind of collecting is that eventually you have to confront the monster you have gathered. Am picked up the investigative pile and started sorting through it. Among the fallout was the copy of Les Moore's medical questionnaire. While Am wasn't particularly interested in the details of Moore's demi-demise, he was interested in the questions on the form. Judging from the questionnaire, it appeared the doctor was looking for common denominators in both the pre–near-death and near-death experiences. Kingsbury's inquiries did seem to be excessive—sixteen pages worth of questions. Why had the doctor felt the need to probe so deeply? And what was the point of his exploration?

Am questioned the questionnaire. It was divided into three sections, including general background (a hodge-podge of social, political, and religious questions); medical history; and the near-death experience itself. There were a number of psychological questions, enough of the "leading" variety to make Am wonder if Kingsbury was trying to make a case that those having "near-death experiences" were mentally unbalanced to begin with. There was even greater emphasis, though, on the subject's physical history, in particular the "death." Kingsbury's hematological roots were evident, with several questions dealing with blood, one of which Am had hoped he would find. His pale theory still had some flesh—or blood, as was the case.

Dreading it though he was, Am knew that the only possible way he'd get a look at the UNDER questionnaires and Kingsbury's notes was through Detective McHugh. The information wouldn't come cheap. For the detective to grant that boon, he'd have to think he was on the serious receiving end of getting more information than he was giving. Am dialed the detective's number with the same enthusiasm reserved for making a dental appointment, and was half-relieved when he was told McHugh wouldn't be returning until mid-afternoon. He left his name and number, and the message *"Please* call." Already he was having to truckle.

Am hung up the phone, not gently. Its revenge was that it almost immediately started ringing. The display identified the call as coming from the utility room. Why would anyone be there?

"This is Am."

"This is Cotton."

The maintenance man's voice was low. He was still in his secret-agent mode, probably would have preferred if they had communicated through decoder rings.

"What is it, Cotton?"

"Were you aware that the efforts to neutralize the Neptune Room have been countermanded?"

What the hell was he talking about? Am stifled a sigh. "I don't understand what you're saying, Cotton."

"The engineering department," he said, "has orders to make the Neptune Room operational by oh-eleven hundred hours today."

There was an echo to Cotton's words. In his mind's eye Am could picture him hunkered down in the darkness and confines of the utility room, his whispered voice playing off the concrete walls. "Are you telling me," said Am, "that engineering is fixing up the Neptune Room this morning?"

"Shit," muttered Cotton, the enclosed utility room doing a good job of shouting the word around. But Cotton remembered that Am had once been a manager and probably couldn't help himself. "That is affirmative."

The repairs didn't make sense. The Swap Meat wouldn't be checking out until tomorrow—unless the Hotel's tactics had finally gotten to the swingers and they were all leaving early. "Thanks, Cotton," said Am. "I'll check it out."

"I also have it on good authority that the normalization of the occupation rooms is occurring today."

That translation, Am supposed, was that the swinger rooms were being put aright. "I'll find out about that also," said Am.

"You should know that the Neptune Room could easily be"—Cotton paused dramatically—"deactivated again." Then he hung up.

Deactivated, thought Am. I've created a monster.

Kate Kennedy was apparently well over her waterworks, judging by her overly (even by her standards) effusive greeting.

"Kate," said Am, cutting her good cheer short. "I hear that the Neptune Room is being made—" (to his annoyance, he had to stop himself from saying "operational") "—up now."

"That's right, Am. It appears we overreacted a bit yesterday. The Swap Meat has accepted the fact that they couldn't have the meeting rooms, but even without them, they've been just as happy as peas in a pod."

"I wonder what Gregor Mendel would have said about those peas," said Am.

"Gregor who?" Kate asked very cheerily.

"Nothing," he said. "I also hear that the Swap Meat guest rooms are being fixed up."

"We were going to call you," she said. "It's just that we all agreed this morning that there was no need to treat the group so badly."

The *we* again. "Who's we?" he asked.

"Janet, me, and Melvin. We really think we made much ado about nothing."

Am had a distinct feeling that the first "we" was the unholy triumvirate, and the second "we" was he. "We think we should treat them like normal guests," she said. "Don't you agree?"

It was getting more difficult figuring out which "we"

was which, even with Am's new understanding that he was an overreactor whose draconian measures had been deemed unnecessary.

"You're saying it's time to kiss and make up?" he asked.

"Exactly," she said.

And the Swap Meat would be the last group ever to object to that.

"Why the rush to get the Neptune Room fixed up?"

"We're doing it as a favor to the San Diego Police Department. It's comped."

She offered the last sentence as if she was doing her patriotic duty. Swingers are our friends, she had all but told him, and now she was saying the same thing about the police. Am wasn't sure which supposition was easier to accept.

"Why do they want the room?"

"Apparently they're having a press conference."

The bad feeling, the one that had temporarily left him after figuring out who was hiring all the young GMs, returned. "Who's in charge of this press conference?"

"Detective McHugh," she said happily. "He's in our office now . . ."

What better place for him to announce that Dr. Thomas Kingsbury had been murdered than at the very Hotel where it happened? Maybe the "we" sentiment was right. Perhaps Am had overreacted. A simple orgy didn't sound like such a bad thing now, at least not when compared to a more public humiliation.

Chapter Forty-Two

McHugh was just leaving the sales and catering office when Am arrived. He was chewing on something, no doubt one of the food samples left out for prospective clients. "Did you tell them," asked Am with righteous indignation, "why you wanted the meeting room?"

The detective appeared amused at Am's anger. "Of course I told them. I said we were having a press conference."

"Where you are going to announce that Dr. Kingsbury was murdered?"

"That's right. And I would have told them that, too, except they never asked."

Damn, thought Am. Sales still wasn't asking the right questions. You'd think by this time they would have learned. He didn't make their same mistake. "What was the cause of the doctor's death?"

"Show up in a couple of hours, Caulfield. I'll save you a ringside seat. Hell, maybe I'll even introduce you to the media."

"I don't think the Hotel is the proper place for your press conference."

"Why not?" asked the detective. "This is where the investigation is taking place. Besides, it's publicity for you."

"Sure," said Am. "Maybe you can announce our two-for-one May Murderer's Special. Two people check in and only one leaves."

"You'd probably make a killing," said McHugh. His wit inspired him to smile momentarily. It inspired Am to fantasize about giving Cotton orders to "deactivate" the room during his press conference.

"Now, you'll have to excuse me, Caulfield," he said. "I have to go and make myself pretty before the media arrives."

"I can understand the necessity of that," said Am, "but we need to talk."

"I doubt that."

"You have some information that interests me. And I know some things that could prove useful to your investigation."

McHugh pretended he wasn't interested. "I gotta run," he said, offering his statement while standing still.

"I'll walk with you."

The detective shrugged, then started walking. Am fell in beside him. "What is it you want?" asked McHugh.

"A look at the case file," said Am. That really wasn't of interest to him, but he wanted to throw McHugh off. "And Kingsbury's interview notes of the UNDER participants, as well as all of their questionnaires."

McHugh mulled over Am's requests, tried to figure out why those things were important to him. His inclination was to just say no, then watch Caulfield pout and plead some more. But he had to put personal pleasure aside. Caulfield had said something about having information that might be useful to the investigation. Since his team hadn't yet turned up anything of significance, McHugh was ready to grasp at any straws. He didn't like going into press conferences without a few good possibilities. The jackals were good at knowing when he was bluffing, at exposing the thinness of the standard "pursuing several leads" line.

"Tell me what you got."

"Do we have a deal? Do I get what I asked for?"

Sure, thought McHugh, everything you want. But next week. The detective nodded.

"Today?"

It was almost like the jerk-off had read his mind. Well, he didn't have to make it easy for him. If he expected everything brought to him and handed over on a silver platter, he had something else coming. "Downtown," said McHugh. "Four o'clock. Don't be late."

Don't be late, the detective thought, because I'm going to be. At least two hours.

"I'll be there," said Am. "Where?"

McHugh tossed him a business card. "Now shoot," he said.

Am didn't want to identify Marisa as an accomplice, so he made it sound as if he had worked alone. He told McHugh about Skylar and Brother Howard, and the reasons the men had for wanting to see Kingsbury dead. The detective kept an expressionless face, but he was surprised. This sounded like good stuff. Maybe he'd only be an hour late for their appointment.

"We'll check it out," said McHugh, evincing the faintest of interest.

Am had hoped for a little more enthusiasm and gratitude, but then this was Detective McHugh he was dealing with. They were almost to the lobby. "I'll see you at four," said Am.

Five, five-thirty, thought McHugh. He nodded.

"I demand satisfaction!"

The shout made both men look up. Down the hall they could see a man wearing red pajamas waving his fist under the face of Felipe the shoe-shine man.

Bradford Beck wasn't going to take it anymore. He liked the way Toyota was cringing and acting afraid. The little Jap wasn't going to get away with a few empty promises this time.

The morning hadn't started well for Bradford. He had awakened with a terrible hangover, had learned that champagne and tequila are not a very good mix. And then there was this damnably annoying itch in his groin area. Though he scratched and scratched, he couldn't seem to find relief. Bradford kept telling himself the symptoms were psychosomatic. He had worn protection, after all, but things had gotten a bit racy—very racy, in fact. Out of hand, some might even say. That Missy was some wild woman. But the morning after he was repenting those few hours of pleasure, and not only because of the itch. If he had given Cleopatra all of his attention, then maybe her nose wouldn't have gotten out of joint and maybe things wouldn't have happened the way they had. He'd been courting Cleopatra for too long to give her, and all her money, up. The best-laid plans, he thought, then scratched furiously and gave up on the rest of the saying. Cleopatra, he had thought, suddenly awakening. I've got to help her. Then he noticed something. All of Cleopatra's luggage was gone.

Bradford tried to call the front desk, but his phone was still broken. He threw on some pajamas and some shoes (he had neglected to bring his slippers) and stormed over to the elevator to make his call. The front desk didn't seem to know anything about Cleopatra's whereabouts.

"Your bellman made a fucking citizen's arrest on her!" Bradford screamed to the operator. "Someone there better be able to goddamn tell me where she is!"

The operator had politely suggested that he "sleep it off," and then had hung up on him. That's when Bradford went ballistic. Toyota was going to make everything right this time.

Wearing only his red silk pajamas and his calf-skin loafers, Bradford stormed down to the lobby. Screaming "Toyota!" and "I demand satisfaction," he ran up to the shoe-shine man and pushed him up against the wall.

"Yesterday you made a lot of promises," Bradford said. "Well, my room still looks like shit. Nothing's been done, that is if you don't count my girlfriend's being kidnapped. Your bellman did that. I've encountered nothing but rudeness and buck-passing. The buck stops here, Toyota. Got it?"

Felipe was terrified. He started pleading his fear and innocence in Spanish. Bradford wouldn't hear anything of it. "Talk in English," he said. "I don't speak Japanese. This is still America."

The shoe-shine man kept babbling. "English, I said," yelled Bradford, then kicked him hard in his backside. Even though he had applied a lot of boot, Bradford noticed the shine on his loafers was still untarnished. The Nip should stick to shoe-shining instead of managing.

The lunatic's crotch-pulling and shouting were bad enough, McHugh thought, but he could almost overlook them, just as he could his wild talk about kidnapping, and his interpreting Spanish as Japanese. But the kick couldn't be ignored. He had Bradford on the ground and tied up in about four seconds, then stood up to admire his handiwork. As a kid, McHugh had wanted to be a rodeo performer.

Am was attending to Felipe. The shoe-shine man was shaken up, but not hurt. Bradford had done a lot more bullying than pummeling. "Are you okay?" Am asked him.

"Okay," said Felipe, using one of the few English words he knew.

"I'm arresting you for assault," McHugh said to Bradford. He didn't bother to Mirandize the kook. This one was probably just going to get kicked over to county mental health.

"Are you a police officer?" asked Bradford.

"Yes."

"I mean a real San Diego police officer?"

McHugh flashed his badge and nodded.

"Good. Maybe you can tell me where Cleopatra is."

"I can do even better than that," said McHugh. "I can take you to her barge."

Chapter Forty-Three

Before the press conference, Am didn't know much about potassium cyanide. Now he was only too familiar with the chemical compound. As far as Am was concerned, the medical examiner was entirely too enthusiastic on the subject.

"Quite, quite fatal," Dr. Simpson had told the assembled press. "Two tenths of a gram will kill you within fifteen minutes. We estimate Dr. Kingsbury had about twice that in his system."

The press asked their questions and the ME answered. It was a primer on poisoning. Potassium cyanide was "very, very (Dr. Simpson invariably emphasized his statements with two adverbs) easy either to obtain or to make." There was "simply, simply nothing" complicated about making such a poison. The component parts didn't have to be purchased at a chemical lab. They could be obtained at a photography lab, or a craft shop, or even a neighborhood store ("though it would be necessary for anyone trying to create a proper poison to carefully read the labels," the doctor admonished, "to make absolutely, absolutely sure that a fatal toxin was manufactured.")

Someone had read their labels well. The potassium

cyanide, Dr. Simpson said, could have been administered in either liquid or powder form, but it appeared the murderer had opted for liquid. It was the better choice, in his opinion.

The ME's demonstration included a chalk talk on the chemicals of death (KCN was the chemical abbreviation of potassium cyanide), and how different proportions of other products could have approximated that lethal combination.

Why, said Dr. Simpson, any layman could make a very effective poison from any number of over-the-counter supermarket offerings. And when you considered what anyone could buy in a hardware store . . .

Detective McHugh chose that moment to thank the medical examiner and direct him to his seat. There was a reason, he thought, that the man just worked with corpses. But most of the media weren't paying any attention to Dr. Simpson's closing remarks. Being enterprising journalists, they had assiduously avoided organic- and physical-chemistry courses in college. They were humanities majors, for God's sake, and hadn't been much interested in his hieroglyphics (who cared that potassium carbonate—K_2CO_3—was used in making glass, pigments, ceramics, and soaps?). Besides, there were other matters more pressing, like food.

Am had worked out a set of signals with Cathy Cleary, the banquet manager. Cathy was waiting on his calls like an anxious pitcher. Whenever Am thought there was something being said that was particularly damaging to the Hotel, he signaled the banquet manager to send in food. Though poison recipes didn't affect the Hotel per se, Am still wasn't keen on seeing them printed up in the local newspapers. They might give some ideas to San Diego's no-growth advocates. He motioned to Cathy, who sent in a waiter with a tray of shrimp. The quantity had been agreed upon ahead of time, a full platter, but not nearly enough to feed a roomful of hungry journalists. This was the third tray to be sent out at an opportune time (miniquiche had been the first course, and scallops wrapped in bacon the second). Pavlov's dogs never responded so well as the press. The appearance of the shrimp caused an immediate queuing up. Am hoped that the continued interruptions of "alternate feeding frenzies" would keep the media from getting too worked up over the poisoning.

McHugh tried to vie with jumbo shrimp, but learned that on the media food chain, detectives apparently rank below such crustaceans. Most of the haphazard questioning was done by those who already had shrimp on their plates. They called out with full mouths over the din of those still jostling in line. Marisa was one of the few journalists who hadn't been seduced by the fare. She stayed seated, taking notes and asking questions. Am sidled up next to her, wrote on a piece of paper: "Dinner Tonight?" She saw his message and nodded. "What Time?" he wrote. Marisa held up seven fingers and Am nodded.

"Could the poisoning have somehow been inadvertent?" asked one reporter. "Could Dr. Kingsbury have somehow taken it accidentally?"

"No," said McHugh. "I'm told that's highly unlikely. The scientific consensus is that it was introduced in his food or drink."

That announcement didn't stop the media from eating as many shrimp as possible.

"Where did Dr. Kingsbury dine—"

Before the reporter could finish asking where Kingsbury's last meal had taken place, Am signaled for the next tray to be brought out. Why did everyone have to know that Kingsbury's final repast had been at one of the Hotel's restaurants? Next they'd want to know how much he tipped (16 percent, if Am remembered correctly).

It was a small side of roast this time, served on the opposite side of the room as the shrimp. Some of the media started running, beating the server to the carving table. Detective McHugh found that he was talking to himself.

"Clever," said Marisa, the word less than sincere.

Am tried to look innocent. "What do you want to eat tonight?" he asked.

"Lobster," she said, "unless you're planning on bringing some out on the next tray."

Am didn't comment. "Got a restaurant in mind?"

"We'll decide later," she said. "Let's meet in the lobby at seven. I have a six o'clock follow-up interview with Lady Death. She's promised a whopping thirty minutes this time."

"Why a second interview?"

"Believe me, I tried to beg off, but this country's decided Angela Holliday is big news. Her book has only been out three days and already it's a best-seller. My editor wanted a follow-up piece, something more in-depth than my last *Architectural Digest* copy. Or did he say in-death? I can't tell you how much I'm looking forward to her hourglass again."

"You make her sound like a black widow." That wasn't how Am thought of her, not at all. Like all men, he thought that any woman who was receptive to him showed remarkably good taste. "Off the record, you should know that she's been having some death threats. I was called up to her room last night, just after you left, to investigate one."

"Oh?"

Was that suspiciousness Am heard, or only his guilty conscience? Not that he should feel guilty, he told himself. Hadn't he been virtuous? Rather than fully answer that question in his mind, Am told Marisa about how McHugh had agreed to let him look over the questionnaires and Kingsbury's notes, and what he had traded to get that concession. She should have been consulted, he told her, but opportunity seemed to be knocking. Then, uncertainly, he told her why he wanted to look at the questionnaires. In the telling, he became that much more convinced it was a tenuous and silly thread to be following. But Marisa didn't see it that way. She agreed with him that it was a lead, however unlikely, that needed looking into.

They didn't get a chance to talk any further, as the mostly disappointed media were taking their seats. The shrimp and the roast beef hadn't lasted very long.

"See you later," said Am.

Marisa nodded, and he returned to the back of the room. McHugh's questioning started anew. Am listened carefully. In his bullpen he still had baked ham, two desserts, as well as chilled beer and wine. Was the Hotel safe? one questioner wanted to know. Was the poisoning random, or had Dr. Kingsbury been singled out for death?

Am signaled Cathy for the ham.

Chapter Forty-Four

Annette's gears ground again. Am could feel the grating in his fillings.

"So sorry," said the Fat Innkeeper.

Am faked yet another smile and waved his hand. He should have just called off their little drive, and not only because of the damage done to Annette. Am had thought he could kill two birds with one stone, both give Hiroshi his driving lesson and make a necessary stop, but he hadn't counted on the killing including his car. The gears ground again.

"So sorry," said the Fat Innkeeper.

Annette's bucking shook both of the passengers. So this is what epilepsy is like, thought Am. "W-why d-don't y-you p-p-p-pull o-over there?" he said, pointing.

Hiroshi complied, but not smoothly. Learning how to handle the three-speed manual transmission wasn't proving an easy task for the Fat Innkeeper, but even after a shaky and abrupt stop he looked anything but defeated. The man was beaming. He had managed to get half the car in a parking space; the other half had jumped onto a concrete island. Their testing ground was a parking lot near the University of California at San Diego's BioMed Library. It was a pleasant enough place to learn how to crash a car, with stands of eucalyptus surrounding the lot and only students to run into.

Having no inclination to play car-pachinko anymore, Am managed to say with a straight face, "Since you seem to be getting the hang of this, why don't you keep practicing while I run over to the library. I shouldn't be more than five or ten minutes."

"No problem," said Hiroshi.

Am felt a slight tinge of guilt. "She'll operate better," he said. "if you head her west toward the ocean."

"The ocean?"

"Never mind. I'll be back soon."

Am ran off. Hearing the grinding of gears made him run away that much faster. He was out of breath when he walked through the library's doors, had to stop and take in several deep breaths. His hyperventilating attracted the attention of a student, who looked upon his deep breathing with undisguised disdain. Was I ever that young? thought Am. Was I ever that arrogant, ever that smugly immortal? Breathless, he continued to chase death.

He approached the computer catalog with some trepidation. When Am had been a UCSD undergraduate, there had only been card catalogs. He looked at the prompts, saw that he could conduct his search through author, title, words, or subject. Am typed "blood" and the search was on. He looked at the bewildering array of articles and books cited, most with incomprehensible titles. I need a bloodhound, he thought.

Am decided on an author search, and typed in the name of Thomas Kingsbury. Several of the doctor's books were in the library, and Am went looking for them. He quickly scanned the texts, marked some pages that were of interest to him, then went and made some hurried copies. Despite his rushing, everything took longer than he expected. He literally ran out of the library, started sprinting to the parking lot only to be stopped by a familiar honk. Annette glided to a standstill in front of him, this time without any grinding of gears. Hiroshi looked as if he had won the Indianapolis 500.

Am checked the time. He was supposed to meet McHugh at four o'clock, and it was already a quarter to. "I better drive you back to the Hotel," he said.

Hiroshi reluctantly gave up the driver's seat, moving his bulk over to the passenger seat. Am handed him his pile of copies to hold, and quickly pulled Annette away from the curb. His hurried movements didn't go unnoticed.

"I have no need to get back to the Hotel," said Hiroshi, "if other matters demand your attention."

"I am running a little late," Am admitted. "I'm supposed to be meeting with Detective McHugh at four o'clock in downtown San Diego."

"You will be discussing the death of Dr. Kingsbury?"

Am nodded.

"Then we had better hurry."

"It could be several hours before we get back," warned Am.

"My afternoon is clear."

"If you're sure . . ."

For once, Hiroshi didn't try and outpolite him, just nodded, got himself comfortable, and looked the picture of someone out for a drive in the country. Am steered Annette along La Jolla Village Drive, then turned onto Interstate 5. She bucked a little, and Hiroshi looked concerned.

"It's okay," said Am. "She just doesn't like traveling away from the coast. Makes her cranky." Then, louder, to Annette more than Hiroshi, "But we're going to be driving to a building that's not very far from San Diego Bay, and we might even cruise back along the harbor."

Annette's ride steadied. Her behavior seemed to intrigue Hiroshi all the more. "Have you," he inquired gently, "considered selling this vehicle?"

As far as the Japanese are concerned, everything in America is for sale. It's an opinion that Americans themselves are responsible for, having chosen to withold virtually nothing from the auction block.

How many times had Am threatened to give Annette away? To have her towed to a junkyard? By no stretch of the imagination was she reliable transportation. But for whatever misplaced reasons, he still hadn't gotten rid of her. "She's not for sale," Am said.

The Fat Innkeeper nodded, as if that was the answer he expected, as if that was the only appropriate response, and went back to enjoying the drive. He swiveled his head frequently, taking in the sights along the freeway. Am didn't think most of the route was particularly scenic, but then he wasn't Japanese. A friend of his had once driven cross-country with a student from Japan and said that what had impressed the foreigner most were the open stretches of land.

"I hear Dr. Kingsbury was poisoned," said Hiroshi.

Am nodded, then told him what he knew, which made the Fat Innkeeper look unhappy. "Being poisoned is not a good way to die," Hiroshi said with some vehemence. "I was poisoned once. It was not pleasant."

The Fat Innkeeper smiled at Am's startled look. "I dined on a fugu fish," he explained. "Just as I was telling everyone how delicious it was, the numbness set in."

Am had heard about the tropical fish, and how it was considered a delicacy in Japan. There was a potentially very high price to pay for eating such fare, though. Deaths had occurred when the poison sacs of the fish had not been properly removed. Chefs had to be specially licensed by the government to prepare the fugu fish. Even so, sometimes poisoning resulted.

"Did you feel you were going to die?" asked Am.

The Fat Innkeeper nodded. "Yes," he said, "but the paralysis passed after a few minutes, and then I only felt foolish."

Hiroshi shook his head, as if that movement would rid him of the memory, then he stuck his head out the window, and for a minute or two looked as happy as a dog catching a breeze. When he reentered inside the car, he smoothed his hair and said, "Mr. Takei came and visited me today."

Without overtly condemning or probing, with saying very little, he still managed to say a lot. Am responded in the same minimalist format. "He won't be troubled again," he said confidently. "That's a samurai promise."

Hiroshi raised an eyebrow, then nodded, accepting the good news without question. "A samurai used to have the right of *kirisute*," he said, "to use his sword on those who did not show him the proper respect. He could legally kill, with no questions asked."

"In this instance, there wasn't that need," said Am, "but I would like to reserve that right for the future."

The Fat Innkeeper gave him a questioning look, then re-

alized Am was joking, and with a little smile of his own
went back to looking out the window. Mission Bay, and all
of its colors, seemed to fascinate him. There were tanned
bodies running around in Day-Glo shorts, a skyful of rainbow kites, and a bay crowded with windsurfers racing along
blue water.

"Do you surf?" asked Hiroshi.

Before I became a serf, thought Am. "Yes."

"I would like to learn."

Am wasn't about to volunteer that "maybe later" he'd
take him out. Helping an obese Japanese man navigate the
rigors of a surfboard wasn't something he wanted to do.
How could you translate "my wave" with the right emphasis into Japanese? Banzai? Kamikaze pilots could learn a
thing or two about single-mindedness from a surfer claiming a wave.

"Excuse my foolish talk," said Hiroshi. "This land offers
too many diversions. This is my time to prove myself as an
ii hito, a good person. My family thinks I have been *waga-
mama* far too long." He remembered Am wasn't Japanese,
offered the one word translation: "selfish."

A deep breath, and then another explanation: "On several
occasions I have not agreed to a *seiryaku kekkon*, a strategic
marriage. As the *choonan*, the eldest son, this kind of obedi-
ence was expected of me. What made my selfishness worse
is that I'm a *shachoo-no-musuko-san*, the son of a company
president. My family expected me to be the *atotori*, the successor, but I never proved reliable. I have always been diverted by useless studies, and travels, and thoughts, and
distractions.

"Like wanting to take up surfing," he admitted. "I am
considered the *fukoo mono* of the family, the unfilial child."

The admission was personal, and unexpected. Am had been told that the Japanese rarely revealed themselves to their own countrymen, let alone *gaijin*.

"My sister Reiko had to bring in a *muko-yooshi*," he said. "She took a husband so that the family could have an appropriate successor. He gave up his name and took ours. There is an expression for what my sister had to do. It is called *kazoku no giseisha*, and it means Reiko sacrificed for the household. I should have been able to do that on many occasions, but never did."

Sharon had told Am about how the Hotel California was a proving ground of sorts for Hiroshi. The Hotel had been likened as the beachhead for Yamada Enterprises. The company was now in the process of building *maquiladoras*, industrial plants along the border of the United States and Mexico, and had purchased other commercial real estate for a variety of enterprises. Hiroshi was supposed to be the company standard-bearer in this part of the new world.

"I came here to change," said Hiroshi. "I keep reminding myself about the tale of Rosetsu, and that gives me inspiration."

Am looked interested. There was a story here. Maybe even a folktale. "Who is Rosetsu?" he asked.

"A painter," said the Fat Innkeeper. "He lived over two hundred years ago, was an apprentice under the great master Okyo—Maruyama Okyo in Kyoto.

"It is said that Rosetsu was Okyo's worst student. For three years he tried hard, but he did not get better. All the other students quickly advanced, but not Rosetsu. Okyo could offer him little encouragement, and Rosetsu became more and more distraught.

"He left Okyo's school one cold winter evening, walked away from being a painter. Rosetsu wasn't sure whether his journey was to kill himself, or to try and make it all the way home to his distant village. He only knew that he was giving up on art, and life itself.

"He walked all night, and then all day, and then into the night again. He had no food, and no sleep. A few hours before dawn he collapsed under some pines, fell down into a pile of snow. Rosetsu thought he was lying down to die, but his final rest was denied him. He kept hearing this noise of splashing water, and he had to see what was making the sound.

"Rosetsu crawled forward and saw a large carp jumping out of the water. It was trying to reach some food lying on the ice. For three hours Rosetsu watched the fish struggle. Time after time the fish jumped, bruising and bloodying itself on the ice. It tried all ways to get the food. The fish pushed at the ice from underneath, and jumped on top of it. Finally, the carp's persistence paid off. Its valiant leaps broke down enough ice for it to reach the food. Bloodied, with broken scales, it gained the hard-fought prize.

"This was Rosetsu's inspiration. He resolved that he would be like the carp, and give his all. He would, if necessary, die trying.

"Rosetsu returned to Kyoto. He told Okyo the story of the carp, and said that he would be as determined as the fish to succeed. He was as good as his word. In time, Rosetsu became one of Japan's greatest painters. On his paintings you can always see the Rosetsu trademark, the crest of a leaping carp."

Every nation has its stories of perseverance. Am was

going to tell Hiroshi about Bruce of Scotland, who had drawn inspiration from the persistence of a spider, and eventually won his throne, but Hiroshi was not yet through with his musing.

"I think Rosetsu's symbol of the leaping carp was a wonderful reminder to him," said Hiroshi. "In his every painting he reaffirmed that turning point in his life."

He looked at Am. "I understand I have you to thank for my new badge, my emblem."

"What do you mean?" asked Am, confused.

"You have provided me with my leaping-carp crest, my bond with nature."

Am still didn't understand.

"I am considering having it placed on all my stationery. It would probably be too presumptuous, though, to have a signet made of it."

No, Am thought, not that. Not now, not ever.

Hiroshi pulled out a folded piece of paper from a coat pocket, spread the paper out for Am to see. It wasn't exactly the fearsome lion crest of Richard the Lion-Hearted. It wasn't even a carp, for God's sake. It was a sea worm, *Urechis caupo* to be exact.

The Fat Innkeeper.

"I have heard," said Hiroshi, "that I bear an amazing resemblance to this."

There was a long silence, and a long worm, between them. Am thought of a lot of explanations. He looked at the drawing, then looked at Hiroshi. What would Ikkyu-san have done?

"It is a damn good-looking worm," Am said.

Chapter Forty-Five

The San Diego Police Department headquarters wasn't exactly on the Bay, as Am had alluded to Annette, was in fact over a mile inland from the water. Downtown redevelopment hadn't spread as far as its 1401 Broadway location. The in-vogue restaurants, luxury hotels, and upscale stores weren't part of its neighborhood, but then neither were the tattoo parlors and adult movie dens. It was situated in a neighborhood in transition, but one that looked undecided as to which way it was heading.

"To Protect and Serve," read Hiroshi. The caption was printed on all SDPD black-and-whites. "Perhaps I need a slogan along with my crest. What do you think?"

"*Mozukashii ne*," said Am. That had been one of the first phrases Sharon had taught him. She said that as a round-eye, he would be frequently hearing those words. The translation was "a difficult question," and usually resulted in the avoidance of an answer. Am and Hiroshi seemed to be reversing roles.

Nothing else had been said about *Urechis caupo* for the rest of their ride, and Am had been content to let a sleeping worm lie. He couldn't tell whether Hiroshi was teasing him, truly angry, or for some reason actually taken with the idea of a worm logo. The Japanese had their own reasons, and aesthetics, for everything. Where else but in Japan would a dove be considered a messenger of war?

To his own way of thinking, Am believed a fat worm was not likely to draw the walk-in crowd. It wasn't cuddly like a sleepy bear, or inviting like an apple. Am considered all the hotel logos used by the various chains, and then decided a fat sea worm wasn't such a bad thing after all, but he didn't tell Hiroshi that.

They were twenty minutes late even before having to take on the police bureaucracy. Their way forward was blocked by an officer sitting at a desk. After dutifully making a few calls, the sentry informed them that Detective McHugh had not left word for them to be admitted, and that they couldn't get by without a pass. McHugh wasn't in, and there was no word when, or even if, he would be back. The officer pointed to a waiting area, said that they were welcome to wait for Detective McHugh, or that they could leave a message for him.

There were several messages Am was tempted to leave, but chose instead to wait. Am suspected a delaying action on McHugh's part, or a power play, or both. As time passed, Am fumed all the more. Hiroshi was content to watch the cast of characters come and go. He engaged, even initiated, a few conversations with passers-by. Am was tempted to tell him to act more Japanese, having read of a Japanese government poll where two-thirds of the Japanese stated they had no desire to associate with foreigners. Hiroshi was all but flagging them down.

"I have to go feed the meter," Am said. He had anted up for an hour, not expecting their visit to take longer than that, and there was still no word from McHugh. Hiroshi nodded, and Am went out to feed some quarters. The way of the world, he thought. You pay the city to talk with their so-called public servants.

He didn't come back empty-handed, which made him feel better for having something to do besides just waiting. Am brought along the copies he had made at the library, and to his surprise found the reading interesting. One of Kingsbury's books documented the distribution of human blood groups around the world. "Strange is it," Kingsbury quoted from Shakespeare, "that our bloods, of color, weight and heat, pour'd all together, would quite confound distinction, yet stands off in differences so mighty." In the Bard's day, no one knew about the four blood types, A, O, AB, and B. Kingsbury's book scientifically documented the "differences so mighty."

Am read how anthropologists had traced migration routes through the genetics of blood-group inheritance. The "trail of blood" could be followed along the Bering Strait and other migration routes, the gene markers identified by types and factors in blood. It wasn't light reading, with passages dwelling on phenotypes, gene frequencies, graphs, genetical shorthand, and mathematical formulas, but Am wasn't willing to be deterred. He was on his own trail of blood.

Preoccupation always draws attention. Hiroshi started reading the pages that Am had finished with. Though he never inquired directly as to Am's interest, his curious glances were finally rewarded.

"It's probably nothing," said Am, putting his last page of reading aside and answering Hiroshi's looks, "but I'm wondering if Kingsbury didn't announce his murderer when he died."

Am sighed, wishing he had something more dramatic to announce. It seemed a tenuous supposition even to him, but it was his only potential lead. "Dr. Kingsbury's last words were 'Be positive.' We've all operated on that assumption. But were those really his last words? Kingsbury was a hematologist, a blood doctor. Among his peers his last words might have been interpreted very differently. A fellow hematologist might have assumed he was saying, 'B positive,' as in a blood type."

"Be positive," said Hiroshi. Or was he repeating, "B positive"?

"Part of this investigation has been to get to know Dr. Kingsbury," said Am, "to try and understand how he thought and acted. What was he thinking as he lay dying? Did his medical background come to the fore? Facing his own mortality, I imagine he was scared and confused. Gasping for breath, paralyzed, he might have been at a loss to even remember his murderer's name. That's where his training might have taken over. Kingsbury the research scientist might have identified his killer in a way that made perfect sense to him."

Am didn't sound like Perry Mason making a point. Spoken aloud, he thought his theory sounded thin. In this instance, he wasn't even sure if blood was thicker than water.

"How would Dr. Kingsbury have known the blood type of his murderer?" asked Hiroshi.

"My guess is through his medical questionnaires," said Am. "I was able to obtain one. It's extensive, goes so far as to ask for the blood group, and has a box to check positive or negative."

"What medical questionnaires are you referring to?"

Am explained how the UNDER conventioneers had filled out medical questionnaires for Kingsbury prior to their gathering, and how Kingsbury had selected sixty of them to interview during the conference.

"B positive," said Hiroshi. "Is this blood type that uncommon?"

"Not in your country," said Am. "Japan has twice as many B genes as in America. In Japan, seventeen percent of the population has type B blood."

Am thought about Hiroshi's interest in the case, and for a moment felt a little paranoid. He had to ask the question: "Do you know your blood group?"

"O," said Hiroshi, "although I couldn't tell you whether it's positive or negative."

"Probably positive," said Am, then glumly added, "It would have been a much better clue if Kingsbury had said, 'B negative.'"

"Not necessarily," said Hiroshi. "Everyone might have just assumed he was being fatalistic at his end. From what you have said, it was his optimistic final words which surprised everyone, and drew attention."

There might be something to that, thought Am, but he still wished the doctor had done a better job of identifying his murderer. While a B positive blood type was relatively uncommon in San Diego, a B negative would have been much more rare. He had learned how all blood types are either Rh positive or Rh negative. The determination of Rh factor was done through red-blood-cell tests (they were originally done on rhesus monkeys—thus the Rh) whereby if the cells clumped, the blood was identified as Rh positive, and if they didn't, the blood was Rh negative. The designation was particulary important in pregnancies. If mother and fetus have different Rh blood factors, complications can result. In the United States, Am had learned, only 15 percent of the population has Rh negative blood.

"Caulfield," announced Detective McHugh. "Sorry to have kept you."

The detective managed to say those words with a straight face, even if there was some giveaway in his eyes. McHugh would have preferred finding Caulfield red in the face and stomping around, but having made him cool his heels for ninety minutes was almost good enough.

Hiroshi was already standing and bowing. "This is Hiroshi Yamada," said Am, "of the Hotel California."

The Fat Innkeeper presented McHugh with his hand, and then his business card. The detective halfheartedly shook hands, but didn't offer his own business card, merely pocketed Hiroshi's card and looked unimpressed. He knew the Jap was the big Hotel cheese, but that didn't excite him. As far as McHugh was concerned, the sooner the Hotel fell into the ocean, the better.

The detective led them to an elevator. "Ground rules," he said. "You can look over the case file, as well as Kingsbury's notes and the questionnaires, but no copies. Not even any notes."

"Why?" asked Am.

"Because this is an active homicide investigation," McHugh said, though by the tone of his voice he might just as well have said, 'Because I said so.'

On the ride up, the detective decided to elaborate a little more. "This information is sensitive, and nothing is attributable, even to that reporter you were playing footsies with at the press conference.

"Speaking of which, Caulfield," said McHugh, "couldn't you have been a little more generous with that food you served? Those reporters didn't even leave crumbs for me."

They got out of the elevator and the detective led them to what must have been an interrogation room, told them to sit there, and went to get the promised material. When he returned, McHugh dropped the stack of questionnaires, loudly, onto the table. Then, ignoring Am's outstretched hand, he tossed the investigative reports and Kingsbury's notes atop the questionnaires. He also tossed a bone.

"Talked with your two birds this afternoon," he said. "That's why I was a little late. I'd say they're both guilty."

It took Am a moment to figure out that the detective was referring to Skylar and Brother Howard. "How could they both be guilty?" asked Am.

"Guilty of being con artists," said McHugh. "Guilty of being liars. Guilty of being greedy slugs. And it wouldn't surprise me if one of them is guilty of murdering Doc Kingsbury."

He walked to the door of the conference room, warned Am and Hiroshi once more not to make notes, and said that if he suspected them of trying to smuggle anything out they'd be subject to full body searches, "including any and all cavities." He closed the door firmly behind him.

Hiroshi, for one, believed him. "Please do not try to leave with anything," he said.

"Only my dignity," said Am, even if he suspected that was wishful thinking.

Chapter Forty-Six

Bradford Beck had gotten a glimpse into a world very different from the Scottsdale country-club set he was used to. It had scared the hell out of him.

He hadn't known that the police had no intention of booking him. They had put him in holding (along with mostly drunks), ostensibly as a preliminary to processing him. In reality, he was under observation of sorts. If he acted truly bonkers, they'd take him for a ride to county mental health. If he acted no crazier than most who were behind bars, they'd kick him.

Bradford tried to make himself invisible to everyone in the holding tank, or as invisible as possible with bright-red pajamas. He sat in a corner and came to life only when someone resembling SDPD came around, at which time he was extremely unctuous. That was probably one of the reasons he got kicked early. Cops aren't very fond of gratuitous ass-kissers. Better to be cursed, in their opinion, than to get too many "Yes, sirs" and "Thank you, officers." Bradford's release didn't come quite in time. Before he left, one of his roommates threw up on his calfskin loafers. Though Bradford tried to wash the shoes at a water fountain, he couldn't seem to rinse off the smell. The damnedest thing was that despite the vomit and rinsing, the shine on the shoes was still something to behold.

People's idea of heaven can radically change at any given time. After his experience, Bradford couldn't imagine anything more pleasureable than taking a bath. He didn't care if his room was a shambles. He didn't care if the staff at the Hotel was insolent and uncaring. After being thrown in with hardened criminals and felons (so he thought), and being afraid for his own life, he was ready to be more accepting. And besides, that itch in his groin area was driving him crazy. He had been afraid to scratch in the holding tank, afraid to give others ideas. But a bath and a good scratch—that was heaven. That was all he could ask for.

He had a hell of a time getting a taxi to stop for him, had to show his cash and promise a sizable tip before the driver would consent to take him, and even then the man had an attitude. The cabbie kept pointedly sniffing the air, and made a point of opening his window and keeping his nose out of the cab as much as possible.

Bradford was probably the first person in the Hotel's history to be dropped off wearing pajamas. He ran ashamedly up to his room. When he opened the door, Bradford immediately sensed something was wrong. The room smelled . . . nice. There was a spring scent in the air, the fragrance of pine needles and lavender. Afraid that he was walking into the wrong room, Bradford double-checked the room number to make sure he wasn't breaking and entering. It was 212.

Everything was immaculate. This was the room he had expected the day before. The sliding glass doors were so clean as to be almost invisible, and beyond them was the ocean, blue, and immense, and inviting. For a moment Bradford forgot about his itch. He went to the sliding glass doors, girded himself for a mighty tug, but only had to use his index finger to throw the doors open. The ocean breeze kissed him lightly. The sun was getting lower in the horizon, was already casting a red tint to the clouds. A spectacular sunset was in the offing.

Bradford walked back inside the room and looked around. There was a fruit basket, by God, on the table, with a card which read "Compliments of the Management." Bradford remembered how hungry he was, and quickly chewed down an apple, then sucked on an orange. He walked around the room and was amazed at the difference. It was now light and cheery and bright and . . . expensive. The trappings were those of glossy magazines: solid wood and comfortable chintz and live plants and original artwork, with the backdrop of the immense Pacific. It was the picture postcard he had so wanted.

Somewhat dazed, he ran a bath. It was like one of those fairy tales, he thought, where the elves had come and in a very few hours had transformed a setting. The sunken tub filled with water. The Hotel offered not one, but two kinds of bath gelée. Suds frothed everywhere. Before easing himself into the water, Bradford removed his offensive lizard-skin shoes and placed them on the balcony. He wanted to let the ocean breeze work its wonders on them, had the distinct feeling that in a few hours they'd smell as good as they looked. Bradford took off his soiled clothes, threw them in one of the valet bags, then sank down into the tub. This was beyond ecstasy. He scratched and scratched. Almost, he was able to relieve himself of that damned itch.

He had no desire to get out of the tub. Periodically, with a twist of his foot, he treated himself to some more hot water. When he had left the room that morning, the bathroom hadn't even had a towel (not to mention any toilet paper). Now there was a rackful of thick towels, and two full inviting terrycloth robes. A fat amenity basket had magically appeared, whereas before there hadn't even been soap in the room. There was even a telephone in the bathroom, Bradford noticed. And it was apparently working, to judge by the flashing red message light.

Bradford reached for the phone, dialed 0. "Hotel operator," said a pleasant voice. "How may I help you, Mr. Beck?"

This was the service he had expected. This was the pleasant and mellifluous voice he had wanted. The last twenty-four hours now seemed like a bad dream.

"I have a message," he said.

"One moment, please," said a voice. The hold music played Mozart, pleasant and sweeping passages. He didn't have to wait long, though, which was almost a pity.

"Thank you for holding, Mr. Beck," she said. "The message was from a Ms. Cleo Harris. She called at eleven-fifteen this morning, and left no forwarding number. Her message is, 'Don't ever try to communicate with me again, you swine.'"

There was a long silence between the operator and Bradford, before she said, "There are no other messages, Mr. Beck."

Another silence. "Can I be of any other assistance, Mr. Beck?"

"Can you put me on hold for a while?" he asked. "I'd sort of like to listen to that music again."

"Certainly, Mr. Beck."

The damn itch was back. To the strains of Mozart, Bradford scratched mightily.

Chapter Forty-Seven

"It's hard being positive," said Am, "with only one B positive."

Hiroshi didn't seem to be sharing his gloom. They were driving back to the Hotel and the Fat Innkeeper was once again intent on seeing the scenery.

Les ("that's my real name, honest") Moore had been the only B positive in the entire group of questionnaires. Am didn't see how the New Jersy CPA could have had anything to do with Dr. Kingsbury's death. Boring people to death would have been Moore's way, not poisoning them.

Am had thought there would be several B positives (statistically there should have been two or three out of the sixty, dammit), and had hoped the identity of the murderer would suddenly be obvious, would jump out at him. Now the only thing jumping out at him was his gloom. It was time to bring his investigation to a close and hope the police could do better. He'd go through the process of interviewing Moore, probably be forced into hearing more details of his near-death experience, then he'd slip into a deep depression. Intuitively, Am knew Moore hadn't killed

Kingsbury. He wished he'd been as intuitive about B positive.

"The gold rush," said Hiroshi, "occurred in California in 1849, did it not?"

"Uh-huh," said Am distractedly. "Not here, though. It happened in northern California, around Fort Sutter."

"San Diego has no gold?"

"Not too much of the ore variety," said Am. "There are a few tired veins around Julian and Campo. That's about it."

"How is it then," asked Hiroshi, "that in Dr. Kingsbury's room they found traces of gold?"

Am looked at the Fat Innkeeper. While he had been busy going through the questionnaires, and trying to decipher Kingsbury's illegible handwriting, Hiroshi had started reading the investigative reports.

"Traces of gold?" Am repeated.

Hiroshi nodded.

"Where were they found?"

"In the carpeting. Several flakes."

Am wished he had read the case file. He had thought his answers would be found in the questionnaires or the doctor's notes, hadn't considered they might emerge elsewhere. "Did the police theorize where the gold came from?"

"There was no conjecture in the pages I read," said Hiroshi.

"The doctor was fond of a certain drink called Goldschlager," Am said. "There's actual gold flakes in it."

"Gold in a drink?" asked Hiroshi. It didn't make sense to the Japanese man, but then he probably wouldn't have understood about pet rocks either.

"You'd have to try it," Am said, but he was thinking

about something else, something he should have considered earlier. Just how had Thomas Kingsbury been poisoned?

"Gold flakes in a drink," repeated Hiroshi. "Isn't gold toxic?"

"It damn well can be," Am said.

Someone must have doctored Kingsbury's bottle of Gold-schlager. No, that wouldn't have been certain enough. Someone must have hand-delivered him a potassium-cyanide cocktail. With all the gold floating around, the doctor wouldn't have noticed a few white flakes. By all accounts, Kingsbury didn't sip this particular drink. He would have downed the poison and the drink in a single gulp.

Annette responded to the gas. The speedometer rose from sixty to seventy, then to eighty, and kept rising. She started to make sounds. For the last ten years she had never been pushed beyond sixty-five. Hirsohi looked at Am with alarm.

"I think I know who murdered Dr. Kingsbury," Am said. Then, to Annette, "We're going to the beach."

The old woody rattled but held. Anyone who regularly travels Southern California freeways is used to seeing unusual sights, but this one was worth taking notice: a woody that was almost half a century old was racing for all she was worth toward home. Most of those in the fast lane gave the right of way to Annette. It was a good thing. Her brakes had always been iffy, and no one would mistake her handling for that of a sports car.

"Why this hurry?" asked Hiroshi, clearly alarmed. His inquiry was voiced just before they took the Ardath exit going eighty miles an hour. Between them and a long drop to some intersecting freeways below was a guardrail, one they came perilously close to slamming into.

Am answered the question after getting Annette more centered on the asphalt. "Marisa is talking with Lady Death," he said.

The Fat Innkeeper had no idea what Am was talking about, looked at him as if he had lost his mind. "My reporter friend is interviewing Angela Holliday," Am said. "The murderer. At least I think so."

"Ah," said Hiroshi. He didn't relax, but at least seemed to understand.

Lady Death had told Am that she had filled out one of Kingsbury's questionnaires, had even described how they had gotten together for drinks before the conference so that they could talk. Her questionnaire hadn't been among those in Kingsbury's room. For some reason, she must have retrieved it. For likely the same reason, she had also murdered Dr. Kingsbury. The doctor had even made a reference to his meeting with Angela Holliday. He had told Skylar he had "a date with deceitful destiny." What did that mean? As for the supposed break-in of her room, Lady Death had probably seen Am and Marisa drinking in the Lobby Lounge and been curious.

Marisa, he thought, more alarmed than ever.

Annette was losing power on the ascent up Ardath. "Come on," said Am, "come on."

She pushed up and over the rise. Glistening far below was the ocean and La Jolla Strand.

"Hold on," Am warned Hiroshi.

The descent into La Jolla is often backed up with traffic. As Ardath merges with Torrey Pines Road, there is the inevitable gridlock. Neither Am nor Annette were going to be denied on this day, though. They didn't slow up, found open spots where none seemed to exist. Am knew the illegal shortcuts and used them, sailed through a gas station's parking lot and then through an alley behind a restaurant. Hiroshi's eyes were closed. He was holding the dashboard very tightly.

Am was afraid of more than crashing. What if Marisa had mentioned to Lady Death that he was searching for their B-positive murderer? It seemed unlikely. Marisa hadn't been looking forward to the interview, had probably kept the casual conversation to a minimum. He doubted it was the kind of thing she would volunteer anyway, but he was still afraid for her. It was a hell of a time, Am thought, to learn just how much he cared.

He sailed through a red light, then, to the loud blaring of horns, turned west toward the ocean. It wouldn't do to park in front of the Hotel, not when every moment might count. The fastest way to the Crown Jewel Suite called for an unusual route.

On the south side of the Hotel is a boat-launching area that's open to the public, where four-wheel-drive vehicles pull their boats out to the water. It's the only place on the La Jolla Strand where it is legal to drive onto the sand, and even at that, the course is very regulated. Am had another path in mind.

His turn into the boat launch thruway was too wide and too fast. In desperation, Am slammed on the brakes. Annette fishtailed, spinning out to a gravel pathway. The woody's gymnastics spared her a collision into a boat trailer by inches. Hiroshi tried to say something to Am, but he wasn't listening. His only focus was on swinging Annette's wheel around and pressing forward again. The Fat

Innkeeper had apparently had enough. He opened the door and jumped out.

Squeezing by the boat trailer and truck, Annette shot ahead toward the sand. The ride rapidly got bumpy. The beach was covered with seaweed. Too late, Am realized the reason. The tide was high. Very high.

He steered Annette toward the seawall, but not in time. A wave crashed into Annette's side. Her beloved ocean pushed into her. For a moment, Am let up on the gas pedal, and that was a mistake. The water pooled around the wheels, and Annette sank into the La Jolla Strand equivalent of quicksand. Am pushed hard on the gas, but her tires only dug deeper holes.

Am jumped out of Annette, gave her one last forlorn look. She reminded him of something. Then he remembered. She looked like another beached whale.

Chapter Forty-Eight

The interview had gone far better than Marisa had expected. Angela Holliday had opened up to her, had given her more than sound bites. She hadn't pulled out her damn hourglass, and hadn't acted as if Marisa were just one in a line to get a few quotes out of her. They had far exceeded the half-hour time limit, but weren't close to running out of things to say. Their talk wasn't a one-way conversation. Angela asked questions of Marisa, learned about her life outside of her stories ("Sometimes," Marisa had said, "I wonder if there is one"), and her goals.

By mutual consent, the two women had decided to watch the sunset together. It was, said Lady Death, her favorite time of the day.

"Anthropologists say that among tribal people the twilight is a time for quiet," Angela said. "When the sun is setting, there is a melancholy that comes over them. The term for it is 'Hesperian depression.' It is a time they think about their mortality."

"You've thought about that more than most," said Marisa.

"Yes."

The congruence of water and sun, of boiling horizon, was still a few minutes away. "Would you like a drink?" asked Lady Death. "I've recently become enamored of this rather exotic schnapps called Goldschlager . . ."

"I tried it for the first time last night!" said Marisa. "I'd love one."

The drinks were served, and a toast was made: "To new horizons," said Lady Death.

Marisa had never learned to shoot drinks. She sipped hers, and watched the sunset. The two women were contemplating those thoughts that sunsets bring when the interruption occurred. One moment their attention was on the ethereal, and the next it was on a woody being wildly driven along the beach. A woody. Marisa got up and looked for a camera crew. Sometimes Hollywood comes to San Diego's beaches to do filming. But there were no cameras, just a chariot of the surf-gods mired in the sands.

The driver jumped out of his wood-paneled wagon, and gave it a desperate look. Marisa had expected a teenager, but this was no youth. Even from seven stories up, the figure looked familiar. When he turned around, Marisa knew who the crazy driver was. "Am," she shouted, "Am!"

He yelled up to her, screamed, "Don't," but she couldn't be sure of what else he said. He shouted a second time, but she still couldn't make out his words. Then he yelled, "I'm coming up," vaulted up the beach stairs, and passed from her sight.

"Did you hear what he was yelling?" asked Marisa.

"He said he was coming up."

"No," said Marisa. "Before that."

"I think he yelled, 'Don't drink.'"

"Don't drink?" Marisa was puzzled at the words.

"I guess I won't offer you a refill then," said Lady Death. Marisa's glass was empty.

"I wonder what he meant by that," said Marisa. She was still looking down at the beach. The waves were crashing into the abandoned woody. "Poor car," she said.

Lady Death cleared the glasses.

The fastest way to the Crown Jewel Suite was a service elevator on the south side of the Hotel. Am desperately pushed 7, then, breathing heavily, tried to think about what to do next. The only thing on his mind had been to get to Marisa. It was still difficult to think beyond that. He had been the dog chasing the bus. Now he was about to catch it.

The elevator doors opened. Am ran across a walkway to the Crown Jewel Suite and remembered too late that he didn't even have a pass key on him. He knocked on the door, decided if it wasn't opened within three seconds he would grab an entry key from one of the maids. That, or break it down.

The door opened almost immediately. "Am," said Marisa. She looked bewildered, but he didn't care. Am reached out and hugged her, which might have confused her even more, but not so much that she didn't return the hug.

"Aren't you supposed to save the embracing until after you're out of danger?" asked Lady Death.

It was a good question, especially as she was pointing a gun at them. She motioned the two of them away from the door, directed them with the gun to sit down on the sofa, then closed the door behind her.

"What's going on here?" asked Marisa. Her question was more rhetorical than not. Guns have a way of saying a lot.

"Your boyfriend went mad," Angela said. "Probably a hundred people saw that. He drove his car on the beach and started shouting like a crazy man. Then you opened the door and he pushed his way into this room. The rest, I'm afraid, is going to be an awful blur. And an awful mess."

"Too many people know about B positive," said Am.

"That's not what Marisa said."

Am turned to her, in a quick look confirmed his fears.

"You know what the worst thing is?" said Lady Death. "I don't even know my blood type. I threw away my medical questionnaire without even taking notice of it. I think it's rather rare, Mother said something about it once, but I'm not even sure. Can you believe that? A half hour ago Marisa told me about your theory. She swore me to secrecy, of course. Since that time I've been going crazy trying to remember what my blood type is. And wondering what I'd have to do, if necessary, to keep it a secret."

"You don't want to kill again," said Am.

"No," she said, "I don't. But this isn't a time for rational thoughts. My wagon isn't hitched to a rational star. It is a time to dream. I am on the verge of everything I have ever hungered for. Do you think I can just walk away from the adulation and riches? No, not even walk away. I'd be led off in shackles."

"It," Am said, purposely not elaborating on what "it" was, "wouldn't be worth it."

"I think we disagree."

Marisa had to ask the question that journalists always ask: "Why?"

Lady Death didn't answer, but her eyes grew more focused and her trigger finger grew whiter. Am decided to answer, decided he better keep the conversation going. He had figured out why she wanted her medical questionnaire back.

"The reports of her death," he said, "were greatly exaggerated."

The Twain quote had been floating around in his head waiting and wanting to come out. He had known it, and not known it.

"She overstated the extent of her injuries," Am said. "She had no idea that Dr. Kingsbury would be requesting medical reports and examining her records. My guess is that Angela had serious injuries, but not life-threatening. Her near-death experience was likely just a hallucination brought on by the pain medication. Or wishful thinking. Or was it greed?"

"It was none of those things," she said. "It was the real thing. I died."

"Did your doctor think so? Was there any medical corroboration?"

"The medical community is often blind."

"Including Dr. Kingsbury?"

Lady Death smiled or, more accurately, pantomimed a smile. "He was not so blind," she said. "And he was no saint. He wanted me exposed in more ways than one. The doctor wanted to make an example of me, and at the same time he wanted to bed me. Without saying it, he implied that if I was amenable to his attentions, matters would go easier on me. When I went to his room the night before last, he thought I was his lamb for the slaughter. He never suspected it was the other way around. I brought two drinks, his and mine. He swallowed his in a gulp."

She didn't continue. But Am needed to keep her talking.

"And what about you?" he asked. "Did you finish your drink?"

"Yes," she said. "The knocking at the door frightened me, of course, but it wasn't totally unexpected. I left with the glasses as soon as the hallway was clear. The doctor was almost dead. I actually wanted to stay to see him die, but I knew I couldn't."

"If I had been a fraud like you," said Am, "I probably would have wanted to see a firsthand death, too. Grist for the mill, right?"

His remark stung, made her angry, which is what he wanted. He had kept her occupied while the Fat Innkeeper silently opened the door and crept up behind her. For a big man, Hiroshi was agile and fast. He grabbed the gun, wrenching it from her. During the quick tug of war he said, "Please." Then, with the gun in his own hand, he said, "So sorry."

Polite even to a murderer.

Lady Death collapsed on the floor, and there, she cried for a minute. If Hiroshi sympathized, he did it with the gun pointed at her. It was a good thing the suite had two phone lines. Am called the police with one of the telephones, and Marisa called the paper with the other.

With the necessary phone calls made, everyone gathered again in the sitting room. The silence, and the waiting, grew more uncomfortable. Lady Death spoke first, her voice small and tremulous.

"May I watch the sunset?" she asked.

Hiroshi and Marisa looked to Am for an answer. "From inside," he said, "not from outside."

He was afraid of her leaping. "Thank you," she said quietly, then walked toward the floor-to-ceiling window and looked out. She stood there and stared for a minute, then broke the silence again.

"May I have a drink, please?" she asked. She made her request to the window, didn't turn back to them.

Am hesitated. "I'd like the gold," she said, "to toast the dying of the light."

There was another ocular consultation between the three of them, then Marisa quietly said that both of them had already had a glass of the Goldschlager. Deciding that there was no harm in her request, Am poured from the opened bottle at the bar and brought Lady Death her potion. "Thank you," she said.

The sky was mostly red, but there were many colors tinting the horizon, subtle hues radiating out of the clouds. "It's beautiful," she said.

Lady Death raised her glass to the sunset. "Be positive," she said. She turned to them, smiled, then shook her head and added, "Damned if I really know."

Later, Am would wonder about her reference. Was she musing about life after death, or her blood type?

She swallowed her drink Kingsbury-style, with one gulp. A few moments later, she started convulsing.

"There must have been two bottles," shouted Marisa. She was right, but it was too late to be right.

They watched her die. It wasn't *seppuku*, but it was close enough.

Chapter Forty-Nine

Am didn't feel much like a hero, even if Marisa's articles made him sound like one. What seemed to be forgotten among all the PR was that Am had done just about everything wrong. It was Hiroshi who had remembered about the high tides, who had been smart enough to jump out of Annette and get a pass key so that he could walk into the Crown Jewel Suite unobserved. And though Am had figured out who the murderer was, and why she had killed Kingsbury, and even how she had murdered him, he was dissatisfied with how he had reached his conclusions. It was like getting the right answer to a math problem, but solving it the wrong way. His answers had resulted from using the wrong formula. They worked, but they shouldn't have.

"Damned if I really know," Lady Death had said. And damned if he did. As it turned out, her blood group was AB, the rarest of the four blood types. So much for his inspiration, his clue from beyond the grave. Lady Luck had delivered him Lady Death. There was bitter poison to consider, and bitter irony to swallow. But still, he reminded himself, for having gotten everything wrong, there were still things that had turned out right.

Between Am, Hiroshi, and Marisa, a triangle of under-standing had emerged. Am wasn't sure which of them had suggested the ceremony, but they had all known it was the right thing to do.

A day after Angela Holliday's death, the three of them walked in procession from the central Hotel gardens to Am's (and Hiroshi's) special place. It was twilight when they started, but the sky grew progressively darker. Hiroshi led the way with a lantern. What they were doing was somewhat eastern, and somewhat western, but it was mostly Californian.

Hiroshi had told him that during the Festival of the Dead, during *Obon*, family members led the dead forward with lanterns to the temple graveyard. Hiroshi, with his lantern, was leading Dr. Thomas Kingsbury and Angela Holliday to their place of rest. The dead were supposed to be appeased by members of the household. The three of them were that household. The Hotel had always been gen-erous that way with extended family. Hirsohi considered what they were doing was more than ceremonial. He thought of it as insurance of sorts, a way to ameliorate the curses and placate the *gaki* at the Hotel California. Maybe they should have included Stan the ghost in the ceremony, but he seemed to be having too good a time haunting the place.

Am had never been to his special place at night. It was even quieter than he expected. Hiroshi's lantern illumi-nated the setting, but around them was more shadow than not. The three of them stood in front of the rock. They had brought nothing with them, no memorial markers, carried only their feelings. Without having discussed it, Am knew he was to be the speaker for the dead.

"Thomas Kingsbury's last words were 'Be positive,'" Am said. "I'd like to believe that he didn't die angry, that he had a last momentary glimpse of insight and found his dying peace in that. His words are best accepted at their face value. It is not necessary to interpret them as the words of an afterlife, for they work just as well as being wonderful advice for the here and now. It would have been better had Thomas Kingsbury and Angela Holliday come to this revelation earlier rather than later. Let us hope they have both found this peace now."

Brother Howard wouldn't have given a similar talk, thought Am, but the words seemed right for everyone, and everything, there.

Hiroshi extinguished his lantern. He didn't want the spirits to follow him. They were home. The three of them found the path through the light of the moon, walking in silence and contemplation. No one spoke until they entered the lobby of the Hotel.

"I need a minute of your time, Am-moo," said Hiroshi.

Am knew that the Japanese liked to add an "oo" to any word that ended in a consonant sound, but he wasn't sure if it worked with his name.

Hiroshi bowed to Marisa. "Hotel business," he explained. Marisa was grateful not to be included, and excused herself to go and sit near one of the fountains.

The two men went to Hiroshi's office. Even before they sat down, Hiroshi asked, "What is her prognosis?"

The tow truck had arrived soon after the ambulance had left. In the dark night, hauling Annette out from all the mire, she had seemed like another body being dragged away.

"They tell me Annette's going to be just fine," said Am. The unsaid part: For about three thousand dollars.

As if reading his mind, Hiroshi said, "The Hotel will pay for her repairs."

Am hadn't expected that kind of generosity. "They are not insignificant," he said.

"The only terms," said Hiroshi, "are that I would like to drive her every so often . . ."

Am could live with that, though he wasn't sure if Annette could.

". . . and she must be available to use in promotions. I have decided Annette is better than a sea worm."

They both smiled, but Hiroshi wasn't through with his surprises. "Mr. Takei is leaving," the Fat Innkeeper said.

Am felt a surge of excitement that he tried to suppress. All too nonchalantly, Am asked, "Did you tell him that no more imposters were going to be showing up looking for his job?"

"He knows that," said Hiroshi. "But he is not happy here. He wants to go home."

The Fat Innkeeper pressed his fingers together. "I think you are the right person for the job."

Am refrained from getting up and dancing a jig. Hanging over Hiroshi's head was a map of the world with oversized Japan still centered.

"I am not sure if I am that right person," said Am. "I think you have already noticed that I am not very Japanese."

Hiroshi refused to argue, but then anyone Japanese wouldn't have anyway.

"I haven't liked some of the changes going on at the Hotel," Am said, "and I'd find it hard not to speak up.

"There are some hotels that were never meant to be a Marriott, or a Hyatt, or a Hilton, or a Sheraton. There are some hotels that don't operate by the same set script, and shouldn't operate by that script.

"I think of the Hotel as an eccentric relative, a crazy but wonderful old aunt who is loved all the more because of her quirks. Would you like your beloved relative to suddenly be humorless, to wear only dark clothes, and act formal and proper to the point of being boring?"

Could eccentricity translate to the Japanese mind as being something positive? Am had read that the Japanese lived by the social standard that the nail sticking out should be hammered down.

"Our guests expect this wonderfully different aunt," said Am. "They have come to love her. Who wants an old friend to change?"

Hiroshi didn't say anything for a minute, seemed to be immersed in thought. By the time he answered, Am was already kicking himself for having gone too far and said too much. "I will listen to any of your concerns," said Hiroshi, "but I think they should be voiced in private."

Am kept the smile off his face. His major worry had been answered. "What will my salary be?" he asked.

"The same," said Hiroshi. "You are the most overpaid security director in the country."

And I'll be one of the most underpaid managers, Am thought. "At least I won't have to worry about security anymore," said Am.

The Fat Innkeeper shook his head. "For the foreseeable future," he said, "you will assume both positions."

Hiroshi spoke before Am could speak. He left no room for argument. "The Hotel needs its samurai," he said.

Chapter Fifty

"We better celebrate tonight," Am said to Marisa, "before I realize how much work's waiting for me tomorrow."

Klaroshi, he thought. Death by overwork. It was a Japanese phenomenon, a way of life—and death. It was one Japanese import he hoped America would not buy into.

Am felt good. Impending doom had been staved off for at least another day. All the swingers had checked out (and had left with smiles, according to the staff). Most of them had even announced that they were looking forward to visiting the Hotel again. Am tried not to dwell on that future threat.

Only one guest had expressed unhappiness with his stay. Upon paying his bill ($483.24), the man had said the Hotel had "ruined his life" and "cost him millions." It was the same guest that had attacked Felipe the shoe-shine man. The poor fellow was obviously psychologically unbalanced.

The staff had seemed unusually cheery that day. Jimmy Mazzelli, for one, had been positively glowing. He had told Am he was off on a vacation tomorrow, going to Arizona to see a "special someone." Romance was definitely in the air. Am was not immune to it himself.

He had his arm around Marisa. They were walking aim-lessly around the Hotel smiling at one another. "How do you want to kick up your heels?" she asked.

Am considered her question, then stopped walking. "This," he said, " for starters."

He kissed her. It was a long time before either of them came up for breath.

"I think," she said with a happy sigh, "that's a question I'll ask you more often."

"Let's celebrate with dinner," Am said, "and maybe a movie, and . . ."

How did he want to kick up his heels? Am remembered something.

"There's a grunion run tonight," he said.